# NO NUMBER IS GREATER THAN ONE

*By David Weiss*

SACRED AND PROFANE

NAKED CAME I

THE ASSASSINATION OF MOZART

THE SPIRIT AND THE FLESH

NO NUMBER IS GREATER THAN ONE

# NO NUMBER
# IS GREATER THAN
# ONE

## DAVID WEISS

COWARD, McCANN & GEOGHEGAN, INC.
NEW YORK

First American Edition 1972

Copyright © 1972 by David Weiss

Library of Congress Catalog Card Number: 70-188729

Printed in the United States of America

To

the poetry of

STYMEAN KARLEN

"One voice with this book"

# Contents

# NO NUMBER IS GREATER THAN ONE

# I Speak to Myself and Say

I speak to myself and say
There is but one country
The world

I speak to myself and say
There is but one people
All of the people

I speak to myself and say
There is but one color of people
Each is a different shade
of the same color

I speak to myself and say
There is but one commandment
Hold no cause greater than one
of the people

I speak to myself and say
Kill the cause before you kill
one of the people

I speak to myself and say
There is but one prayer
And one religion
This is the prayer and the religion

I speak to myself and say
There is but one god of nature
over all of the people
One people

Now I speak for myself and say
There is but one wisdom
for one people, all of the people
This is the wisdom

STYMEAN KARLEN

# I Speak to Myself and Say

"Kid, this assignment is easy," said the sergeant. "All you got to do is to count the enemy dead. It's better than risking your ass in a search and destroy mission."

Maybe, maybe, thought the private, but he was silent. He wished he didn't itch so.

The sergeant, a middle-aged career soldier, assured the twenty-year-old draftee, "You won't have to stay out there long. We give Headquarters the figures they want, I'll see to it that you finish your year here as a file clerk." The sergeant was proud of his detail. He had collected bodies from all over the Territory and he had ordered them deposited in a large muddy ravine as if he were putting money in the bank. He pointed out, "You will be out of the direct line of fire."

But not completely, thought the private. The pit, as his fellow soldiers called the ravine, was also within range of the enemy guns.

However, the sergeant was positive that the enemy wouldn't shoot their own dead. He said, "They may be nuts, but they ain't crazy." He laughed.

Only the private's itch got worse. Some of the bodies were a mess.

The sergeant added, "This is important, kid. We got to make a respectable showing. The competition is getting tough."

Besides, the private realized, he had no choice. If he

3

refused this detail today, tomorrow he would be in the bush and his chances of getting to be twenty-one would become less and less. And the bodies were piled neatly and clearly, considering. Most of them were whole. And there were more than enough to warrant a count. But which was which? How many of the bodies were enemy dead? In many cases he couldn't tell, for many had died from burns and bombs. He wondered if the sergeant in his enthusiasm had thrown in a few of their own bodies. Or maybe he should. Nobody would know the difference. As their own casualties rose, so did the demands from Headquarters. Headquarters insisted they must maintain a ratio of at least ten enemy dead to one of their own, to prove they were achieving Pacification, but with the steady increase in their own casualties a little lying was becoming necessary. And with so many burnt to death it was often impossible to tell the civilians from the soldiers. If they would allow him to count civilians it would help.

Ass-deep in mud and bodies, he wished he could avoid the stench.

"You got everything you need, ain't you," the sergeant said.

"Sure, sure." The non-com, who was in the army for life, wasn't asking, he was telling.

"Then what are you waiting for, kid?"

"It's the flies. They sting."

The sergeant wasn't listening. The stink was giving him a headache.

Alone now, for the non-com had some booze he had to sell, the private tried to focus on his assignment. Some of *them*—he couldn't think of *them* as *we* or *us*—were so badly mangled it was difficult to be accurate. And how much of a body constituted a body? And two legs that seemed to match, what about *them*? Was that something wriggling? He could have sworn one of the bodies had flopped over and was pawing the air. The possibility that someone was still alive in this sea of mud gave him such a cruddy feeling that for relief he thought of some of the girls he had laid. He was proud he had gotten into several nice girls; there was even one girl who did not make him feel she was doing him a favor; he didn't trust whores—he was afraid they would give him the clap. Then he sought to think of the bodies as sandbags and that helped. By the end of the day his count had reached four hundred.

The trouble was, the sergeant wasn't satisfied. Headquarters said they had to have at least two hundred more to reach their quota. Otherwise, they would never achieve a ratio of ten to one.

The sergeant, who disliked the private for being a draftee but who hated the major at Headquarters in charge of the body count because the major was an appointee, had a favorite reverie. Some day this thin-lipped, stiff-necked ex-accountant, who operated like an I.B.M. machine, would have to come to him for a favor. But today he was still the major.

As the major examined the sergeant's figures as he would a profit and loss statement, his frown grew frightening and he snapped, "You must be more efficient and inventive. My charts show a definite falling off of enemy dead last month. Perhaps you don't know where they are. If you can't do better than this, we will have to assign you to the bush."

So the sergeant ordered the draftee to check the bodies hanging on the barbed wire above the ravine, stating, "We need every body we can get. It's urgent. What about the village we hit yesterday? There must have been at least a hundred and fifty dead in it. And what about that corpse against the tree? Is it theirs or ours?"

"I don't know, and anyhow, it's been there a while."

"Use it. And don't forget the village count. That should push us close to six hundred, our quota for the week."

"What about the children?"

"Kid, you've got to count everything that's dead and doesn't move. The village will help. There's nothing left in it that is alive. There's nothing to panic about. This is your job. Don't forget the tree and the wire. That is what you're getting paid for." The sergeant strode away.

The village did help. When he finished, he was close to the quota.

And now he was running out to the tree in the special gait known as the coward's crouch, which everybody used, a running, weaving, bent over run to make sure he was the smallest target possible. But after he reached the body, with only an occasional burst of fire, he couldn't tell whether it was an enemy body or their own it was burnt so. He couldn't even tell whether it was a person. He pushed it over with his foot and as he turned it around he saw a penis, somehow still intact.

Muck the count, the whole mucking business. Suddenly he felt sorry for the poor bastard, whoever's side it had been on—it would never get another piece again. Ah, what the hell, what was the point of getting worked up, he had his own ass to worry about.

The private didn't go all the way out to the barbed wire, for that was in the direct line of fire—he was risking his ass as it was, being out in the open—but lying in the mud, once he could make out all the bodies hanging on the wire, he included every one of them in his count, although he was not sure they were all enemy dead. But nobody should catch him in such a little lie and he wasn't hurting anybody. He felt proud when he reached five hundred and ninety. Then he was upset. The sergeant had said they must have six hundred at least.

He saw a shell hole a few feet away with some bodies in it. He felt he had made a great discovery and he crawled forward to ascertain the correct number. By now the private was so absorbed in his determination to show the sergeant that he was as much a man as anybody, it didn't matter whose dead they were.

As the private crept into the shell hole he counted ten bodies. They were so caked with mud he couldn't tell whose side they had been on. They had been killed by the same mortar burst, but they looked so grotesque he assumed that they were the enemy. He added quickly: six hundred! What a nice, simple round number! But would the sergeant accept such an even number? Suddenly he was scared. He was stuck up to his waist in the goo. He remembered how he had made mudpies as a child, and that his Mom had given him hell for coming home dirty.

Then his body shook violently. There was a little hole in his chest, no larger than a dime. He had forgotten to use the coward's crouch.

And as he fell face downward in the mud, indistinguishable from the others, he wondered if the sergeant would include him in the body count. He tried to cry out. But his mouth was full of mud, suffocating him.

The sergeant assumed that the draftee had deserted and he ordered another private to finish the count. This one, a soldier who was two weeks away from going home to the world, did it with field glasses, and he reported the ten bodies in the shell hole and the one near by as if they were a bonus.

It was an excellent body count, thought the major. He felt like a success story. His luck was improving. The general might even unbend enough to congratulate him and promote him. He informed the sergeant that if these figures were maintained the sergeant might be decorated. These numbers gave him such joy. Just wait until the President saw his figures! They would prove that Pacification was prospering. They had achieved another fine week. Six hundred and one.

The next day the Pacification Program announced proudly: "*The body count of enemy dead last week reached its highest figure this year, six hundred and one. While our losses were only sixty. At the rate we are going we expect total Pacification to be achieved soon.*"

There were some mornings when Alexander Grant felt that he really had made a mistake in being born. This day was one of them. Alex was in his fifties, but a few more mornings like this one and he would feel eighty. While he was preparing his breakfast he turned on the news in the hope the news would give him a subject for his newspaper column and each item depressed him more, for death by war, riot, airplane, and murder followed each other like one two three four, and now, just as he expected relief, the Pacification Program was on.

The voice spoke as if it were announcing a score.

"Our casualties—sixty dead."

"Allied casualties—one hundred and twenty dead."

"Enemy dead—six hundred and one."

Real, real, real reality, he wondered, what was really real? He closed his eyes, but when he opened them a moment later, although the voice had stopped speaking, the figures were still there. He cursed his vivid imagination, but the figures became bodies. He must be mad, he thought. He could not tell which of these bodies in front of him were enemies and which were not. Was it because the bodies were so battered, he asked himself, like flies?

He took another doughnut, although he had eaten two already and this would mean an extra effort on the tennis court to keep his weight down, and a second cup of coffee, and then he turned another station on and heard: "It was revealed today in Athens that a second tomb containing the graves of soldiers who died fighting alongside the Athenians against the Persians at Marathon almost 2,500 years ago has been unearthed by Greek archaeologists in the Marathon plain. The tomb is assumed to be that of the slaves who fought with Athens, for it is a hundred yards away from one which contains the skeletons of the free Athenians who died with them. Moreover, the archaeologists are even more sure that the second tomb contains only slaves, for the free men were buried with their weapons and robes—whatever, it was believed, they would need in the next world—while the slaves were buried as they had died, layer by layer, without any possessions or individuality."

"The history of man!" he cried to himself. The news had become a loud hurdy gurdy and he switched it off with a bang.

Yet when he sat at his desk and felt his typewriter under his fingers and tried to start his column no words came. Instead, the body count and the ratio, *six hundred* and *one* to *sixty*, dominated his mind. He thought angrily, Of such felicities are our days born! Did the Pacification Program think he was that stupid? That he would believe a *ten* to *one* ratio?

Alex decided it was the terrible insistence on numbers that irritated him so much. He thought, The news shouldn't upset him, the news wasn't any worse than usual.

He was listening with only a small part of his mind until

the Pacification Program came on while he was reflecting about his newspaper column. He was wondering whether he should write about taxes or the economy, generally safe subjects, or whether he should assume a philosophical posture and suggest a moratorium on controversy in an effort to foster a mood of reconciliation in the country. That should please many of his readers. But the Pacification Program was a jolt. Suddenly to write about taxes or the economy seemed worthless and to seek reconciliation futile. He glared at his typewriter; it had become an antagonist, defying him.

And now there were the two letters that arrived with the news.

After he read them, and he did so carefully, he was so shaken by their contents he sat in a state of shock. He felt as if the walls of his study were tumbling down. Was he really living in a never-never land, as one letter suggested, where everything was measured, comfortable, and known? Or afraid to offend the establishment, the other letter implied, because he was an essential part of the establishment?

He stared out the window of his apartment where the view, when there was sunshine, was cheerful and stimulating, with a fine profile of the Capitol, which he liked, for that gave him a sense of solidity and permanence. But today even the dome was blurred by a gray, watery sky that seemed to stretch interminably and the color of the Capitol was a candy white, a pretense, he thought, much less sturdy than it appeared.

Should he write that? Words formed in his mind: "To put a crown upon our capital is not to give our representatives infallibility...No one is always right...*Are you really your own master?*"

But the last phrase was what his son had written!

He was going soft, he thought savagely, using someone else's idea. Yet he felt fit; he had played three strenuous sets of tennis yesterday and although his opponent had match point three times and was twenty years younger he had won. Only the two letters made him feel so old.

Alex rose suddenly, abruptly, and eyed himself in his full-length mirror. He preferred to work in his shorts and sports shirt, and as he looked at his reflection he felt a little less

edgy. His legs were just as muscular as a young man's; his
shoulders were wide and strong; his flesh was unwrinkled;
his hair was still brown, without a trace of gray; and his
features were firm, and, as he had found out on many
occasions, attractive to a considerable number of women.
Today, however, that was not sufficient consolation.

Perhaps music would improve his mood. He went to his
large collection of classical records and selected a favorite
composition, Mozart's 'Jeunehomme' Piano Concerto, for
his record player. But while he loved this music, and the
realization that Mozart had created such a glowing, incom-
parable melody at the age of twenty-two filled him with the
wonder that was Mozart, it did not settle his mind or his
stomach.

His son had written: "You can't have it both ways,
Alexander!"

The other letter had suggested that he was like an ostrich
with its head in the sand.

Suddenly he felt very vulnerable. Alex returned to his
typewriter, but nothing he thought of seemed right to him.
It was the fault of his typewriter, he told himself, it was such
a self-sufficient machine. And so attractive he was certain it
had fallen in love with itself. Now if he could only give it
bread and water and tell it to go to work. But no matter
how he sought to flatter it with his emotion it was im-
movable.

He could not write what his son had asked him to write,
it was too personal. Yet he picked up James's letter and
started to reread it as if he were having a dialogue with his
son.

When he had seen that the letter was from James, Alex
had expected that his son, who was a senior in a near-by university, was asking him for money—James was always over-
spending his monthly allowance—or was telling him about
the latest girl James had fallen in love with and wanted to
marry. James was almost as fickle as his father, thought
Alex, except that his son confused sex with love and desire
with marriage. Or had James gotten a girl in trouble, Alex
wondered, his son's tone was so urgent? When he had been
his son's age that had been a constant problem and had

forced him into his first marriage, but today, with the pill and the open use of contraceptives that shouldn't be a problem.

But from the start of the letter Alex realized his son's purpose was different. James addressed him as Alexander, a tone he assumed when he wished to speak to his father as an equal.

"No rubbish, Alexander," James said. "I used to think we had much in common, but now I am beginning to wonder. For I can hardly believe my eyes that the vacancy still exists in your columns. Don't you realize that today most of my friends, especially those who are students, feel we live in a heartless world. No matter what opinions we express, the government ignores them. And you do, too."

But this was preposterous, Alex retorted, he worked for his readers.

"Alexander, you can't pretend that students are voiceless, our protests must not fall on deaf ears. We are the ones who are most involved in the Pacification Program. It is our blood that is being shed. I wonder how the government would feel if they were being shot at."

Alex paused, smiling. The prospect of some of the senators he knew squirming on their fat bellies to avoid being hit by enemy fire was amusing.

His son wasn't interested in being funny, writing, "If you would say this, it would be useful. Your opinions are heeded."

By some in government, yes—but I can't carry the world, James.

"I have read that you have so much influence you are referred to as 'another State Department'."

Only that sounded like an accusation, for his son added, "But now you use your influence in the wrong direction. You are always trying to be a moderator, but it is too late for compromise."

One should try to see both sides of a question.

"Alexander, the fooling has got to stop. The Pacification Program is not a friendly tennis match."

As if that was ever truly friendly, Alex reflected acidly.

"Pacification is a graveyard."

This time Alex did not answer.

"And you have to use sense in your column. You are not stupid."

Alex paused, thinking this was the price he paid for bringing up his son to question.

"You can't continue to support the Pacification."

But I don't, Alex's mind ran on.

"I know you don't support it openly. But you support the Pacification Program by your silence."

James was shrewd; James knew how to hit him where it hurt.

"You are as guilty as they are. Unless . . ."

James had left a space in his letter to stress what followed.

"You challenge the legality of the Pacification."

But that would embarrass the government!

"Unless . . ."

James was being too dramatic really.

"You are afraid to risk offending your friends in government."

Irate, Alex knew he should stop rereading this letter before he lost his temper completely. Yet in the same situation he would have shouted at his son, "Good heavens, James, why don't you listen! The least you could do is listen!" And because he had an image of himself treating his son as an equal, although he realized in practice it didn't work that way, he read on, trying to listen as he read.

"Or is it that you can't afford to criticize the government?"

Perhaps, perhaps, and yet . . .?

"Who are you loyal to, Alexander?"

That was a good question, James.

"But one can betray things more important than countries."

Here's looking at ourselves, thought Alex, but at fifty it was rather late in the day for self-discovery.

"Alexander, it has been very difficult to write this to you, but something has happened that has forced me to say what I feel. When I entered your university, I entered with Sid Virgin, a close, wonderful friend, my best friend from our high school football team. Each of us lived in the shadow of the university where you made such a name for yourself as a quarterback and my dream was to follow in your footsteps, although I knew I would never be as good as you were. But Sid and I had played together for three years and as a quarterback who preferred to pass I appreciated his ability as a catcher of my passes.

"By the time we reached the university Sid had grown into the ideal build for a wide receiver, six foot three, very fast, with great hands and reflexes, all I had to do was to hit his finger-tips or lay up the ball where he could jump for it, and he could go sky high. We had beautiful dreams of becoming the best passing combination in the country. And that seemed as if it might come true when we were chosen to start the opening game in our junior year. You were there, remember, Alexander . . ."

Indeed, he did remember and how proud he was of his son.

"I was elated and scared stiff. I might get hurt, I had escaped any serious injuries so far, but this was the big time, the men I would be playing against would be much bigger than me, they would concentrate on me, quarterbacks were considered fair game, and I might let you down. Football is a damned serious business at the university, you know."

He did know, Alex reflected, he had gone through this himself. Yet one of his treasured hopes was to see his son follow in his footsteps. And now, as Alex read on, James seemed to be standing before him, shorter and stockier than himself, but older than he was at the same age. Only James was no longer arguing with him, but as he made out his son's angular, lean face—James had inherited his mother's features—James was telling him what the letter was truly about.

"Alexander, it was my favorite time of the year, a sunny Saturday in late September, and as I prepared for this game with the knowledge that I was starting, I recalled all the Saturdays you had taken me to the football games. It was our ritual of being together, of being father and son even when I was living with mother the other six days of the week and you were allowed only visitation rights. And this

Saturday seemed the best of all Saturdays. Ever since I could remember I had dreamt of the day I would be playing quarterback for your university.

"As we trotted on the field and the home crowd roared a loud welcome, I was most conscious of the fragrance of the cut grass, the autumn leaves, the cool, crisp air, so good for breathing, giving me the sensation that this was an afternoon invented by God. But we were also expected to win. There was a large crowd in the stadium, and for most of them there was just one image: victory. But I didn't mind, for as I concentrated on our opponents they looked ugly and nasty, and I felt very decided and dedicated about that.

"A few minutes before in the dressing room Head Coach Butch Borborg—you know him, too, he was your coach—viewed us with a patriarch's indulgence and then, with his jutting jaw quite prominent, declared, 'This is a game of kicking hell out of your opponent. The thing that infuriates me, kids, no shit, is guys who smile during the game. I despise kids who fool around, who are friendly. Either you beat hell out of the other guy or he'll beat hell out of you. Kids who don't believe like I do, I get rid of them, no shit. You don't hurt your opponents, they'll hurt you. You gotta rack them up before they rack you up.'

"But when I went into the game the first time we had the ball I didn't feel ferocious as I was supposed to, but even more scared.

"All my life I had waited for this day and now I had a terrible empty feeling in the pit of my stomach and I longed to throw up, but please God, not in front of all those people. Only there was nothing in my stomach to throw up—I had done it in the dressing room latrine—and before I could flee as I felt I should, I had to call the signals, I had to handle the ball. Then, while I handed it off to someone else, an enemy linebacker hit me with an abusive violence that left my head ringing. But it also made me so mad I didn't worry about being hurt; I had to hurt him.

"Coach had ordered me to control the game, which meant grinding out the yardage slowly, carefully, while I would continue to fake and get hit without being able to hit back. But when I got hit again when I didn't have the ball and I

noticed their defensive halfbacks playing too close to the
line of scrimmage, I saw a way of getting even.

"I called a down and out pass to Sid. It was almost absurd. Sid, with his speed and faking ability, was ten yards
ahead of the defensive halfbacks when I passed to him, and
then he was so fast he had a touchdown without a hand
being laid on him.

"I felt like a hero when we came to the sidelines to an
ovation from the crowd, but Coach Butch Borborg
glowered at me and muttered, 'If it hadn't worked, kid, you
could be in the shit-house now.'

"But it had worked, I thought to myself, and screw you,
Coach, I don't have to take your crap, not after that.

"The next time we had the ball I saw that the enemy had
put two men on Sid. So I didn't pass to him. Then, late in
the second period, when we were tied 7-7 and I noticed that
Sid was back in the basic confrontation of one-on-one
between wide receiver and defensive halfback, I had him
fake another down and out and instead I sent him straight
down the field. As I expected he got a step on his man, I hit
his finger-tips and we had a second touchdown. It was a
glorious feeling, especially when Sid and I came off the field
and our side of the stadium stood as one to cheer us.

"For an instant, however, I felt guilty for getting so much
attention, the rest of the team was being ignored, but that
didn't last when Coach Borborg said, 'A smart play, kid,
you sure had the bodies counted then.'

"I felt like a giant killer. Football was alive with possibilities. Sid and I would fashion a brilliantly successful
attacking duo.

"Early in the second half, when I saw that the enemy were
playing Sid one-on-one again, I called the play that had
worked so well before. But as Sid jumped for the pass I
floated just ahead of him, a play we had practiced many
times, he didn't see the two defensive halfbacks converging
on him from behind. They ignored the ball; they had a ten
yard run on him; they knew they really had him. By the
time they reached Sid they had tremendous momentum and
a savage shot at him. One halfback hit him in the knee with
calculated ferocity, while the other jammed his ankle from

the other side and ruthlessly hammered him into the ground.

"Sid held on to the ball for a considerable gain; the enemy was penalized fifteen yards for pass interference; but Sid didn't get up.

"While the enemy stood around in their huddle during this time out nonchalantly discussing their next defensive maneuver, Sid was carried off the field on a stretcher.

"On the next play, still shaken by what had happened to Sid, I overthrew my receiver and I was intercepted. When I was intercepted again the next time we had the ball, I didn't play any more that day.

"However, we held on to our lead, winning 14—7, but I had no feeling of victory. I heard in the dressing room that Sid had been taken to the hospital with a torn cartilage in his knee.

"But you were considerate with your congratulations, Alexander, you didn't overdo them and you expressed the proper regrets over Sid.

"Yet I was let-down. I wondered whether my regard for football was adolescent and I felt guilty about Sid—if I hadn't called that particular play, partially to show off, he wouldn't have been hurt.

"When I visited Sid in the hospital the next day he pretended to be brave, but his eyes never left mine and there was a tortured look in them and my guilt increased, for I knew he was horribly depressed. He was finished for the season and we couldn't make jokes about that.

"Most of his physical pain had ebbed, but his anxiety had increased. Sid was in the university on a football scholarship; he couldn't afford it otherwise, his father was a truck driver, and football was a necessity. Yet when I said, 'You'll be back soon, fellow,' he gave me a wan smile and replied, 'Sure, sure, as good as new.'

"But when the doctors refused to give Sid a clean bill of health after he left the hospital, saying that his leg would be a risky business from now on, that it was too unreliable to take the punishment of football, his scholarship was taken away from him and he was forced to quit school.

"Meanwhile, I was the second-string quarterback until the end of the season. Then, in the last game of the year, when the first-string quarterback was knocked out early in the game, the biggest one of the season, Coach Borborg had to use me. Still thinking of Sid, I didn't give a damn, I was loose, relaxed, and when I threw two touchdown passes in the last minute to win *The Game*, my past mistakes were forgiven and I was regarded as a champ, with a vested interest in football.

"You were proud of me, Alexander, and you were surprised that I wasn't excited about becoming a campus hero, but I was thinking about Sid.

"Once Sid had to quite school the Pacification Service picked him up. As far as they were concerned, he had flunked out of school. And while he didn't want to go into the Service, he had no choice. He was drafted.

"I didn't hear from him for a long time, and then, a few months ago, I received a lengthy letter from him, almost as lengthy as this one I am writing to you. Evidently Sid had to get some things off his chest. He wasn't a big talker, but he had a lot of feeling."

Alexander paused. Now the voice he was listening to was not his son's, but his friend's—James was quoting Sid Virgin word for word.

"Kid, I've been assigned to the Territory. Unwillingly. Practically nobody here is a volunteer, and while it is never said openly, it is almost automatic for a guy who has been in college to end up at a firebase. And I've had to smuggle this letter out of the Territory with a pal going back to the world, for what I've written would never get by the censor.

"But what bugs me most of all is the detail I'm on. It's an ass-hole detail, I'm looking up the enemy's backside. I've got to count asses. Yeah, that's right. The stench is awful, it is like you are in a human garbage dump, sometimes you work in mud and bodies up to your armpits, but it is supposed to be a safe detail, with a low casualty rate. But it isn't absolutely safe, like pushing booze at the base bars.Once in a while a dead enemy isn't dead and ambushes you. Yet that isn't the worst thing we face, it's keeping up with the body count. I got a sergeant who reminds me of

Butch Borborg, who has the same jutting jaw, the same bark in his voice, who gives us our assignments like one of Butch Borborg's pregame locker room fight talks. He can smell a body count a mile away without ever risking his own ass. And he doesn't believe in prisoners—he can't include them in his body counts.

"Our detail has strict orders to keep firing until everything in the Kill Zone is killed. We got Kill Zones and Pacified Zones and Liberated Zones. They are all marked out and defined like a football field. The Kill Zones are where we kill everything that moves; the Pacified Zones are where we count bodies and announce our 'victories; Liberated Zones are where we spread freedom and everything is dead.

"Most of the time I don't get to the Kill Zones, but the other day, when I was in a Pacified Zone something happened that really bothered the guys on my detail. Four of us were counting bodies because this had been a big Kill Zone and there were lots and lots of bodies, all kinds. I was paired with Larry Wilbur, a high school dropout, who had the usual basic attitude—to cover his own ass. Wilbur had the days counted until his year in the Territory was up, and now he had only twenty-three days left and he was beginning to think that he would make it back home. But he was proud of his body counts; in the time he had been in the Territory his personal body count had risen to ninety-nine; and he kept that record with the days he had left to serve.

"What bothered me, however, was that there were women in our body count and children. When I found two small children, a small girl of about five, and a larger, older boy who lay over her in a protective posture, as if he had tried to shield the younger child, and there were six bullet holes in the boy I grew numb and puked.

"The sergeant hurried over to see what was wrong and he yelled, 'Jesus Christ, you don't get them, they'll get you, Virgin!'

"But when I couldn't stop puking, he got mad and he snapped, 'You'll lose your breakfast and you ain't in the line of fire. What are you so scared about? You ain't gonna die before your year is up!'

"There was the sound of a shot and the sergeant hit the

ground like he had been hit, his teeth chattering, and he screamed that we should go into the bush and grab the bastard. The other pair assigned to the body count figuring, I guess, that the sergeant would appreciate the favor, crept into the bush, although the shot had come from the opposite direction and probably was a nervous draftee aiming at an imaginary enemy, and besides, we were supposed to be in a Pacified Zone on the verge of being liberated. They emerged in a moment with a prisoner, a frail old man who cried out that he was a farmer.

"He looked like a farmer to me, but the sergeant, standing again, towered over the cringing old man, joy, relief, triumph on his rocky features, and shouted at us, 'What's the count?'

'Fifty-five,' my partner whispered.

'It's fifty-six now!' barked the sergeant.

"The old man pleaded in a piteous voice, 'No! No!' and fell to his knees, pointing to the flag and crying out, 'I believe in it, I do, I do!' but the sergeant yanked him to his feet and yelled, 'He ain't gonna outsmart me! I'll blow this bastard away!'

"He put a rifle to the old man's head and pulled the trigger. When it failed to function he corrected it, then to be certain this time, he placed the rifle between the old man's eyes and fired. And as the corpse lay at his feet he fired a complete round into the inert body.

"He muttered, 'You gotta make sure he ain't just three-quarters dead.'

"Then he turned to my partner, who had become a sickly green, and asked, 'What's your body count now? Your personal one?'

"Wilbur mumbled, 'Ninety-nine, I think.'

'Now you got a hundred.'

"James, it was awful. I hadn't done a goddamned thing to stop the sergeant. Should I have? Could I have?

"The sergeant kept acting like there was nothing more beautiful than the sight of the old man tumbling over in a heap, and I was thinking of the time I caught one of your passes with my finger-tips—what else could I think of to stop myself from going nuts? The sergeant must have seen

how shook up I was, for suddenly he said, 'I was carrying
out orders. We got to shoot all prisoners who try to escape.
It is the only way we can liberate the Territory.'

"When the sergeant was gone and we were back at the
base, Wilbur warned me not to mention this incident to
anyone. He said, 'Virgin, the safest thing is to forget it.
Otherwise, they'll send you into the bush. And it's almost
impossible to keep your ass covered there.'

"Ten days later, when Wilbur had less than two weeks to
go before going home to the world, he stepped on a mine. I
found out when the sergeant asked me, 'What should I write
Wilbur's mother? The kid was only twenty.'

"I shrugged. What I was thinking I couldn't say. By now I
had to cover my ass, too. Once you are in the Territory all
that matters is staying alive. Then suddenly, I couldn't resist
saying, 'Maybe you could tell her that you used him in our
body count. So that he didn't die in vain.'

"The sergeant glared at me as if I were nuts, but when he
saw that I was serious, he said, 'Wilbur would have liked
that. He was proud of the size of his body count. He had
reached one hundred and seven. But I can't tell his Mom
that. I'll say he got it defending the detail against enemy
attack. Poor fish! I warned him to keep his ass down!'"

Sid seemed to pause to gather breath, and then he
resumed with a new passion, "Kid, when a guy gets his ass
blown off, you keep thinking it could be you."

Alex wanted to console him, but how?

"If somebody would only explain why I'm here? What the
hell I'm fighting for?"

Alex wished he could speak to Sid directly, but the latter
was fading from view as his letter was concluding.

"Kid, if I ever get back to the world, I'm going to say as
loud as I can that the Pacification isn't worth an inch of
dirt, it doesn't make sense, it stinks. Wilbur got his ass
blown off for nothing. And if it should happen to me, ditto."

James underlined what followed in his own lengthy letter.

"Alexander, Sid Virgin never made it home. They had his
funeral here last week, in a cemetery behind the stadium,

but I kept seeing him running down the field for a pass, with those wonderful hands of his and his great speed, going up, up through the roof of the sky. I heard that he was hit by one of our tanks while he was on a body count detail. I even heard someone whisper, 'It was his own fault, flunking out of school,' and I thought, So this was Sid's contribution to peace with honor.

"Alexander, I've quit the football team. I know this will hurt you, you take such a pride in football, but I can't go on with it after what happened to Sid. And if they try to draft me, I will refuse to serve."

Alex wondered whether this would damage his own situation.

"I can't support something I don't believe in. Can you? Or can't you afford to criticize the government? Your friends in power? Or does your publisher and the establishment have the last say in such matters? Are you really your own master?"

That was ridiculous; James should know better. It was simply that he preferred to take the long-range view. Yet he was quite moved by what his son had written. It was natural for his son to be upset.

"Alexander, are you always going to temporize, play it safe? Or are you going to speak out and denounce the Pacification Program for the pious fraud it is? We can no longer live on the assumption it will end soon and take refuge in that comfortable illusion. It has been going on for a long time and if we don't stop it now it could run us all over. You must challenge the Pacification Program before it is too late.

"The night after Sid's funeral I went to the cemetery and put my football letter on his grave."

While his son's letter was written with an up and down angularity, as if he were climbing a mountain, the other letter was written precisely, in a clear black script that caused each word to stand out.

My Dear Mr. Alexander Grant:
I have never written to a public figure before, but there is

a time and a circumstance that demand some rules should be broken. I have read your column for years, and on the whole, I have found it humane. But lately you seem to have put your head in the sand. Don't you know murder is going on? Each day our young men are being slain shamelessly, flouting our constitution, and yet you continue to write optimistic articles about the state of the world. It is shocking.

For while you never approve of the Pacification Program, you never actually express any disapproval. Somehow, you always manage to suggest that everything will turn out satisfactorily in the end.

But will it? Do you have a son of draft age? I did.

Christopher was twenty on his last birthday. When he was drafted, I was desolate, for I am a widow and he was my only child. He didn't want to go, he was a fine pianist, whose favorites were Bach, Mozart, and Beethoven. He hoped to become a concert performer, he was in music school, but this was not sufficient to defer him. His draft board said, Who needs music? and shipped him into the Pacification Program and the Territory. And Christopher, whose phrasing of Bach was beautifully clear, we'd argue and argue over the respective merits of Bach and Mozart, for me, Mozart was the loveliest thing I knew, wrote me: "No one listens to me here, the accents here are harsh and strident, there is nothing lovely here, death is everywhere and all we think of is to survive."

A few weeks ago there was a knock on my door and a tall, gray-haired sergeant stood there and I thought my heart would stop, I could hardly breathe, I knew what he was going to say before he said it. After he expressed his condolences, he added, "Of course there will be insurance benefits, gratuities based on the deceased's base pay, and remember, your son died bravely, in the service of his country. It is natural that you should react very emotionally."

I didn't say a word. Ever since Christopher was drafted I had expected this. I stood stunned while the sergeant bowed himself out.

Some time later a coffin arrived. But it couldn't be

opened because it contained unrecognizable remains. I was given an official document as proof. The receipt for the coffin said: *Non-viewable remains.*

I received also a statement of explanation: "We regret the circumstances of the deceased's death precluded restoring the remains to a viewable state. But before shipment the remains and the casket were inspected and found to be in a satisfactory condition. Yours sincerely, The Pacification Program."

But suddenly I was possessed with a feeling that the coffin didn't contain my son. If I could only touch his wavy hair, long at the back. I loved its curl, so pretty and yet so natural. Christopher didn't believe in futile sacrifices, he was the smartest boy in his class, and he was tall and the box was small. He was very definite about music, fun, living. I could imagine Christopher saying, "They have a hell of a nerve telling you that I am dead." But the casket was sealed.

And I was brought back to reality, for a friend of Chistopher's in the Pacification Program wrote me: "There wasn't much of the body left, we could only restore what remained with hope and faith. He was on a body count detail when he stepped on a mine. If it wasn't for his dog tag, he would have been totally unrecognizable. But he was lucky. At least he didn't get barbecued, like so many of the enemy."

There was also a letter from Christopher, only to be delivered to me if he were killed. He had written:

"Mother dear:

"Weep with me on this, the most unhappy and dreadful moment of my life. For when you read this, you will know that I am no more. The obscenity they call the Pacification Program has murdered me. I am no longer a person. I have become another number in the body count. Yet I had no voice in my fate. It was predetermined by those in power who were more concerned with protecting their privileges than my life. They must approve of what is happening, or they would have halted this senseless slaughter. And now I lie dead: Only you can speak for me. Only you can grant my final request.

"Please, inform the people—the silent majority and the

silent minority and all those who are silent—that their
silence is allowing this murder to go on. I wonder if they
really know what is happening. Do they actually see what is
taking place here? They must speak out, anyway they can,
to stop this murdering Pacification Program.

"Otherwise, mother dear, my death will have been in vain.

"Your eternally loving son. Christopher."

Alex halted. It was difficult to read on. But he couldn't be
that cruel, he told himself, this mother had nothing else left.

So, Alexander Grant, you must speak for Christopher. It
is the least you can do. No one will listen to me, but you
have a large audience. Already there are too many old men
telling young men murderous lies. We can no longer say to
our children they must kill the enemy. The eternal enemy.
What would these old men do without the enemy? Yes, they
are old, whatever their age, for they are against life. They
cannot exist without enemies. But we must. Or nothing will
be left.

Suppose the ice of the Arctic began to melt, or the sun's
heat began to diminish and all of us were suddenly struggling to survive together, who would we kill? Who would be
the enemy? Perhaps then, we would remember that we
belong first of all to humanity, to mankind.

What I propose is peace. Not peace through the Pacification Program, but peace because we believe in it. It is a
belief I pray that you share.

Christopher has no one else to speak for him. Will you?
Or do you think he died in vain?

                    Mrs. Christine Lister.

When Alex was a child he had frequent nightmares that
he would not live long enough to know love. He had
thought about this often, especially during his own wartime
service. And he had vowed that *his war*, as he referred to it,
must be the last war, yet war had been going on somewhere
in the world ever since. He had written a column about this
once, called *You Name the Year, I Will Name the War*.

But no one had heeded him. Staring at his typewriter, reflecting about this, he whispered to himself, "I am but one man, what does she expect of me." Yet titles formed in his mind such as: *In Memoriam. The Dehumanization of Youth. Why There Isn't Any Good News.* Only it were as if his typewriter was stuck and none of its keys would move.

At such moments, and they occurred often, Alex had a habit of arguing with his typewriter, calling her "old Stone Face," or "old Cold Face," or "old Iron Face," depending on his mood, and he was sure that his typewriter was a she, she was so contrary, and yet, in a way, *his girl.*

When nothing came from his writing that he liked, he snapped at his typewriter, "Go ahead, write. You don't need me, old Iron Face, I'm the one who needs you. You're the one who can't keep a secret. Go on, tell everything. But if people don't have some lie they can believe in, they'll hang themselves from the first tree or start walking around naked, as they're doing already. Marijuana, that's for infants, real old-fashioned now."

As Alex examined what he had written, he thought, It wasn't what he wanted to say in his column, but it was relaxing.

Or a way of saying nothing, he decided, in a sudden change of mood.

He banged hard on old Iron Face and wrote: "*Man Was. Man Is. Man Will Become. When Will Civilization Start.*"

No, no, no, these were not the titles he wanted.

"*Next. Next Next. Next Next Next. Next Next Next Next.*"

At least, he reflected, he was typing correctly. Old Iron Face was stiff this morning. Was it that he was afraid to commit himself? He believed the two letters he had just reread and he agreed that Sid and Christopher had been sacrificed needlessly, but he said to himself it was beyond his ability to alter anything. He felt lost in his speculations, and so he tried to find a realistic subject, perhaps an essay on the value of a civilized burial service in the Pacification Program. Those body counts were a perversion, he was convinced of that, the government didn't have to keep score that way.

Gradually old Iron Face seemed to be hearing what he

was saying, and he wrote a title he thought might work.

"*Hereafter Is Now*," had a sound he liked and it triggered his feelings.

He added, "We keep thinking about ending the Pacific-ation Program next year, or the next, but why don't we try to end it now."

Yet as he continued he began to equivocate. In his mind he wrote, "We must have peace now, whatever the price," but in his column he said, "However, we must not pay any price for peace, but we must examine all the possibilities."

Even so, when he finished this column he felt better. He knew he was not as outspoken as his son and Mrs. Lister urged, but he had brought the subject of body counts into the open. And one thing he stressed. At the end of his column he wrote: "As a parent I share with many parents their distaste for the government's growing obsession with the counting of bodies. We cannot use this as a measure of success. We cannot accept this practice with indifference. The Pacification Program's use of the body count as a proof of victory is offensive. If we cannot think of each human being as a unique and vital expression of life, our society has ceased to have any justification."

Now, Alex told himself, he could go with a free con-science to the dinner party which was being given this evening for two of the President's chief advisers. It would give him an opportunity to talk to them.

While he was finishing his column it started to rain and he was irritated. He had allotted two hours for tennis this afternoon and now that was impossible. He cursed the rain, and then decided—even though he didn't really believe it—that the rain was for the best, now he could answer the two letters immediately.

But as he searched for words that would be consoling yet sensible, he felt old Iron Face was grinning at him wickedly and whispering, "I can keep a secret. You didn't tell every-thing."

"Who would listen?" he replied. "Man is hostile, Man is a creature of action, Man will never change, Man is a killer ape,"—who had written that?—"Man will always be violent. History will always be the same, we can't change history."

Instead of writing this, old Iron Face was saying, "You temporized, played it safe."

No matter what he said, old Iron Face kept writing, "You temporized, played it safe." Old Iron Face, Alex thought, Self-Sufficiency herself. He could think of only one thing to change her rhythm, writing, "Let it be known that from now on this day is the birthday of my typewriter and I name her: Self-Sufficiency. Happy Birthday until her next."

But she answered, "You did temporize, play it safe."

Or was it Sid and Christopher saying that and old Iron Face was speaking for them?

# Submit the Dimensions

Submit the dimensions
Height and weight
Of the quality of air

The numerical quantity
Of the breeds of life
Birds or
Tigers or flowers or
Dust or

If you want
People there
Or just yourself
Or one other or

If you want
God there
Or

Would you promise
To live
There,
Not
Return here

Then I would create
The world
You ask for

One question first
Would you be
Sure,
Doubt
Is not allowed now since

Death
Will not exist there

STYMEAN KARLEN

# Submit the Dimensions

"Alex, there will be people here who will be useful," said Marcia Moderin, his hostess. "All you have to do is ask the right questions. I have invited some people of importance."

Good, but dinner parties were notorious for superficial conversation and Pacification was a sensitive subject. He wished he hadn't come to care about it; then it would be easier to discuss. Yet he mustn't be critical; Marcia was proud of her ability to attract important guests.

Marcia, a middle-aged widow, whose husband had acquired his fortune in chemicals and a wonderful collection of modern art—which he had bought as an investment—had invited Alex to her large colonial house in the suburbs as an expression of her esteem.

That is, she called it "esteem," Alex reflected, but he sensed it was something else. Now she stood at the foot of her wide, palatial staircase, her favorite spot for commanding attention. Marcia was tall and tanned and radiant with outdoor health, a handsome woman who used her charms carefully. She was unusually slim and attractive for forty, with a lithe body he associated with sensuality.

"I invited you early, Alex, so we could arrange for you to talk to the right people."

"Thank you. It was considerate of you."

"What are you doing this weekend, Alex?"

"Why?" She placed her hand in his in an instinctive gesture of friendship and he felt her warmth and affection.

She said in an appealing voice, "I have a secluded retreat in the hills. I thought you might enjoy seeing it. It is quite attractive."

"I would be delighted, but it depends."

"On what?" Marcia's voice, usually pleasant, sharpened.

"On whether I learn anything important tonight."

"You will. That is why I invited Graham Graves and Roger Shipmen."

"I thought you were giving the dinner party for them."

"I am really giving it for you, but I had to say it was for them. Otherwise, they would have been offended and they wouldn't have come. After all, they are presidential aides. Graham is his chief foreign policy adviser, while Roger, whatever the title, is his chief investigator. They could give you confidential information for your column."

"As long as I don't quote my sources."

"None the less, you will know *what* is true."

"But they can't stand the sight of each other. They are the leading competitors for the President's favor."

She beamed and said, "That will make it a fascinating party."

"Even if they end up disliking each other more?"

"It will be very amusing. You wouldn't want my evening to be a bore."

"Who else is expected?"

"Senator Upshaw and Senator Cotterick."

Alex whistled.

"You are surprised!" Marcia was delighted.

"Parry Upshaw is an ardent supporter of the Pacification Program, while Silas Cotterick is one of its harshest critics."

"Exactly. I told you it would be an interesting evening."

"Is there anybody else coming I should know about?"

"A few diplomats, several wives."

Nobody else that would interest you, she really meant, he thought, but he said, "With the two presidential aides and the two influential Senators it sounds like a session of a government committee."

"Possibly. I hope I have been helpful, Alex."

"It can't do any harm. I may get something out of it."

But Alex didn't respond as Marcia had expected, and

suddenly, looking disappointed, she withdrew her hand
from his.

Yet the dinner party started enjoyably. Alex knew most
of the guests and he was greeted cordially by them. He liked
being with people of importance, it gave him a feeling of importance. Marcia sat at the head of the table in a doge's
chair of Venetian red and gold, and everything in the dining
room was bright and shiny under the chandelier she had im-
ported from Europe. Alex was pleased that she sat him
across from the two guests he desired to talk to the most,
Graham Graves and Roger Shipmen. But he was surprised
that she placed them next to each other. Surely they would
suspect something devious in this arrangement.

Instead the two presidential aides acted as if they were
firm friends and gave little attention to anyone else, except
Senator Upshaw who sat on Graves's right and Senator
Cotterick who sat on Shipmen's left.

The four men, as if to disprove the rumours of hostility,
chatted animatedly throughout the dinner. For men who
liked to hold forth, reflected Alex, they were being attentive
to each other. There seemed to be a common flow between
them, as if they had found a conversational bond. And now,
in the art gallery of Marcia's spacious colonial house, they
were still carrying on their animated discussion.

He wondered how to interrupt them. While all of them
knew him, he couldn't afford to risk offending any of them.
He pretended he was admiring the original Monets,
Pissaros, and the Rodin on the end table.

He studied the eighteen-inch-high Thinker; he didn't like
it as much as the life-sized original he had seen many times,
which he felt was the most powerful figure he had experienced, that struck him as a reproach to what *Man Was*.
But who would give a damn here? Whatever Rodin had
done, no one was noticing. The discussion had become so
spirited, they must be talking about affairs of state. The
view through the picture window was of a magnificent
grassy lawn, a beautiful garden, splendid oak trees, and it
was being ignored.

As their conversation grew more intense, Alex thought

there was no handsomer man in the government than Graham Graves, but he was small, five foot four, a self-made professor who had risen from one scholarship to another, until now, he had won the most potent scholarship of all.

Roger Shipmen, who was ten years younger at forty, was the athlete in the government; he took great pains to cultivate this aspect of the presidential personality, he was large, rugged, thick-chested.

Senator Upshaw, the one man at the party who rivalled Graves in good looks, was an elder statesman. Seventy, with elegant white hair which sat upon him like a crown, his regular features were shaped with a perfection that was arresting. When he stretched out his hands for attention, he looked like a biblical prophet with an amazing appearance of sincerity. Yet when he became passionate in discussion, as now, Alex noticed he had a habit of scratching his crotch, a nervous twitch that was like an unconscious leer.

Senator Cotterick was an attractive man also—Marcia preferred good-looking men, her women guests were inclined to be plain—and he was tall and broad-shouldered. His dark eyes stressed his skill as a questioner. Every line on his deeply lined face was etched as if it had come from careful thought, as if nothing in his appearance was superficial.

Suddenly, feeling desperate at the way he was being ignored, Alex picked up the Thinker and brought his arm back as if to throw the statue through the window. "Oh, no!" cried Graves. "You don't pass that way."

When he saw Alex's surprise he was apologetic. "I'm sorry, Alex, I shouldn't have criticized you, you were one of the finest passers I ever saw. As I was telling them."

Alex realized with surprise the intense conversation they were indulging in was about football.

Graves added, "I was telling our friends that you were the most deceptive quarterback of your time."

Alex put the Thinker down and suggested, "Because I ran, too, when I played quarterback?"

Graves said emotionally, "I will never forget your ability to fake."

"Yes," said Alex. "I wasn't bad at faking."

"You were a master. When you started on an end sweep I don't think anyone knew for sure whether you were going to pass or run."

"Sometimes I didn't know either."

Cotterick said, "That is what I liked about football in our day—one could improvise. Now however, everything is cut and dried."

Shipment asked, "You played varsity football, didn't you, Senator?"

"Guard, if I remember," Alex interjected, "and was Phi Beta Kappa."

"That will get no votes," Upshaw grunted, "but football might."

Cotterick said, "Guards weren't exciting, but Alexander Grant was."

Shipmen asked, "Grant, why didn't you play for money?"

"The war came along."

"And young men didn't try to get out of it as they do now."

"Perhaps, sir, that is because of the Pacification Program."

"What is wrong with the Program?"

"Couldn't we move a little faster towards peace, Mr. Shipmen?"

"We are. We have established a kill ratio of ten to one."

"But how can we justify a policy based on how many bodies we kill?"

"Don't you trust our figures?" Shipmen looked quite forbidding.

Alex felt uncomfortable, but he had to venture on. "I'm sure they are accurate, if you say so, Mr. Shipmen. But that is not the point."

"What is?"

"Mothers fathers brothers sisters husbands wives sons daughters."

"We love mothers as much as anyone," declared Roger Shipmen.

"That is why I'm interested in your view. If you could explain why we need a body count to justify the Program it would be helpful."

"We have to accept things as they are."

"Nonsense, Shipmen," said Cotterick. "I've received a number of letters from the Territory pointing out how vicious this practice is."

"Rubbish," retorted Upshaw, scratching his crotch with a new vigor. "They're traitors. Everybody gets these crackpot letters today."

"Have you, sir?" asked Alex.

"Of course." Upshaw's irritability grew. "I burn them. Peace must be enforced at the end of a gun barrel. Do you think everybody is muddle-headed like my good friend, Cotterick? Are you a peace monger, Grant, like the wet-behind-the-ass college students?"

"Sir, I am merely raising a few questions."

"Don't."

"None the less," said Cotterick, in his rumbling bass, "the Territory isn't exactly the garden spot of the world."

"What is?" said Upshaw. "Is your constituency? Your party would vote telegraph poles if they had to. But I find your opposition to Pacification offensive. Peace, at this point, would be an indulgence."

The two senators squared off as if to attack each other and Shipmen stepped between them and said, "In any event, Pacification is a fact of life and we have to live with it. Correct, Grant?"

Before Alex could reply Graham Graves took him by the arm and away from the others and said, "Let them squabble, they'll settle nothing."

"What is your view, sir?"

"Alex, I was delighted to hear you were coming. I have been eager to talk to you about the university's prospects this season. I am told your son is going to be the varsity quarterback. That sounds encouraging. He must have inherited some of your talent."

"Are you sure, sir, he is going to play?"

"Graham, Alex. We know each other that well, at least in private."

"Suppose my son doesn't play?"

"He must. He is the best quarterback we have. I have

heard from the best sources. I can't quote them, not officially, but that's true."

"I didn't know football mattered this much to you, Graham."

"It is one of the things the President and I have in common. He is an ardent fan. He would love to talk football with you. He has always admired you as a football player."

"That was a long time ago."

"You still look like you could play. You haven't grown old or fat."

"That is why I'm concerned about the Pacification Program."

"So am I. When I was in the university—I am a graduate, and I am still on the teaching staff, with leave—my great ambition was to make the team. If I could have played quarterback in just one game . . . !"

Graham Graves was ecstatic at the idea, but it was different than the chief adviser imagined, thought Alex.

There had been moments when he was hit so violently he expected his fingers to be torn from his palm, his palm from his arm, that he would shatter into many pieces. It was easier to talk of instant success that came after weeks of driving work. Sometimes he was so scared of the cheap shots the opposition took when he wasn't looking and the officials were engaged elsewhere. When after a necktie tackle he feared his neck would break or his head would fall off and his eyes blurred and his thighs became so heavy he was unable to stand. Or the times his metal jock supporter was so bent by a deliberate kick in the groin that if he hadn't worn it protectively he would have been damaged for life. It was easy to be romantic and nostalgic, afterwards. Then, savoring the pleasures of victory, out of the muddy pants and away from the dirt, football was a recipe against anonymity, old age, death. It was easy to brag then, to look backwards with a loving remembrance. But he had never loved football playing it as he did leaving it. Football had been a duty, like war; it was something he had been frightened doing, and more frightened not to do. He had gone out for football originally to prove to himself that he could play, that he could make the team, no matter how he was terrified, and he spent the next six years of high school and university football proving himself and hiding his fears. Running wide, running fast, running elusively, bringing his knees up to smack back, proud of his straight arm which was like a left hook, or passing just as he was about to be hit, he thought only the sadists and masochists on the team enjoyed it. But there were times when a rage rose in him that drove him to hit back with anger; moments when he got so mad nothing mattered but to hit back. He wondered if the President and his chief adviser would have loved football so much if they had played. But perhaps they needed their dreams.

"Alex, you were one of the best quarterbacks we ever had."

"I was quick, I had good peripheral vision, and I was lucky."

"I doubt that. Alex, the last time you won *The Game*, did the enemy really try to knock you out?"

"Of course. They tried to kick the shit out of me."

Graves looked thoughtful, then he said animatedly, "But they didn't. You really put it to them. You beat them 35–7. It was the worst licking they took in many years. It is the spirit we need now."

"Is that why we are using the body count to prove we are winning?"

"Alex, don't you want Pacification to succeed?"

He hesitated; he wasn't sure. Then he said, "I want peace."

"Of course. So do I. I am passionately interested in peace. Anything that will improve our chances of peace I will listen to."

Peace with victory, thought Alex, peace by a score of 601–60, and dreams of power and glory, and sometime in the twenty-first century perhaps? Zoom bang! Would the kids be playing with rockets then instead of toy pistols? When James had begun to walk he had given his son a toy football instead of a gun.

"I've an abiding interest in peace, I've been studying it for years."

Marcia was standing beside them, exclaiming, "I'm

delighted you two are getting on so well! Now I know my party is a success!"

"Indeed!" replied Graves. "I've admired Alex for a long time."

Graves looked so proud that *he was* the confidant of the football hero, Alex realized the chief adviser like so many men who had not been good at sports had an inordinate regard for those who were. Shipmen and the senators had followed Marcia and they were thanking her for such a charming evening when her son burst into the room.

Stan was looking for his Mom. He needed money. He had decided to cut his classes for the rest of the week when he had gotten a lift home from the university. Bearded, long-haired, Stan was dressed in his uniform, Levis, Army fatigue shirt and sandals.

"No, I'm not hungry, Mom!" he shouted, anticipating her question. "Got some change? Some kids are waiting outside for me but they're broke."

Marcia smiled embarrassedly but Graves said, "How much do you need?"

"Ten bucks will do it."

As Graves handed him ten dollars, Marcia said, "You know, Mr. Graves, of course, and Mr. Shipmen. And I would like you to meet Senator Upshaw and Senator Cotterick."

"Hi!"

But when Stan saw Alex, he paused on his way out the door and said, "You're James Grant's old man, aren't you?"

"Yes. Why?"

"Didja know he was quitting the team?"

Alex tried to appear surprised and exclaimed, "No!"

"Yep. He claims it ain't relevant."

"Relevant to what?" asked Graves, frowning.

"All this crap that is going on."

Marcia cried out, "Stanley, I can't imagine what you're talking about!"

"Hell, I'd better get out."

"Stanley, aren't you going to thank Mr. Graves for his loan?"

"Hi."

Stan was almost out the door when Shipmen's voice, harsh and demanding, halted him. "You are certain that James Grant is quitting the football team as a protest against the Pacification Program?"

"That's what he says. He claims it's a dead bag. He's got it bad."

"Got what?" questioned Shipmen.

"The protest scene, man. He says if the Pacification Program doesn't stop soon he's going to parade naked on the football field."

"Are you sure?" Alex asked. He was startled.

"Sure! It'll be wild!"

Shipment asked, "When is this supposed to happen?"

"He hasn't said. If he told you, you could stop him."

Upshaw declared, "I take a quite serious view of nakedness. There is entirely too much undressing taking place these days."

"Oh," said Stan, "I don't think it is such a big thing. What is so important about being naked?"

"It's obscene!" yelled Upshaw.

"Why? James ain't got any lice on him. He's just psyched-up these days. He says the Pacification Program stinks." Stan was gone before anybody else could stop him.

There was a deathly silence as Alex felt that everyone was accusing him. Then he mumbled, "I didn't know anything about this."

Graves said sadly, "But evidently your son has been a little less than honest with you."

"James didn't lie about it. He just didn't mention it."

Upshaw stated, "Your son should have told you. There could be unfortunate consequences."

"Do your children tell you everything, Senator?"

"They're grown up."

Shipmen asked, "Grant, what are you going to do about it?"

"I don't know."

Upshaw declared, scratching his crotch, "Grant, young people need discipline. They have to be told what to do. They don't always appreciate this, but you should. Marcia, I am sure you are aware of this, too."

She said ruefully, "I'm aware that if I question Stanley, he won't tell me anything. It's better to have some of his confidences than none at all."

Shipmen said, "Grant, you ought to talk to your son."

Graves added, "Before he does anything rash. It would be tragic for him to give up such a promising career. You must talk to him, Alex."

"I'll try."

Upshaw said contemptuously, "You don't sound very hopeful."

"Did your children tell you everything when they were twenty-two?"

"They didn't have to. They didn't do such obscene things."

Cotterick said, "At least, none they told you about, Upshaw. Alex is right. We can't blame him for what his son does. And we shouldn't blame the boy either. He is not the only one who is offended by the high-handed way the government has sucked us into the Pacification Program without consulting the people or their representatives."

Upshaw looked outraged; Shipmen smiled a chilling smile that said absolutely nothing; but Graves said in a fatherly tone, "It is natural to be rebellious at that age, but the boy will get over it. I'm sure he will see the light when Alex explains to him the facts of life."

After the other guests were gone Alex, who remained at Marcia's request, told her that he would love to visit her mountain retreat but he must see his son first. If Marcia was disappointed, she didn't show it. Instead, as she escorted him to the door she said, "If you want Graham Graves's approval, you've got to like him."

"I tried, but he acted as if the Pacification Program was inevitable."

"He was gracious to you. He took possession of you and turned his back on the other guests."

"He has a thing about football."

"And you have a thing about the Pacification Program."

"I didn't criticize anybody. I merely raised a few questions."

"But criticism was evident, whatever you didn't say. Alex,

you ought to be more careful. There are some things you shouldn't say."

"I've already done so. In the column I wrote this morning."

She shook her head sadly, "Alex, you are too sensitive. You can be very sweet, really, and amusing, and your feeling about politics is often excellent, but there are some things you feel too deeply. If you allow them to dominate you, you will never get on with Graham and Roger."

"Perhaps we can arrange something next week."

"Perhaps. Give me a ring, Alex."

"I will." But what was he waiting for, he wondered. He noticed that her servants were gone, that they were alone, and that behind her concern was passion. Her vivid blue eyes glowed with desire; she was letting down her light brown hair which was bleached blond by the sun; her tall, enticing figure had such a slant it seemed to be beckoning to his arms. At this instant he realized the place, the moment, the situation, the need, and her appeal harmonized. Her expression said why waste this lovely opportunity. Better still, she understood what he was thinking. Before he could do anything clumsy, she took him by the hand and she led him upstairs to her bedroom.

It was a seductive chamber, spacious and fragrantly scented, and remote from anything else. The bed was large, which Alex preferred, and the crimson quilt was suggestively sensual.

This was a familiar situation to Alex and he undressed swiftly.

Yet as he penetrated her easily and expertly, he thought, Her breasts were squashy as if she had been fondled too much. For a moment, too, he was comparing her unfavorably to the three women he had married and the two he had loved. Then her body called him with an extreme, abrupt urgency, to pleasure, to triumph, to an instant of ecstasy, and now he didn't need any reasons for what was happening.

Later, as Marcia fondled his powerful, muscular arms she commented on his vigor. But it was more like frenzy, he thought. For a brief time he had been driven by an overwhelming physical craving. The vital thing had been not

Marcia, but his desire. After the tension of the dinner party sexual release had become a necessity. Marcia had been not the worst woman he had known, but she had been not the best either. And now, as she lay in his arms, he wondered who else had occupied her bed. Was she using his sexual efforts as therapy? Or for relief? Marcia, with all of her passion, had been remote.

As he sat up to get out of bed, she said, "Don't go. Not yet."

"I must. Before my son does something irrevocable."

"One's emotions are intensified when they are neglected."

"An attractive woman like you must have many admirers."

"You're the first man I've known in a long time. When you've been accustomed to love, it is very difficult to do without it."

After they had been joined to each other again, she murmured this was an improvement, and he thought, Now I am there, I have completed the circuit, replaced the irreplaceable, my self has fitted her self, and any improvement in the situation would only make matters worse.

"I was wondering when you would show up," said James.

Alex stood in the doorway of his son's room at the university.

"Well, what are you waiting for?"

"I hope that I am not intruding."

"Would that stop you, Alexander? Would you leave?"

Alex glanced around the room to get his bearings. There were pictures on the wall of James in his football uniform, which was a good sign, and his books were piled neatly in a corner as if they were being used and music records were stacked carefully in a wall cabinet of obvious importance. This was all that was tidy. Clothes and papers littered the room where James had dropped them. He had been reading a newspaper when his father had entered. It was the night after the dinner party and Alex had driven all day, often above the speed limit, to get here. But now he asked himself if his sense of urgency was necessary.

James looked casual. He was fully dressed. Like Stan, he

wore Levis, an old Army fatigue shirt, and sandals. Alex was relieved that his son had not grown a beard yet, although James's hair was much longer than it had been when they had seen each other last.

James said, "To what do I owe the honor of this visit, Alexander?"

Alex said, "I thought there were some things we could talk over."

When they faced each other as James stood up, Alex was taller, as always, and he wondered if his son still resented that. Both of them, actually, up to this moment, he reflected, had said nothing that mattered.

James's lean, angular face grew taut and his brown eyes became somber as he stared at Alex, and then he did something Alex remembered from early childhood. James unconsciously began to curl his already curly hair with his fingers, a habit that indicated tension.

"Did you get my letter, Alexander?"

"Yes."

"I thought so. I've been reading your last column."

"James, it was influenced by what you suggested."

"It still tastes like baloney."

"I questioned the Pacification Program and the body count."

"What you wrote won't change anything."

"That would be idyllic to expect. At least, right away."

"How many fellows are dying *right away*? Sixty, they said last week."

"James, I sympathize with your feelings. I want to be on your side."

"As long as I don't embarrass you. I know why you've come. You want me to return to football. Carry on the family name and all that jazz."

Alex smiled despite his son's seriousness.

"You don't think I can?"

"I didn't say that."

"I know you don't expect me to live up to your feats. You were varsity quarterback three years in a row, the only one to win *The Game* each year. They still got your number in the trophy case. No one has worn it since."

Alex burst out laughing.

"What's funny?" James looked indignant.

"I was a pacifist. The only reason I played well was to save my skin."

But James thought his father was making fun of him and he stated, "Today, that isn't funny. I can't go on the field to kill, kill, kill, and still be against the Pacification Program. I'm not returning to the football team, whatever you say."

"This isn't why I'm here."

James didn't believe him.

If he told his son how scared he had been, perhaps that would convince him. But he couldn't. His football record was one of the few things James seemed to respect. He said, "I am concerned about the story that you are going to parade naked on the football field."

"Clothes, that's a fetish."

"Then why do you think parading naked will halt Pacification?"

"Who told you?"

"Stan Moderin."

"Stan talks too much. He's stoned most of the time. He's on The Great Detour. He's copped out. He's put a blanket over his head. But it's too soon to talk about what's going to happen here."

"Yet you want me to express your point of view?"

"I spelled it out, and so did Sid."

"I'm still not sure what it is."

"We don't want the world to be a complete failure. Our Students' Union is asking that Pacification be stopped in a year, and they want the university to join them, but I want Pacification halted now."

"Parading naked on the football field will accomplish that?"

"Maybe I should fly over their heads on a swing like I used to in the playground when I was a kid."

Alex smiled in appreciation of that idea, then said, "But all that will happen is they'll throw you in jail for indecent exposure."

"At least some people will realize how strongly we feel."

"Do the authorities know about your proposed protest?"

"They may. The campus police are watching me, and they have put a plain-clothes man in several of my classes."

"You're kidding, James."

"Not on your life. I'm one of their public enemies."

"Who? You just can't accuse the air."

"The university. The government. The establishment."

"Then you shouldn't risk your education."

"You mean, risk your situation."

Alex was silent.

"Besides, this is *my* education. I've grown up, I don't want to inherit the world your generation has given us."

Matters were getting out of hand and Alex, to regain his composure, asked, "May I sit down?" They had been standing ever since he had arrived, as if they were in a gym seeking to outdo each other in fitness. He was tired and stiff, and that was affecting his thinking.

"Suit yourself."

"Where? Everything is littered with clothes and papers."

"Oh, you'd rather have me waste my time cleaning up." James kicked dungarees off his bed, said, "Put your ass there. If it fits." But as Alex sat, his son added, "But don't get set. I've a meeting to attend and it could take the rest of the night and you wouldn't want to go."

"Should I wait?"

"Not unless you want to write your column here."

"And you will dictate it?"

"Why not. At least I would speak out."

"No thanks." Alex stood up wearily, feeling he had wasted the day, perhaps even a vital part of his life.

As James saw the weariness spread across his father's face, for once not the attractive, assured, perfectly groomed man whose surface was like a smooth stone, he forgot to set his jaw or to glare and he said less belligerently, "It is true you have disappointed me so far, but your last column was an improvement. At least, you did question a little. But you didn't speak out enough. You are too inhibited."

Alex had to avoid James's eyes. How could he tell his son about his extensive sexual life? Or explain that James had been the result of an accident, that he had married James's mother only when she had become pregnant without his wanting her to. His son was staring at him with a strange look in his eyes. Did James know? Had Rita told their son after all to spite him? She had always thought it monstrous of him to resent marrying her, and even worse when he had divorced her. He didn't have the courage to ask James; James would never forgive that.

"I'll swing over their heads with a rhythm of my own."

"What?"

"Naked. On a swing. As I told you before."

James was putting him on. He must be, anything else was unthinkable. But he said, "Are you prepared to take the consequences?"

"Yes. Are you?"

With that, Alex stood up.

"Alexander, as I said, *Hereafter Is Now* was better, but not good enough. You are, I repeat, too inhibited. I'll be seeing you."

"When?"

"When you write something I can trust."


Alex almost went off the road on his drive home. Of all the words to choose! It rained all the way and as his window wiper moved back and forth with a monotonous regularity it seemed to be saying over and over, "Inhibited ... Inhibited ... Inhibited ..." Yet when he shut it off he couldn't see clearly and he hit the shoulder and almost lost control.

He had to turn the window wiper on again for safety and as he drove through the night he felt he was hurtling through a great void. Most of the time he was the only car on the road and except for the lights on the highway everything was dark and he was dreadfully alone.

To quiet his nerves and the scrape of the window wiper he turned on his car radio and instead of the music he desired, there was the inevitable news on the hour and he was confined by a lewd, malign voice, announcing murder rape riot flood and always the Pacification Program and its body count. Their figures were announced each hour. Alex had decided to drive through the night, pushed by a need to flee from his son's facts, but there was no escaping them. By the third news broadcast he knew the numbers by heart.

"Our weekly casualties—fifty-nine dead."

"Enemy dead for the week—one thousand and eleven."

Weren't they satisfied with a ten to one kill ratio, he thought angrily. Whatever radio station he turned on, the news arrived each hour. Wasn't there any place where a man could find privacy?

At four a.m. there was an addition to the news.

"The Pacification Program is happy to announce that our casualties are the lowest in several years. While the total of our losses in the last ten years is just fifty-two thousand, and one hundred, we have liberated six hundred and sixty-six thousand, six hundred and one of the enemy."

Seconds later the commercials came on, the detergent, the mouth wash, the deodorant, and the announcer sounding like the Messiah.

Disgusted, Alex snapped back, "Buzz ... buzzz ... buzzzz ... buzzzzz ..."

The noise didn't stop. If he could only hear some Mozart, he thought in his desperation. The only music he could get on the car radio was loud, raucous country music and he turned it off angrily.

So he drove on in an agonized blur of time, filled with a sense of shame, feeling even more alone in this wet and dark and cold, and wondering how conciliation could ever succeed.


Alex was still dejected when he fell asleep the next morning at his apartment. And he didn't find any peace as he had hoped.

As he tossed restlessly it was still raining, the echo of guns sounded everywhere, he was in a nightmarish haze, and he found himself sitting in a ghostly auditorium. There was a fanfare of drums and the lights became a blood-red and he saw the President, as if in a news conference, standing on the stage behind a podium, saying, "It is just a question of time. Time will take care of everything. Even the Pacification Program. Any shit-ass can understand."

Yet suddenly the President's dark suit with its delicate gray pin-stripes and its painfully proper design fell off him and he had nothing on. It was rather silly, reflected Alex. For the President, naked, had one of the most uncomplimentary bodies that Alex had ever seen.

Alex thought that if he were as skinny and bony and thin-chested as the President he would never reveal himself to anyone else. But the President didn't speak but waved his penis at Alex like a gun and Alex expected him to ejaculate bullets. Instead the penis grew and grew until it was a huge automatic carbine pressed against Alex's throat with the muzzle under his chin. He closed his eyes to shut it out, and then he heard a shot, and when he opened his eyes he saw a burst melon at his feet, or was it a shattered head?

"Who threw this up on stage?" he heard someone cry. "This doesn't have a face!"

However, the man who stood on stage now was not recognizable, although he was fully dressed in a military uniform. Alex couldn't tell what his rank was because medals covered every inch of his body, they were even on his fingers and toes, and there wasn't any trace of the President.

The officer stood in front of a giant computer and his face kept changing. At first it wore Graham Graves's amiable smile, then it contorted into Roger Shipmen's stern expression, and now suddenly, it was leaning toward Alex with Marcia Moderin's pleading expression.

But the voice was metallic, stating, "I question whether a different body count is necessary at all. We could compute one basic figure each week with a varying total to fit the ratio when it fluctuates. When you get down to it, all the corpses look just about the same."

Alex shouted up from the audience, "What about Sid Virgin?"

"Poor old Sid, that was hard luck."

"What about Christopher?"

"Don't know him. Thank heavens for that."

"My son, James?"

"Is his body decomposed? We don't count them."

"And all the others?"

"This is the largest computer in the world. It can count all the bodies in the universe. Nobody will get ahead of us. Ha . . . ha . . . ha . . . ."

"What about all the others?"

"We have the best bomb production is our history, the Territory is a fine target, a great target, we got to take their heads off, oh, nothing personal, we mustn't get nervous, we got enough hospitals and graves to handle everybody."

When Alex awoke from this dream he thought he had been in a kind of madness, and he sought to shut it out of his mind. He sat at old Iron Face trying to decide what to write for his next column and she said, "Describe the President naked," and he replied, "I don't dare," and disgusted with old Iron Face's obstinacy, ignoring the news, desperately needing to feel cheerful, he titled his column, "*Come the Millennium*," and half facetiously but also half seriously, he suggested it would be healthy for the country to take a vacation from politics for a little while, and then, perhaps, everybody could practice the virtues of moderation and conciliation.

He felt better when he finished this column, although old Iron Face was resisting him and he made more mistakes than usual.

She kept saying, "I told you so!" but when he retorted, "Told me what?" the answers he got were wrong keys like $q$, $y$, $x$, $z$, keys he tried to avoid as much as possible.

He was rereading his column for possible mistakes, when he received a second letter from Christine Lister. Very curious, Alex opened her note at once and read:

"I want to thank you for speaking out against the body count, although I wish you had quoted my son's letter. But under the circumstances, perhaps that was too much to expect. Christopher is just one of a multitude of dead boys, and you must get many letters on this subject. You are a public man . . ."

Naturally, he nodded as he read on.

". . . and since you have not experienced the loss of a son yourself . . ."

How would she know that, he wondered.

". . . or you would have written about it, I could not

expect you to feel the way I do. But I am grateful that you spoke as a parent, and spoke for other parents. It is a good first step, even if it is only a small step. At this point I appreciate whatever is done in behalf of life."

Alex answered this letter, although ordinarily he never answered letters from readers. He thanked Mrs. Lister for her interest in his views, and added, "When I wrote that column I sought to write it with your feeling, to put down as much as I could of what you expressed."

He was congratulating himself on how sensibly he had behaved in this situation, when there was a long-distance telephone call from James. For a moment he was tempted to hang up on his son; then, hearing a note of urgency in James's voice, he had a feeling of hope—his son must have changed his mind about his column or about quitting the football team.

James said, "Alexander, you forgot to give me my allowance."

"No, I didn't. It isn't due until next week."

"So you're being vengeful now. You're going to keep me waiting."

"Are you returning to the football team?"

"I can't even get into the stadium if you don't give me some money."

"To protest? To parade naked?"

"Stan has a thing about walking around bare-ass."

"What about my column? Does it still offend you?"

"Do you know how many words there are in the English language?"

"No."

"About three hundred thousand."

"So." Alex wasn't sure that James was right.

"Why don't you use more of them!"

"James, you want to smash things before you know what you are going to put in their place."

"Peace would be a start. Or aren't they giving that away these days?"

"How much money do you want?"

"What you owe me. My allowance."

"I'll put it in the mail today."

"Could you wire it? I need it quick."

"Is it because of a girl?"

"You are old-fashioned. I'm not like you. It is not a girl."

"What do you mean like me?"

"You've been married three times. I wouldn't try to keep up with you. Do I get the money right away? You always say, I don't have to tell you what it is for."

"I'll send it on immediately."

"Okay." James hung up.

A second later the telephone rang again and as Alex picked up the receiver, thinking that his son had decided to say thanks, Marcia said, "Your column surprised me. Graham and Roger could be quite offended."

"I said nothing that hasn't been said before."

"But they are your friends, Alex."

"Marcia, when is your son being drafted?"

"He's got a medical deferment. Nerves, I think. But what has that got to do with it. You mustn't rock the boat."

"Have Graves or Shipmen spoken to you about my column?"

"Of course not!" Marcia was indignant. "I'm your friend. I'm expecting you at my mountain retreat this weekend. Just the two of us."

"Thanks. Will you excuse me? I have to finish my column."

"I hope it is more sensible this time."

"It is what I call *A General Purpose* column. One about conciliation and moderation that should please almost everybody."

"That should be of great interest. You do know what readers like."

But as soon as Alex put down the telephone it rang again. This time it was Graham Graves, which was unusual, and what was more unusual, the President's chief adviser didn't want to talk politics.

"The purpose of my call," he said, "is personal. The President is sneaking off tomorrow to my country place to play some tennis with me and Roger, and he thought you might like to join us. The President loves a fast game of tennis, and you play quite well, you are especially good on the back-

hand side and a splendid retriever, and he likes that kind of
partner, and he has always admired you as a football
player."

"I'm honored, Graham,"

"I hope you are in good shape. I've got a damned sharp
drop shot."

The sergeant assigning the two privates to the Land
Clearing Specialty acted as if he was doing them a favor.
The square-faced, broad-jawed non-com, who never had
been able to hold on to a civilian job because he had always
gotten into brawls with his fellow workers, assured them,
"This detail is a cinch. Pacification has slowed down, we've
liberated this Kill Zone, there ain't none of the ·enemy
around. All you got to do is make sure that this stretch of
the highway is clean, free of garbage. We don't want any
garbage going off in anybody's face."

"Yes, yes," the first private said uneasily. The sergeant
was scraping his ass so he knew it must be a dirty detail, but
if he objected he would only get something worse.

The second private thought, The sergeant sounds like a
good guy. He was a replacement, new to the Territory and
to this detail, and he felt relieved. His only other Pacification service had been a few days on a body count detail,
and that had been a mess, almost as bad as being in the
bush, where, he had heard, the odds were even money that
he would get his ass shot off. Maybe the sergeant had given
him a break even if he was from Headquarters.

"Nobody will take any shots at you," the sergeant said.
"There ain't any crap around here. We cleaned them out
long ago."

But after the sergeant was gone, the first private, who was
the leader, was in no hurry to move on. At twenty-two he
was the old man on this detail. He had been on this dead-
guy run fifteen times. Maybe this part of the Territory was
free of the enemy as the sergeant had stated, he reflected,
but his mines and booby traps were everywhere. Casualties
were nearly as high as in the bush and often more unpleasant. Even though this bomb and mine clearing squad
was called the Land Clearing Specialty, he thought of it as

the venereal detail. Almost all of the booby traps and mines exploded upwards into the genitals; he had seen two of his buddies lose their balls; it was worse than gonorrhoea or syphilis. So he could only think of the sergeant who had assigned him to this detail as Sergeant Syphilis and the general who commanded it as General Gonorrhoea. And now he had an inexperienced cover, a tall, thin kid with pale blue eyes and blond hair and so naive. Buck Fever believed Sergeant Syphilis.

The second private wondered what the first private was waiting for. He was nervous and he wasn't sure how grown up his voice sounded, but as he stared at the short, stocky red-haired vet he was paired with, who was always humming a tune that made him want to jig, he said, "The sergeant could be right. I don't hear any shots being fired in anger."

"And you won't, Buck Fever, not here."

"Then what are we waiting for, Jazz Boy?"

"For my stomach to settle."

"Are you scared?"

"I haven't been farting for nothing." Jesus Christ, the first private thought, with such a partner who needed an enemy!

"Why does this road have to be checked? It looks okay to me."

"It's another fucking V.P., this is the third time I've had to clear this fucking road for one."

"For General Gonorrhoea?"

"No. It's for the Vice-President himself."

"Spleeno Bludgeon?"

"Yes. I hear he's coming to show how patriotic he is. He figures that it will get him votes back home. And we've been given the honor of making sure he is safe, so he can taste blood without any risk."

"But the sergeant said there wasn't any danger here."

"There mustn't be when Spleeno Bludgeon comes along."

"Did you vote for him, Jazz Boy?"

"No."

"I didn't either."

"Why not, Buck Fever?"

"I'm too young," the second private confessed ashamedly.

"I didn't vote at all. What was the use," the first private said resignedly, "I'm still here." He knew he shouldn't have gone to college. It was too dangerous. If he hadn't gone to college, he wouldn't have gotten this venereal detail. And he should have volunteered instead of waiting to be drafted; then he would have had a decent chance to make Division Headquarters, which was very rear.

"Maybe we'll be lucky," suggested the second private.

"Better to be careful," said the first private. "Let's go." He caressed his anti-personal detector and detonator. He hated this venereal detail; at least in the bush he could shoot back.

They had just started on their piece of the road when they heard a loud whoompf and they both jumped. But it was only the armor-plated bulldozer which was working the vegetation and the trees off the road.

The first private said, "They must have hit some anti-personal stuff in the trees. We don't have to worry about that."

"Do you think anybody got it?" At least it wasn't us, thought Buck Fever, with relief.

Jazz Boy shrugged and muttered, "Keep your own ass down."

"Because of the mines?"

"Yes. It's better to get it in the ass than in the balls."

The next few minutes they detonated two small mines on the road without any damage to themselves, although they left two large holes.

The first private said, "Sergeant Syphilis will be annoyed."

"Why?"

"The road will be bumpy. General Gonorrhoea doesn't like that. He's got back trouble, I hear, a slipped disc from too much sitting."

But the second private was thinking that this venereal detail wasn't as bad as the first private had intimated, although he felt it was funny there were none of the natural sounds of nature around them, not a bird or a bee or an insect of any kind, and he was a country boy and used to such things.

The first private said, "Do you think General Gonorrhoea

or Sergeant Syphilis will give us the time of the day after we make this road safe for Spleeno Bludgeon?"

Before the second private could reply, he saw his partner step toward a broken branch. Yet it wasn't a branch, he realized in the next moment, but a disguised wire. Instinctively he jumped back, and then he yelled, "Look out!" He heard a click—why hadn't he yelled first instead of jumping back, he thought guiltily—and an anti-personal mine blew up under the first private.

He fell face downwards crying, "Jesus Christ, they got my balls. I ain't got no balls . . . Oh, God, it hurts!" Then he slid forward, his elbows digging into the earth, his helmet falling over his ears.

His cover tried to lift him up. But the second private couldn't move. He had been knocked flat by the explosion. Then he realized that it didn't matter. The first private had become a basic statistic.

Suddenly the second private was yelling from pain. The mine had blown steel fragments into his legs and he couldn't get up. Then the pain was so awful he thought there was nothing more beautiful than to end it.

When the helicopter arrived and the medic and his morphine eased his pain, he heard the medic whisper, "You're lucky, you still got your balls." And as the medic, who looked hardly older than himself, loaded him on the litter, he added, "Here you go, on to the butcher block."

The second private saw the medic put a leg next to him on the litter but the medic must be kidding, he decided, it must belong to the first private. His leg hurt so much he could feel every pulse beat, and he put his hand down to his knee and nothing was there.

Soon after Sergeant Syphilis announced that the road was free of garbage and a little later Spleeno Bludgeon was able to ride on it with General Gonorrhoea. The Vice-President praised the quiet; he could hear himself praying that nothing would damage his person.

Although General Gonorrhoea was annoyed that the holes in the road had not been filled and that this part of the road was bumpy and his back was jolted so severely it ached, he replied proudly, "Our Land Clearing Specialty is an essential phase of our Pacification Program. We had a special investigation to be certain that the road was clean. There was considerable danger here not so long ago. This part of the Territory has resisted Pacification stubbornly." But he felt safe, for they were being escorted by tanks and armor-plated bulldozers.

Spleeno Bludgeon, who was proud that he was brawny like the general—he had a secret ambition to be a general—and that his face, too, could be like stone when necessary, said, "You are an extraordinary man, General, to have survived so much."

General Gonorrhoea thought, That was a great compliment, he wasn't as much interested in winning as in surviving. If one had to have a venereal disease it was better to have gonorrhoea than syphilis. And he had survived many Vice-Presidents. He had been a captain when the first had come, a major when the second had arrived, a colonel when the third had done his tour, and now he was a general.

Spleeno Bludgeon asked, "Have you been here a long time?"

"Many years. A millennium. I'm an expert on Pacification."

"I'm sure it has been worth it, General."

"It has been a great honor to serve here." Indeed, he thought. At home he never would have risen in rank or have become wealthy.

"General, if I had my choice I would prefer to be in your shoes. But I must carry out our President's orders, I must be a member of his team. I must make sure that Pacification is carried out." And as he heard the sudden sound of gunfire he felt very brave for he hadn't jumped.

Spleeno Bludgeon spent the next day assuring everyone within the sound of his voice that he would fight to the last drop of their blood. He told the natives that they had moved into the adjoining Territory to get out of theirs. He showed them a massive map to prove that.

He went from palace to palace like a door-to-door salesman. One speech became so popular he repeated it over and over. His eloquence grew so fervent his face became swollen and reddish and specks of blood appeared in his eyes and he brandished his hand as a sword as he declared, "We are increasing the Pacification Program only so that we can end it. We are all part of the same team and when I think of our President, I think of a football coach standing on the sideline of the field, his keen eyes commanding us to fight to the bitter end. He has built our team with discipline and self-sacrifice and love. He knows we must win the game. That we cannot afford to spoil our undefeated record. Shortly before I left home, I had the privilege of talking to him and he assured me that he is behind you to the last man."

Each time the Vice-President stated this, General Gonorrhoea nodded approvingly. He thought, At the rate his guest was going Spleeno Bludgeon would make a great Pacifier.

However, Spleeno Bludgeon's press aide felt that his chief ought to do something more homey to strengthen his image. Dick Dont was an attractive dark-haired ex-professor in his early thirties. "An over-educated intellectual," he liked to say about himself, but actually he enjoyed being close to the seat of power, it gave him vicarious pleasure, it was being lustful without taking any of the risks. He suggested to his chief, "You should visit some of the wounded."

Spleeno Bludgeon took Dick Dont's advice. Protected by helicopter gunships whirring noisily overhead and tanks stationed around him on the ground, he visited a hospital. He checked with Dont to make sure that photographers and reporters would be there, and then he arrived with his entourage: officers in smart boots, military policemen who had pressed their trousers for the occasion, and a jaunty sergeant whose mouth watered at this detail.

General Gonorrhoea introduced Sergeant Syphilis with the statement, "We owe much to this man. He is responsible for the road being safe."

Spleeno Bludgeon complimented Sergeant Syphilis on his solid, earthy build and added, "It is ideal for football. What position did you play?"

"I was a guard, sir." That was an invention; he had never played; he didn't believe in shedding his own blood. But to disagree, he calculated, would displease the Vice-President.

"You look it, Sergeant. You have the porportions for a guard."

"Thank you, sir, thank you."

"May I see one of your more touching patients." One, he thought, that would make an especially appealing picture.

"I have just the one, sir. He was wounded trying to save his buddy. But I'm sure your visit will be a consolation."

Buck Fever lay on a bed in a ward room of the hospital and he felt crazy. At the end of his bed where his legs were supposed to be, there was just one bulge under the sheet, and yet he was surrounded suddenly by many people, and his nurse, very excited, whispered, "You're being visited by the Vice-President. Isn't that wonderful!"

But there were so many men guarding the Vice-President the second private could hardly see him. Then, as the photographers crowded around his bed, Spleeno Bludgeon pushed forward until he stood in front of Buck Fever and still Buck Fever kept seeing Sergeant Syphilis's face.

He must be drunk, he thought. But when Spleeno Bludgeon bent over him, waiting for the pictures to be snapped, he knew what was wrong.

Sergeant Syphilis was introducing the Vice-President with an elaborate speech, and the second private realized the two men resembled each other. Despite the fact they were both large and brawny, they were also paunchy and too old for combat.

Spleeno Bludgeon asked, "Do you like football, Private?"

The second private shrugged. Not much. He was too small.

Yet Spleeno Bludgeon was smiling, for the photographers were snapping pictures of him bending over the wounded private, and Buck Fever thought apprehensively, Mom will find out, it will kill her.

Spleeno Bludgeon said, "I have the latest scores. Who do you think will win, soldier. I go to all the football games when I am home."

The mention of home made Buck Fever so homesick he could have wept. More pictures were being snapped as the Vice-President extended his sympathy and the second private prayed that he would be free of his nightmares. Most of his sleeping moments and many of his waking ones he kept hearing the first private's anguished cry, "I lost my balls!"

The second private was so terrified that he would never get this memory out of his head that instinctively his hand went to his crotch and he thought with relief, they were still there, and his penis stood up like a tree and then he was ashamed—the visitors must be able to see it under the blanket. But no one was paying any attention to him.

Spleeno Bludgeon was consoling General Gonorrhoea, who had hurt his back bending over another wounded private. Then he was congratulating Sergeant Syphilis on the success of the venereal detail.

A note of exhortation crept into his voice as he addressed the entire ward, declaring that he was speaking for their Head Coach, the President. "He and I are profoundly moved by your sacrifices. I am sure you will be reassured to know that the President is a great sportsman, a winner, and first in Pacification."

Now the second private knew where he had seen Spleeno Bludgeon before. The Vice-President reminded him of the salesman who had put his foot in the door, thought Buck Fever, and who wouldn't go away until Mom had bought something.

Dick Dont whispered, "We'll send you a picture of yourself with the Vice-President when it is developed, Private."

He nudged Speeno Bludgeon who pulled a photograph out of his pocket and handed it to Buck Fever, and stated, "But until it comes, this should help you. It is an official photo. Of the President shaking my hand. They are hard to get, you know."

The second private held the huge photo in a trembling hand and felt he should say, I'm sorry, really, to have caused you all this trouble.

Spleeno Bludgeon swept out of the ward, surrounded by a grim phalanx of professional bodyguards clutching sub-machine guns, and the second private sighed with relief, now, at least, he could suffer in peace.

"One can always cut down our horrible death toll by staying off the roads," Graham Graves assured Alex as he escorted him into the helicopter that was to fly them to the tennis engagement.

Graham Graves was in an exuberant mood, greatly pleased that the President was going to honor him with a game of tennis at *his* home.

Alex was anxious, wondering what they really wanted. Then suddenly, the helicopter was climbing and Graham Graves was grinning broadly and they seemed to be flying along a corridor in the sky and a few minutes later they were at Graham Graves's country place.

"Just a modest place, really, Alex," Graves said as he led Alex up a beautifully curved driveway. "I rented it for the President's convenience, essentially, when he needs a hide-away to relax."

Whatever the convenience, thought Alex, it was luxurious. At the end of the driveway he came face to face with an imposing three-story mansion with large white Doric wooden columns in the front.

"Only fifteen rooms, actually," Graves said humbly, "but with six bathrooms. Naturally, there is a lot of going to the toilet."

Alex wanted to see the tennis court, which was in the gardens behind the mansion. It was a perfectly kept grass court, with a small stand for spectators, and a Tudor brick house nearby to dress in.

"My gardener takes care of the court," Graves said. "I hired him because I want the President to be pleased with the court."

"It is lovely," said Alex. "And so private."

"Exactly. A tall stone wall surrounds the entire estate."

With a meticulous thoroughness, like a fumigation squad, secret service men swept through the grounds, the mansion, the Tudor brick house, and across the tennis court. Every inch was checked for possible bombs. Only when they were satisfied that the entire estate was safe did the President's helicopter land.

Graves said, "We have to take sensible precautions."

Alex asked, "Where is Shipmen?"

"With the President." Graves sounded envious.

Shipmen was right behind the President as the latter strode out of the helicopter, but Graves made sure that he was the one who introduced Alex to the President. It seemed unnecessary to Alex, for he had met the President a number of times as a candidate and as a President, but Graves did it with a flourish.

The President radiated a quiet optimism as he shook Alex's hand with a firm, carefully rehearsed gesture and said, "How good to see you again, Alex, you look well, ready for a brisk game," and Alex thought, This was government by relaxation and tailored monosyllables.

But Victor Winner hadn't changed much since Alex had seen him several months ago. Tall, thin, rawboned, the President wore a dark suit that was cut to fit him precisely, to smooth down any differences that might come between him and the electorate. His pale green eyes displayed a genuine interest in the person before him, and his brown hair was carefully pompadoured and cut short. Yet even as Victor Winner focused on him, Alex felt he was scanning the horizon for other voters.

He said, "What a lovely day! Not a cloud in the sky!" His voice was perfectly modulated and reminded Alex of an elocution teacher.

Then suddenly, the President frowned.

Graves and Shipmen asked with the same instantaneous urgency, "What's wrong, sir?"

"Nothing! Nothing! Alex, I see you have let your hair grow."

"A little, Mr. President." But my pubic hair is the same, he wanted to retort, and he said instead, "Does it bother you, sir?"

"Not if it suits your personality. But somehow, I don't associate it with your image. All-American football player, tennis buff . . ."

"It doesn't get into my eyes, Mr. President. It is not that long."

Victor Winner grinned tightly and changed the subject.

As the four contestants strolled toward the converted club house to change into their tennis clothes they were surrounded by secret service men. Graves had broken up the Tudor brick house into a number of small locker rooms with showers and a large bar, and each of them dressed separately. But Alex felt uncomfortable. A burly young man in a heavy serge suit lounged outside his locker room. Even the way he tied his tennis sneakers was being watched.

Alex was the first player to reach the court. He felt trim and alert and proud that his muscular legs and arms didn't reveal his age, but he wondered if that mattered now. Everyone else was so self-involved.

Graves came next, smiling with such sincerity that Alex didn't believe any of it. He arrived at a trot, to show that he was remarkably fit.

Shipment followed, striding briskly to prove that he was athletic, and stood behind the diminutive Graves so that he towered over him.

Then, precisely at four p.m., the President emerged from the club house and marched on to the court as if it were a stage and the sun was a great spotlight. He moved strongly, conscious of his virtue and power. He was accompanied by guards armed with sub-machine guns who came through the lilac bushes and who were placed behind the row of chestnut trees.

Alex found it difficult to adjust to hitting a mere tennis ball as he and the President faced Shipment and Graves for the practice shots. It seemed more like a public performance than a competitive game, and yet as he saw how seriously Shipmen and Graves hit the ball and Victor Winner was tense, too, he sensed this game mattered very much to them.

Secret service men patrolled the grounds; secret service men were posted as linesmen and ball boys; secret service men sat as spectators in the stand; secret service men were everywhere and trying not to be visible. Alex looked up to hit a practice overhead and he saw riflemen on the roof of the mansion; he tried a serve and noticed four helicopters hovering overhead like a flock of hawks.

He found this distracting, and he was worried about his partner. Despite the President's beautifully tailored tennis clothes, Victor Winner's awkwardness was discouraging. Victor Winner was built like a scarecrow; his chest was as flat as a washboard; his shoulders resembled a long, angular clothes-hanger; his legs were scrawny and knock-kneed; his stomach hung over his waist and was soft.

No wonder·he had such a fetish about being athletic, thought Alex.

The President said, "Just one set today."

"Whatever you say, sir!" Graves and Shipmen said in unison.

But when the President saw the look of disappointment on Alex's face, he added, "I haven't played for a long time. Nearly two weeks."

Alex sought to concentrate on his opponents, but he kept wondering whether his partner would be one, also. Shipmen and Graves hit with skill and accuracy, but the President went at the ball as if it had to submit to him, thrashing at it, and he was erratic and inaccurate.

He sensed Alex's disquiet and he said, "I'm not warmed up yet."

Perhaps, thought Alex.

"I'll get better," the President assured him.

Alex hoped so; Victor Winner couldn't get worse. Shipmen was playing on the right, and Alex noticed that Shipmen had a strong but unimaginative forehand with which he tried to overpower his opponents, hitting it to the same spot most of the time. While Graves, a left-hander, was playing on the left, and was tricky, never hitting hard, but clever at getting the ball back, particularly to the most difficult places, and always with a slice or chop or drop shot, making his opponent run and extend himself to the limit.

Yet, at first, Alex's opponents seemed generous. They gave Alex and the President the choice of serve and the President suggested that Alex start off. And Alex realized immediately that his apprehensions were correct. His first serve went in on Shipmen's backhand, which he had detected would be a weakness, and Shipmen hit a soft, easy shot at the President who was at the net. It was a sure point and the President missed the ball completely. On the next serve to Graves, Alex's pace and placement forced Graves to hit an even easier shot at the President and this time Victor Winner smashed the ball yards out of the court and almost decapitated a secret service man who was acting as a linesman.

Alex paused, took a deep breath, and glanced at the countryside. When the game was going badly he had a habit of seeking sustenance from beautiful surroundings. Today, they were magnificent. The tennis court was a fertile island in a great sea of grass which extended as far as the eye could see. The sky was a crystal clear blue and he could distinguish hills in the distance but no other houses or signs of life. He longed to hold this view of bountiful nature tight in his mind.

As the game progressed this became impossible. He lost his service when the President made two more errors after he set up easy winners.

Then, on return of serve, each time Alex won the point with a fine drive, the President lost his return with an error. After this went on for a dozen points, Graves was able to retrieve Alex's hard drive and to pop it softly at the President who knocked it out.

The President seemed surprised by the size of the tennis court. Although it was the regulation length and width, it was too small for him; he kept hitting his shots out. As the score against Victor Winner and Alex mounted to love-three, Victor Winner's constant errors depressed Alex. By now the match had settled into a pattern. As Alex anticipated, Shipmen hit every shot at him with all of his strength to intimidate and overpower him, while Graves subtly and cleverly sliced and chopped and drop shotted and sought to run him as much as possible. Yet when Graves and Shipmen hit to the President, which they did just enough to keep him in the game, they gave him easy shots.

Alex thought, It pays to be President, he got all the good shots.

But he was fair about it, he gave Alex the tough shots to retrieve.

Yet Graves and Shipmen were in a dilemma, Alex sensed, they were torn between wanting to win and wanting to please the President. When Victor Winner finally earned a point on his own, Graves and Shipmen sought to outdo each other in applause and the President beamed with satisfaction.

It was a brief reprieve for Alex. As the match went on and he continued to get the hard shots and the President the easy ones his despair grew. Alex ran and ran to keep the ball in play, hoping somehow, that this would help his partner to establish a decent rhythm, returning the ball four, five, six times in each exchange and then, as the President glowered, resenting that *he* was not in the play, they hit to him and he knocked the ball out and lost the point. Alex felt very frustrated.

And when he was serving at love-four the President's olive and gray helicoper flew over the court. Each time Alex threw up a ball to serve the helicopter circled across his vision, distracted him, and caused him to double-fault. He wondered if this was deliberate. Finally, with enormous self-control, Alex got two serves in and the President knocked their opponents' returns out.

As they changed courts Victor Winner was angry and he said, "Alexander, you are making an awful lot of errors today. I never expected you to double-fault."

The next game, Shipmen, forgetting himself, served a perfect ace on the President and he cried "Let," although the ball had not come within a foot of the net. But Shipmen understood; when he played the point over he double-faulted. Graves followed with a shot that hit the line and the President called it out. As the secret service linesman hesitated, the ball had knocked up chalk from the line, the President shouted, "Out!"

Graves and Shipmen began to make errors. Each sought to outdo the other. But Shipmen had the last word; he double-faulted the game away.

As the President prepared to serve, Alex thought, We could win now, if the President could only get the ball in.

The President did, and Alex was so surprised he missed his return and Victor Winner growled, "Such an easy shot! How could you, Grant?"

The President's next serve hit Alex in the back of the head.

Graves laughed and said, "You will stick your neck out."

Shipmen added sharply, "You ought to keep your head down, Grant."

Alex's head ached—it was the hardest the President had hit the ball all day—but he couldn't quit now, although he wanted to. He bent low àt the net, hoping he could keep out of the way, and prayed.

The President was annoyed at Alex for spoiling his first serve, but his serves went in now and while they were extremely easy balls that Alex knew Shipmen and Graves could put away, they hit them in the net and the score became two-five.

It must be difficult to be a presidential aide, Alex reflected.

Graves and Shipmen's lead dwindled to four-five and as they changed courts Victor Winner told Alex, "I knew their morale would crumble, once I got on my game. You mustn't let me down now, Alexander."

Shipmen gave the President a very easy serve and the President pushed it back weakly to Graves at the net. It was a sure point for their opponents, thought Alex, but Graves was determined not to allow Shipmen to outdo him. He knocked the President's return out.

Alex prepared for his return of service and the President stated, "You must challenge them. Like I did. This is our big chance to win."

Concentration gone, Alex wasn't ready for Shipmen's first serve which came in faster than usual, and the President cried, "Out!"

Even Shipmen frowned and Graves was stunned but no one said anything.

This time however, Alex was ready. He hit the second serve perfectly, and blazed a fine backhand between Shipmen and Graves and the President declared, "We mustn't relax."

For some reason, perhaps because Shipmen was angry at the bad call, he served hard to the President, also. The ball was good, right on the line, and the President couldn't call it out—his eyes were shut as he swung at the ball. It hit on his racquet handle, squirted crazily over the net and out of reach and Victor Winner marched around as if he had done this deliberately.

Alex's return of serve was a strong, forcing shot which Graves hit back at the President with severity, as if somehow, he could not submit totally either, and when the President tried to get out of the way—the ball was coming at his pubic parts—it hit the frame of his racquet and fell over the net for the winning point of the game.

Victor Winner dropped his racquet on the court to indicate that the match was over and said, "I knew he would come back. I always play best when I'm behind. Nothing I like to do more. I'm good on the key points."

The secret service men were still applauding the President when the four contestants reached the club house. Graves and Shipmen declared that the President had played remarkably well and ignored Alex.

Just as Alex finished his shower, the President approached him. He was naked, his towel draped carelessly over his shoulder, and he said, man-to-man, "How about a drink, Alex? To celebrate our victory. It was a victory, you know, considering how we started." The President led him into the bar before Alex could say a word or put on any clothing.

Alex liked the bar's walnut panels, the black leather chairs, the circular glass end tables, the windows cleverly designed so that the occupants of this room could see outside without being seen. But when he sought to view the fountain in the dusk so that he could collect his scattered thoughts—he was very uncomfortable standing naked next to the President—it was impossible to see anything but the secret service men forming a human wall around the club house. They were whispering into their lapel microphones, while the President closely scrutinized him as if to decide whether he possessed a virile profile. Was the President a homosexual, he asked himself. But he couldn't be, Alex thought in the next instant, he was the President. It must be that Victor Winner was determined to show that he was a regular fellow and that he possessed a big penis. He strode around the bar to indicate that one couldn't go wrong with such a man. Alex wondered how many votes it was worth.

The President asked, "Can you make a vodka martini?"

"No." Victor Winner looked so surprised Alex felt ashamed.

"I dismissed the secret service man who is my bartender so that we could have privacy. What can you make?"

"Nothing, sir." He didn't feel he had to wait on the President.

Graves entered with his quick, small steps, his towel draped modestly around his waist, eager for a drink after the ordeal of playing against the President, and when he saw the President naked, he tried to dart back through the doorway from which he had come and the President halted him. "Come in, Graham, this is for men only. Make me a vodka martini."

As Graves did, Alex felt Victor Winner was treating his aide as if he were his dog, and Alex wanted to get Graves a collar with the President's name and address engraved on it. And Alex did not ask for a vodka martini, but when Graves handed it to him, he took it.

The drink was relaxing and gave Alex a chance to put his towel around his midriff, although he had spent a lifetime in locker rooms.

The President said, "You are embarrassed, aren't you, Alex?"

"Not at all, sir." But Alex tightened his towel around him.

"Locker rooms can be great fun. But I always shock Graham when he sees me naked. Good to shake him up a little. It keeps him on his toes. I like to get down to the bone. Embarrass a man and you have him licked."

Graves said, "I'm not embarrassed, sir, but you could catch cold."

"See," the President said triumphantly. "He is embarrassed, as you are."

The President strutted about as if he had won a victory. But Alex was not impressed. Victor Winner's muscleless body, his ugly bony shoulders, his flat chest, his knock-kneed legs were fit only for a scarecrow. Yet Graves regarded him with a kind of respect that verged on reverence.

It spurred Victor Winner into stating, "Graham tells me that you are reliable, Alex. Anyone who loves sports as much as you do, should be."

"Sir, did you play football?"

"I wanted to. Personally, I find there is nothing more gratifying than facing danger and surmounting it."

Alex thought, He found it more gratifying not to face danger at all.

"But regretfully," the President continued, "when I was in college I had to work my way through and so I had no time to make the team. But I enjoyed your career. Has your son returned to the team? I hope he appreciates what a responsibility it is to be the quarterback."

"Mr. President, I have spoken to him about it."

"He must obey you. Look what football did for you. It developed your ability to take punishment, to fight back, to come from behind. Like I did in tennis. It is a great character-builder. I'm convinced there is a genuine working relationship between football and God."

"Sir, what about holding, fouling, and pass interference?"

"Sins. But forgivable, when committed in the heat of the game. That's why I can overlook what you said in your column."

"What things, Mr. President?"

"You are widely read. Even abroad. But you are not always well informed. Graham says that your last column could create discontent."

"You exaggerate my importance, Mr. President."

"Not really. Your column is read by the people who have influence. Even senators and cabinet ministers quote it to me."

"Don't you read it, Mr. President?"

"I haven't the time to get bogged down in details. Graves digests the news for me. He reports to me on what matters.

He informed me that your criticism of the Pacification. Program was offensive."

"Sir, it was the use of the body count that I called offensive."

"To be candid, I would prefer another way of keeping score. But it is vital that it is known we are winning."

"What about peace, Mr. President?"

Long, long ago, the President reflected, when Pacification had begun, Victor Winner, then a loser, had thought it could be ended without victory. But now that he was expected to win, he felt he could not afford to lose. However, he said, "I'm deeply interested in peace. I've been studying it for years. But defeat is unacceptable."

"Yet you agree we must explore all the possibilities for peace, sir?"

"Naturally. But your attack on our program could be used by the enemy."

"Because I said we must stop counting bodies to prove we are winning?"

"It is a bookkeeping exercise. You mustn't be hypochondriac about it."

Graves said, "You must write what you think, but more fairly."

The President said, "Then you could interview me. It would be an exclusive." He wrapped his towel around himself while Graves looked pleased at the success of his mission. "What do you want to know now, Alex?"

"Sir, when do you think the Pacification Program will end?"

"That is classified."

"But you are ending the body count, sir?"

"That is classified, too."

"What isn't, Mr. President?"

"We are winning."

"Is that your personal opinion, sir? May I quote you?"

The President hesitated and before he could reply, or have Graves reply for him, Shipmen hurried in. Shipmen was fully dressed in a tailored gray pin-stripe suit which made Alex feel even more naked, and there was an urgency in his voice as he said, "There is an emergency, sir. A new crisis. And Graves is needed, too. It involves your foreign policy."

"What is it?" Victor Winner asked.

"It is classified, Mr. President. But I think you will have to dress. You are wanted in the Capitol."

Alex asked, "Sir, may I continue this interview next week?"

The President frowned, then snapped, "It depends on what you do with this one. You do ask too many questions. It is depressing." At the door he paused for a final admonition. "And anything I said here was off the record. I will deny it if I don't like what you write."

He rushed off to dress, Graves trailing him, and Alex was surprised that Shipmen didn't follow them. Instead, as Alex started toward his locker and his clothes Shipmen blocked his way. Alex wondered whether he should push the aide aside—it wouldn't be easy, with Shipmen's weight and size—and Shipmen said, "I've something important to discuss with you." His voice was severe.

Alex said, feeling very much at a disadvantage in this situation, "Didn't you say it was an emergency? Aren't you needed, too?"

"There are always emergencies. But this one is Graves's, not mine."

"What about the President?" Alex had a feeling that Shipmen had arranged this situation, so that he could be alone with him.

"He will make the decision, once Graves gives him the facts. Were you able to adjust to the President?"

"Of course. Why?"

"Balls naked. It is an impressive sight, isn't it?"

Alex couldn't tell whether Shipmen was being flattering or critical.

"He thinks it intimidates people, but I have a better way."

"Excuse me. It's chilly in here and I'd like to dress."

"Just a moment, Grant. I've something important to discuss with you." Shipmen pulled down the shades with an air of mystery, closed and locked the door, and when he saw Alex's look of dismay, he added, "You wouldn't want what I'm going to say to be overheard. Sit down."

"Without my clothes?"

"It is appropriate. What I have to discuss with you could leave you just as naked—politically."

Menace crept into Shipmen's voice and mockery. Alex sat down. He wished the leather didn't stick to his backside like sandpaper. He squirmed with discomfort, although he didn't want to, not wishing to give Shipmen the impression that he was annoyed. He had a feeling that would give Shipmen too big an advantage, for Shipmen was bullying him, also.

"I looked up your political record, Grant."

Alex didn't answer; suddenly he sensed what was coming.

"You signed a petition that could be embarrassing to you."

"I've signed many petitions." He sought to sound casual, but he braced himself for a shock; Shipmen's tone was becoming nasty.

"This is a special one," Shipmen said portentiously. "A Communist one."

"What makes you so sure?"

"It is on file."

"You're bluffing."

"I have a photostat in my pocket. Do you want to see it? No denial will destroy it. I always check my facts carefully. Now I know why you were so critical of our Pacification Program. You were a Red."

"You didn't have to be a member of the Communist Party to sign it."

Shipmen replied cynically, "A petition to put the Communist Party on the ballot? Nobody will believe you."

"Even though the law stated specifically that I didn't have to be a member of the Communist Party to sign this petition?"

"Did that help you when you were fired from a state job for signing it?"

Alex didn't answer.

"If this part of your past should be revealed, you will hardly be regarded as a reliable critic of our Pacification Program. Or of anything, as a matter of fact. I wonder what your newspaper publisher will say."

"He will say it happened a long time ago. That it is of little consequence."

"Or he may not trust anything you write anymore."

"Does the President know about the petition?"

Shipmen shrugged.

"Does he?"

"Not necessarily. It is possible. What does it matter? It is known."

"Then why was I invited if you think I am not to be trusted?"

"I didn't invite you. Graves did. With the President's consent. But the President would not like to learn that you deceived him."

"Does Graves know?"

Shipmen grinned sardonically. "It will be an awful nuisance for him. Quite embarrassing. The President could be quite annoyed."

"How do you feel about this petition?"

"I'm doing my duty. Graves will know if it becomes necessary. It will make a very good story. Do you want me to write it, Grant? Leading critic of Pacification supported our enemies."

"I was a young man when I signed that petition."

"That is no excuse."

"I thought the matter was dead."

"Such matters are never dead."

"Perhaps."

"My job is to protect the President from abuse."

Alex added with special feeling and emphasis, "But I signed the petition a long time ago."

"You are creating ill feeling in the country," Shipmen stated pontifically. "But revelation that you signed a Communist petition . . ."

Alex interrupted, "A petition to put the Communist Party on the ballot."

"It was a Communist petition," Shipmen retorted. "That is all people will care about. It will discredit anything you say. You will be accused of giving aid and comfort to the enemy. The President was annoyed by your column."

Alex felt like saying, Do you want me to submit my columns to him before publication, but he said instead, realizing that Shipmen was deadly serious, "What would you like me to do, Roger?"

"Stop beating a dead horse. Nothing you write is chipped in granite. What you write on Monday can be changed on Wednesday and reversed on Friday. Stop being a critic. Be affirmative."

Alex hesitated.

Shipmen reminded him, "I never take chances. I'm always sure of my facts." What he couldn't tell the columnist was that the President was at the threshold of concern. Victor Winner didn't have to say, I want to get that son-of-a-bitch; it was his job to know when the President felt that way. Shipmen was proud of his loyalty; if the President asked him to scratch his crotch, he would, and anything else, besides. "Don't look so miserable, Grant, we're not children. Keep your mouth shut about unpleasant matters and you'll have no problems."

As Alex still hesitated, trying to decide how to reply, he heard sounds on the roof. He asked, "What are those footsteps overhead?"

"Security agents."

"Listening to us?"

"I hardly think so, even with all their devices. I made sure this room wasn't bugged before I started our little discussion."

There was a knock on the door and Graves shouted, "Anybody home?"

Shipmen whispered, "Well, Grant, do you want Graves to know?"

It is none of his business, or yours either, Alex longed to cry out, but he whispered back, "No."

"Good. I'm glad you've listened to reason."

Alex nodded; he didn't know what else to say.

Shipmen unlocked the door and when Graves entered and saw that Alex was still naked, except for his towel, his eyebrows rose automatically, and Alex was sure of what he was thinking, but all Graves said was, "I hope you've had an interesting time."

"We've had quite a chat," said Shipmen. "We've come to an agreement."

"Cheers," said Graves.

Sarcastically, thought Alex, neither of these aides trusted each other.

Graves said, "You had better put on some clothes if you want to say goodbye to the President. I don't think he'd like you to do that naked."

Alex was dressed when Graves came to fetch him. Graves still regarded him suspiciously, but he said nothing except that the President was about to depart and it was advisable not to keep him waiting.

Victor Winner stood beside his helicopter, which had landed next to the tennis court. Four helicopters hovered overhead for protection; telephone lines were draped across the tennis court, defacing it; secret service men were every-where, even more than before, as if their chief purpose was to watch each other.

By the time Alex reached the President he had fixed his tie, adjusted his coat, and he felt nearly normal again.

The President was immaculately turned out and his voice was perfectly controlled as he addressed Alex. "Roger tells me you had a useful chat. He assured me that your head is in the right place after all. I'm glad you got over your sulking. I knew you were a good fellow at heart."

Alex said, "Roger can be persuasive."

"I was, too, wasn't I, Alex?" Graves said suddenly, desperately.

"Indeed," said Alex.

"But we must not have too much persuasion," said the President. "Or our friend won't see our point of view honestly."

"Thank you, sir. Could you tell me about the emergency?"

"Always emergencies. No! It is classified." As the door of his helicopter opened for the President to enter, he shook the hands of the secret service men assembled about him, for after all, thought Alex, they were voters, too. Then he turned to the columnist and said, "Alexander, I still think your hair needs cutting." He stepped into the waiting helicopter and said proudly, "Mine!"

# *I Had to Go*

I had to go

From there to here
From then to now
From when to since

I wondered
Yet I didn't know why

Before
I could live with beauty
And not cry


STYMEAN KARLEN

# I Had to Go

*"Bullshit and Blackmail."*
Alex repeated that title to himself as he typed it on old Iron Face, and then he frowned. He was trying to find a theme that would give birth to a new column, but it was no use. Bullshit and blackmail, with a bit of bullying, was what he was feeling, but his newspaper syndicate would never allow him to use such a title.

It was several days later and he had spent the intervening time thinking about what to write next. This morning he had sat for hours with old Iron Face, defying her to write his next column, and nothing had happened. Inspiration, an attitude he detested, had dried up. As if it had ever existed within him, he thought self-contemptuously.

When he sought to write what he called a genial column, full of soothing generalities, a key stuck, then another, and he snapped, "All right, old Iron Face, I get the point, you don't like what I'm saying. If you're so smart, say it yourself." He got up and walked away. But nothing started in his mind as he strode around his study, his favorite device to stimulate a flow of ideas. He felt ineffectual, which, in some ways, was the worst feeling of all.

His paper lay in old Iron Face like an accusation and she said, "Describe the President naked. As I told you to do before. That is not classified. Now you know what he really looks like."

"I can't," he replied, "they will discredit me."

"Don't you have the courage of your convictions?"

"Courage of *whose* convictions?" he answered. Then he

got an idea. He would advise his readers to stay calm, cool, and collected, and before old Iron Face could stop him, he wrote that, only he hit the *f* instead of the *c* and it came out falm, fool, and follected, and he was filled with resentment at the blackmail, he was not a dog to be whistled home, and he typed, "Come, all you mischief makers, join forces," or was it old Iron Face guiding his hands, "give them morsels mish mash and meaningless—it depends on the situation the country finds itself in—we cannot end Pacification too rapidly—why can't death lose for a change—can't we give life a chance—they never ask us—right—bright—tight?" Hell, he wasn't even a bad poet!

The telephone halted his typing and it was Shipmen, informing him, "I read your column, *Come the Millennium.* It is an improvement. I am glad you listened to reason. Keep up the good work. Graves told the President about it and he is pleased." Shipmen hung up before Alex could point out he had written this column prior to their talk.

But Alex was relieved. He could relax, at least for a little while.

In this mood he titled the new column, "*Football—Our Fall Ritual*," and he wrote about it as a theater, as a circus, as a trial of strength and courage, as a passion that possessed large segments of the public, and for wives a long, lost weekend, and yet this was when many people, but mainly men, felt most alive. He adopted the same tone he had used for *Come the Millennium*, and when he finished he felt better.

"You are a dirty old man," Marcia said to Alex after he asked her what she thought of *Bullshit and Blackmail* as a possible title for a column. They were at her retreat in the mountains for the weekend, just the two of them, for she had dismissed all of her servants, and her attitude was teasing yet critical. "Why would you want such a title?"

"It is just a title. To shake up a few people. I'm not using it."

"I hope not. People are more interested in wholesome things."

Marcia was proud of her simple, little retreat, as she

styled it. They had driven up the long, winding road in her car, since Alex didn't know the way, and it was hidden from the main road and her neighbors by many acres of wild forest. She had chosen this isolated spot because it was private and beautiful. Her imitation Tudor cottage was actually a large two-story brick house with a spacious living room, a fine dining room, an elaborately furnished kitchen, and two bedrooms and two bathrooms on the second floor, for herself and for her son.

"But Stanley is never here," she assured Alex, "any more. He says it is too far from the action, but I love it here. Don't you?"

"It is charming," Alex said. Marcia had decorated her boudoir in pink and it was very feminine.

"Do you have something on your mind?" she asked. He hadn't taken one step toward her or the bed.

"No. It was just that we were talking."

Yet neither of them were really interested in conversation. She received his body with such avidity her sexual involvement gratified him. And she admired the precision with which he entered her and his ability to make her feel it was a special moment.

They were lying next to each other on her queen-size bed, waiting for a renewal of energy for a repeat performance, when they heard a car on the road. "Impossible!" she cried. "Nobody knows this road but me and ..." She bit her lips and was silent.

"Who? Who else knows this road?" Alex asked urgently

"No one, I said. Except Stanley and the servants. And I gave them the weekend off. They wouldn't dare return now. I'd fire them."

"You're sure we weren't followed? Does Shipmen know I'm here?"

"Who would wish to follow us?" Suddenly she was shaking with terror, even as she felt exquisitely pure and righteous. "Are you in trouble? Is that why Shipmen wanted to know if I was seeing you this weekend?"

"He asked you that?"

"He called me about something else. But he did mention that he liked your last column and he thanked me for contributing to your good sense. He said it was nice that you and I were getting to know each other."

"Does he know that you invited me here?"

"Of course not! You're rude. But he might have assumed. Are you afraid of Shipmen?" She regarded Alex suspiciously.

"We're friends. We play tennis together."

"He told me. He said the President likes you as a partner. Although the President does think you could cooperate a little more."

There was a sudden, violent roar from the car, as if it was leaving, then silence. Just as they were sure that the intruders, whoever they were, were gone, they heard a burst of frenzied activity in the next room. The bed creaked loudly, there were many moans; Alex felt he was in a whorehouse and he wanted to laugh, only Marcia was crying.

"I'm so ashamed," she sobbed. "It must be Stanley."

"Your son? Are you sure?"

She whispered, "He has the only other key to that room. But I mustn't be unsympathetic, he is so vulnerable, so sensitive."

It was quiet in the next room now. Perhaps they would go away, Alex hoped. Instead, there was a sudden commotion, the sound of angry voices, and Stan stumbled into the bedroom, followed by his girl friend.

He shouted at her, "I'll find the documents." He tripped over a chair, fell on the bed and as he felt the bodies under him, he cried, "Gladys, there's somebody here. Turn the light on. Before I break my ass."

Gladys obeyed and the room became thick with sweat and sexual smells. She and Stan were naked and Alex thought them an ugly sight. Gladys was short, stubbly-legged, with dull, floppy breasts, and a cloudy expression in her eyes, while Stan was round-shouldered, narrow-hipped, and fat-assed. His skin was hairy and freckled. His pubic hair was fuzzy like his beard and was the most masculine thing about him.

Alex asked, feeling guilty, "What do you want?"

"Oh, James Grant's old man." But Stan didn't look surprised while Gladys shrugged and neither of them made any effort to cover their nakedness. "Mom, where did you put my documents, my draft rejection? I've got to prove to Gladys that I'm safe, or she won't have anything to do with me. She hasn't got time for Pacification bait."

Marcia cowered under her blanket, covered to the chin, and whimpered, "They are in my bureau. I keep them there for comfort."

Stan found them and showed them to Gladys proudly. She nodded approvingly, and they turned to go, only to be halted by Marcia.

"Where did you get the car, Stanley? You didn't . . ."

"Steal it? Nah. It's Gladys's. She's got cash."

Gladys mumbled, "Some drips you can't trust. But Stan is fantastic." She held up his draft rejection as proof.

Alex noticed for the first time that she was a dark blonde and that she might have been pretty if she didn't look so apathetic.

Marcia said imploringly, "Stanley, you mustn't break in on me like this anymore. Ever again. It's very . . . very . . . unfair."

"You got the place to yourself for the rest of the night."

"That's not what I mean."

"What do you mean, Mom?"

"You're very rude. Bursting in like this. Without any clothes."

"It's a great way to shake up your mother."

"You did this deliberately?"

"Mom, you take clothes too seriously. You know what I look like and Gladys ain't any different from you." He grinned at his mother and Alex lying in the bed, both of them a respectable distance from each other now, and said, "Relax. You must have used up a lot of energy. At your age . . .?"

Alex was furious, yet he couldn't move, as if to slip out of bed naked was to expose something he couldn't reveal. But he managed to say, "You think you're pretty smart, don't you, Stan?"

"Not as smart as your kid, man."

"What do you mean?"

"He's gone back to the football team. He rejoined it last

week when the quarterback who replaced him got knocked out for the season with a torn Achilles tendon. They say your kid will be starting soon."

"What about his protests?"

"He says they ain't relevant anymore."

"You're certain?" Alex was puzzled and skeptical; this was not like James. He didn't know whether to feel glad or sorry.

"Oh, he's on the team, all right. He wants to be a big shot after all. Like his old man. Glad, let's get out of this creepy joint." Stan pulled her back into the other bedroom.

A little later they heard the door slam next door, footsteps on the stairs, and the sound of the car driving away.

But there wasn't any sleep for Alex or Marcia the rest of the night. It wasn't possible with so much on their minds. Alex knew he should appreciate what Stan had told him, except there seemed malice in it and he still wasn't certain he could believe it.

While Marcia was deeply shaken by her son's intrusion. It wasn't that he knew she was having an affair; it was that he had witnessed it. She tucked up her knees against her stomach until her thighs rested there, covering her pubic parts so that no one could enter. And although she felt so uncomfortable she could not fall asleep, she stayed this way in the hope it would help her to survive her shame.

The next morning Alex telephoned James long-distance, and his son wasn't surprised to hear from him, but appeared to expect the call.

Alex asked, "How could you let me know through a virtual stranger?"

James replied, "I was going to tell you, as soon as I was sure I would be the starting quarterback again."

"Will you be?"

"The coach is still mad at me, but he's got nobody else. The only other passer on the squad has a bad arm, so he will have to use me."

"Is that why you went back? It sounds like blackmail?"

"Alexander, you are insistent this morning."

"James, why did you return to the team?"

"Why did you write *Come the Millennium*?"

"Because it is what I believe."

"So, I'm doing what I believe."

"I wonder."

"Are you going to see the game next week? It is *The Game*, you know. The seventy-seventh time we've played the enemy. There is great interest in it. It is for blood. We are still undefeated and so is the enemy. They say it is the game of the day, the game of the year, the game of the century, it depends where you are sitting. I hear it is going to be a full house, that several friends of yours will be attending. One of your pals, Graves, who is a graduate of the university, is bringing the President. We are going to be on the Picture. Nationally. The President must expect that to get him a lot of votes."

"James, what are you up to?"

"Up to my neck—in new plays. Coach Borborg is determined to show the President something special. More damn option plays. Did you have them when you played, Alex? I've got a lot to learn and quickly."

"I had the option to run or pass."

"Does the President prefer quarterbacks who pass or run?"

"He prefers those who win."

"Will you be sitting with the presidential party?"

"I haven't been invited."

"You will be. You are their latest convert. See you Saturday."

Monday, as James had predicted, there was an invitation from Graves to join the presidential party at their alma mater's game that Saturday afternoon, and Alex accepted it, although with mixed feelings. He was still skeptical about his son's motives, but he was also curious.

To ease the waiting, Alex devoted the rest of the week to his column.

At first *Bullshit and Blackmail* nagged him as a theme, but gradually, with the passing of time, it dimmed in his mind. When he wrote two amiable columns for publication on Wednesday and Friday which he believed would not offend anybody, he felt he had exorcised *Bullshit and Blackmail.*

*Autumn Almanac* stated that a contemplation of this season put existence into a more soothing perspective. *Mozartians Unite* was a verbal hymn in praise of the music of Mozart, which he had been listening to all week.

These were the kind of columns he preferred to write. Old Iron Face was less recalcitrant than usual, as if even she could not dispute the validity of autumn or the worth of Mozart. Or perhaps she was tired of political subjects, he decided, as he was.

There wasn't any mail finding fault with his views, and not a word from James. He heard that his son was practicing faithfully, that the team was determined to annihilate the enemy, that no one could get into the stadium to watch practice because of the secret plays being devised for the President, and that James was the center of attention.

Stimulated by such hopeful news, Alex wrote two columns in advance, although he did this rarely, for it could be dangerous, events could change so quickly. Yet he felt reasonably safe, for the new columns were on non-controversial subjects, too. *Festive Frolic* said the national absorption with sports was an amusing diversion, and he scheduled it for publication the Monday after *The Game*, which he thought was fine timing. *The Rational Man* stressed the virtues of reason and he planned it for publication the following Wednesday. The only diversion he allowed himself was an engagement with Marcia the Sunday after *The Game* at her country retreat.

But while he was gratified with what he had accomplished waiting for *The Game*, he couldn't fall asleep the night before it. He recalled how each time he played he tossed the night before, reviewing the possibilities, who would get hurt, would *he get hurt*, and would he win?

Whatever he pretended to others, he yearned for James to win. Yet his son's performance would be compared to his own and he was the only quarterback to win *The Game* three years in a row. It was too much of a handicap for James, reflected Alex, and unfair. James's fingers were too small for a quarterback who must pass often, although he had overcome this weakness, for the most part, with constant practice. When Alex finally fell asleep he was wondering whether his son could really excel.

The ex-private had no doubts about his ability to excel. But as the Leader of the Committee assigned him to the rat detail, the Leader sounded like Sergeant Syphilis who had commanded him in the Territory. Uneasy suddenly, the ex-private fondled his seven sticks of dynamite, which he carried next to his skin for good luck, for reassurance.

They were meeting in the front room of a run-down, deserted house on the outskirts of the university that was marked condemned, and while only the ex-private and his cover were in The Committee's headquarters, except for The Leader's two bodyguards, an air of suspicion was everywhere. The Leader stood behind a wall of six-foot-high sandbags so that only his eyes and the top of his head were exposed, and his guards had their hands on their hips as if expecting a shoot-out at any moment.

The Leader declared, "Peace and freedom can only be achieved by destroying the university. We must force people to know we exist. If we can't live in peace, we can't let them live in peace."

"Yes, sir."

"You must not fail, Number One. You must make sure that not a stick or stone is left standing. We must show them that we mean business."

"Yes, yes, sir," the ex-private repeated unhappily. The Leader didn't have to prod him. Ever since he had flunked out of the university for failing in chemistry, his major, he had been determined to blow a crack in the chemical lab that would split the university in half.

"We must show the President that he should not have come here."

"Yes, sir, I'll show The Man. I'll blow his mind. I did this in the Territory. I was lead man on the venereal detail, a demolitions expert."

"That is why I have assigned you to free the chemical lab."

"Is there really nerve gas in it, sir?"

"Who told you?"

"I heard . . . sir."

"You must not talk about what you hear."

"Why sir?"

"Security. But don't worry, you should be reasonably safe. Nobody should take any shots at you. Number Two will keep you covered."

That was another thing that worried the ex-private; Number Two was a girl and girls couldn't be trusted. Yet he didn't want to pull out; he had his heart set on completing this mission. And anyway, it was the demolition job that mattered and he would give them a good one. He nodded, pretending to agree, even as he still felt uneasy about the girl.

The Leader said to her, "Number Two, you know your duties?"

"All of them, sir." She thought, The Leader knows what he is talking about, he speaks with such authority; she wished she could be as positive about Number One. If she could only see The Leader's face! Was he as nervous as she was? She had been in two other bombings, but this was the big one. Number One was staring at her as if she were a freak, when he was with his carefully combed and cut blond hair, his lack of sideburns, his clean-shaven face, his business suit. Then she realized this was a camouflage; no one would suspect such an appearance. And he was diminutive, hardly five foot tall, and certainly not the picture of a revolutionary, she decided. But neither was she, she thought, and she was as dedicated as anyone. She hated authority, too. Now she was glad she was on this detail.

Yet after The Leader was gone, out the rear door so she never did see what he looked like, and she sat with Number One in the back bar of a dingy alley restaurant, a short distance from the campus, she had no appetite for the hamburgers, French fries, and beer Number One ordered.

"Beer makes me sleepy," she explained, when he was surprised that she didn't touch it. Her stomach was nervous enough as it was.

His stomach hurt, too, but he hid that, nibbling the food and gulping down the beer. It had been his idea to stop for beer and food; he wanted to snatch a better look at her and to get to know her better. They were not allowed to know each other's names—The Committee said that was too risky—but the ex-private wished he did. Even in the bad light of the bar she was very pretty, a slim, tall, brown-haired girl in blue jeans and a pullover jersey, and the beer made him yearn for her even more. Did she know, he wondered, that if he made a mistake, just one, this could be another venereal detail? She seemed eager to proceed with the mission.

Number Two wondered what Number One was waiting for. She was even more nervous as the time came closer and she wasn't certain how steady her voice sounded, but she stood up and said, "We must not be late."

Her loose, braless breasts dangled in his face and he had an impulse to fondle them, like he fondled his dynamite. He noticed she was as long and narrow as a fashion model. He wondered if she was a tight Virginia, with the kind of a vagina he preferred, and now he had a powerful desire to enter her like a stick of dynamite. Maybe afterwards, he thought, when he proved how valuable he was to The Committee.

"What are you waiting for, Number One?"

"You think I'm chicken? What are you doing later?"

She backed away as he leaned towards her. She didn't like his vibrations, whatever his credentials; they were bad, even if he was The Committee's choice. He was raping her in his mind. "Let's go, Number One."

He followed her out of the bar, and then he led. On a clear day the stadium could be seen from the chemical lab and he gloated at the thought that after he finished there would be such an uproar they would have to cancel *The Game*. One of his cherished dreams was to play quarterback in *The Game*, but no one was using five foot, one hundred and twenty pound quarterbacks, and that was another good reason for hating them and getting even. He wondered what her bag was and suddenly he asked her.

She whispered, "We have to crack open the university so they can see that it covers an empty shell. How far is the lab from the stadium?"

"A few hundred yards. There is a parking lot between us

and a small park they are converting into another parking lot for the crowds."

Yet when he paused a short distance away from a red-brick building, which was an indistinct shadow in the darkness, she asked skeptically, "Are you sure this is the right place? I expected someone to be guarding it."

"I studied here a year. Before I was drafted for the Territory." He would never forgive them for that. "They never have guards here. The campus has been quiet. We will show them. But you must not get too close, in case ... You must stand at least fifty yards away, behind the bush, and if you see anyone coming, whistle. Can you whistle?"

Her demonstration was satisfactory and he nodded approvingly.

"When I blink my flash twice get out and I'll meet you at the bar."

She agreed, pleased with his efficiency, and he approached the building. He was grateful for the shrubbery he could hide behind while he made his final preparations. Then he was puzzled; he didn't recall any shrubbery around the chemical lab. Could he be in the wrong place after all? The night had become chilly and dreary and he felt he was at the edge of the earth. The moon vanished and the stars grew dim and a mist clung to the ground, and although he knew he should appreciate that this hid him from sight, the night was too dark and gloomy for comfort and his eyes were weary of trying to detect the objects around him. They took on an eerie glow. It was hideously quiet. He strained to hear something, anything; he hated silence; it was too much like death. If only something would move he would know what to fear; it was the objects that were motionless that ambushed one in the Territory. But there was nothing but shadows, reminding him of the booby traps in the worst parts of the Territory. There was a sudden staccato burst and for an instant he thought it was machine gun fire and then he realized it was the backfire of an automobile.

Was somebody playing a cruel joke on him? Wasn't he ever going to forget? He had done only what he had been ordered: "Destroy everything living, everything that moves, that breathes, we got to make the Territory sanitary."

Christ, why should he have to remember it, it had been
going for a long time, maybe forever. They were the kind of
nights he wouldn't want to wipe his ass with. He must
exorcise them now, he swore to himself, or be everlastingly
damned.

The ex-private fumbled for his flash, and when he lit it he
jerked it nervously, as if in a spasm. But it told him that it
was almost one a.m., the appointed time, and now the red-
brick building looked familiar and he could start his final
preparations. He wasn't taking any chance of failure. He
had brought three possible explosives with him.

The first, The Committee's choice, was a pound of plastic
explosive he had extracted from mines in the Territory and
had shipped home in small packages with his souvenirs. He
had rebuilt the explosive into a bomb that put against the
side of a building should blow it up with the most damage.
But as a back-up precaution, in the event this device didn't
work, The Committee had given him a plastic carton containing an inflammable liquid, which should set the lab on
fire. But Number One was proud of his thoroughness and
without telling The Committee or anyone else and certainly
not his cover who could squeal on him, he had brought his
favorite explosive device, seven sticks of dynamite. He loved
dynamite. The sticks gave him a virile feeling, as if each
were a penis he owned. He placed them close to the
building, with the homemade bomb and the inflammable
liquid, and caressed them. He was sure they wouldn't disgrace him, let him down. Fertile dynamite, he reflected,
when it spoke everything became rubble, everything became
less than himself. He was not a savage, to use second-rate
material.

Come the millennium, he thought, he would level all labs
to the ground so that man could start from scratch again.
At least he had learned something from the venereal detail,
he smiled to himself. The Leader hadn't fooled him, he
knew there was nerve gas in the lab as The Leader had in-
tended him to know. The Leader's denial had been a come-
on; he admired his cleverness. He would liberate the lab;
when he finished it would be pacified. He would blow such
a loud noise they would have to listen to him. He would get

attention only if he were outrageous. And he would be winning, and it would be exhilarating to win, to get a lot of publicity, even is he—personally—had to remain anonymous.

He squatted in the crouch he had acquired from his years in the Territory, but which he thought of as his football crouch, uttered a pledge of allegiance to the dynamite, lit the fuses and ran.

Flame illuminated the target and the ex-private was stricken with horror—it was the wrong building after all! And he wasn't far enough away! A tremendous roar shattered the stillness and he thought, My precious dynamite has betrayed me, it has gone off too soon, it will get me, too. He remembered how his cover on his last venereal detail had stepped on a mine and then had tried to walk on two broken legs to prove that it had never happened. There was a second, huge explosion, an enormous blast, and he felt a violent blow and a sensation of moving away from everything.

When he recovered consciousness he was sprawled against a twisted tree, many feet from where he had been, and the building was lit up like a Christmas tree. A female was bending over him and at first he thought it was his Mom, he couldn't see her face; Mom always gave him something for Christmas, even when they had nothing, which was most of the time. One year it was a football, the next a baseball glove. Then she was asking, "Are you okay?" and he realized it was his cover, Number Two.

He nodded, but he couldn't move. She was crying and in that moment he hated her; she felt sorry for him and he couldn't endure pity. He mumbled, "I'll be able to get up. Soon. Did the blast reach you?"

"No," she sobbed. "I was just far enough away. I never saw such an explosion in my life. It's terrible. It was so powerful it demolished the building to the ground. I'll never do this again."

"What is your name?" he whispered. Suddenly he had a compelling need to know her name, as if an identity would make his pain bearable.

"I can't . . ."

"Can't what? Where do you come from?"

"I can't tell you."

He didn't want her to go away angry and he said, "I'm sorry."

"Sorry? For what?"

"I put you in danger. You must get out before the creeps come."

"What about yourself?"

"I'll manage, Number . . ."

"Lydia."

"Lydia who?"

There was the clamor of police sirens and she was gone even as he kept repeating, "Lydia who?" He closed his eyes but it didn't ease his pain. His hand went to his crotch and he felt a little better that his penis and balls were still there. But he didn't dare reach for his legs, afraid of what he might find. He felt something crawling over him, and he was grateful he still had feeling, and then he was revolted, for it was furry, it must be a rat, and he couldn't stand rats. The thought of a rat touching him made him sick. He remembered the fifty-five vitamin pills he took each day, but the bottle was smashed—he felt the scattered pills in his pocket—and now the rat had company, for other small, furry animals were scampering over him, poking at his vitamins, and suddenly he felt relief, they were not rats after all, but mice, many of them. That was good, he thought; he had liberated them. But as they ran around him aimlessly they didn't seem to know where to go. Several kept running into him as if he were a wall and he realized they had been blinded by the explosions.

The next thing the ex-private knew there were the flashing red lights of police cars and voices that seemed far away, although they were bending over him as he mumbled, "It was the chemical lab, wasn't it?"

"No," the first voice replied.

"It used to be the chemical lab," said the second voice, "but it was moved last year. Now the cellar contained mice for cancer experiments and the ground floor was used to store football equipment. Everybody knew that. It is why it wasn't guarded. What have you got against football?"

The ex-private tried to twist around to see if they were telling him the truth, but it were as if a vast weight lay upon him and he still couldn't move. Had The Leader assigned him to the wrong building? Deliberately? The Leader must have; The Leader knew the campus by heart. That idea shocked him and now the creeps— he knew they were creeps because they were wearing uniforms—were asking his name.

"Number One," he muttered, "I'm Number One."

"Who else was in on this?"

If he could only urinate, he had a wild desire to go, if they would only let him urinate! His hand felt his face and it seemed the same, and there were two leaves on his face. He caressed them and he was pleased they were long and slender, like Number Two, and he loved autumn, it was the best time of the year. Then the two leaves crumpled under his touch and he was angry.

The first voice said, "Don't worry, he won't run away."

His legs were gone. He didn't have to ask. He could see it in the second creep's eyes; he had seen that expression many times on the venereal detail. Terrified, he cried, "I will not die. I must not die. Please, don't let me die!" Tears streamed down his face.

"Why not? You demolished the building to the ground."

"To the ground," repeated the ex-private, reviving a little.

"Everything. Nothing was left standing."

Now it didn't matter which of the creeps was talking. They were in uniform and he had a contempt for uniforms, treating him as a little scroungy nobody. He felt an itch at his waist and his hand went there, grateful that he could feel anything. He had a surge of emotion and he stopped crying. It was a stick of dynamite next to his skin that was itching and now he felt potent again, although he still couldn't move.

"What is you real name, Number One? We will find out, you know."

"If I tell you my name, will you tell me what happened to me?"

"You were stunned by the blast. But you should be able to walk."

He still had his legs, he could feel them now, and his precious dynamite.

"What is your name? I've never seen such a demolition job in my life."

"The Demolisher. I'm The Demolisher," Number One repeated proudly. "When I do a job, I do it down to the ground."

An enormous black limousine that reminded Alex of a funeral hearse picked him up the next morning and delivered him to the airport where he joined Graves on the latter's plane. It was the largest private plane Alex had ever seen, even more pretentious than the black limousine, and the cabin, except for the pilots' quarters, was like a luxurious apartment with a fine living room, spacious dining room, and lavish bar.

But Graves was somber as he greeted Alex. They were barely off the ground when he asked, "Did you hear what happened at the university?"

"No." Alex hadn't turned on the news, to keep himself in a good mood. Graves looked so ominous he was certain James had committed a crime.

"A building was blown up."

"On the campus?"

"Near the stadium." Graves sounded as if that was the worst sin of all.

Could James have been involved? Alex's heart sank and he was silent.

"Where they store football equipment. How could they be so spiteful!"

"Where there any casualties?"

"When?" Graves was disturbed. Casualties was an unmentionable word.

"As a result of the bombing?"

Graves smiled with relief. "Just some mice. Stored in the basement."

"Do they know who did it?"

"They caught one of them. He calls himself The Demolisher, but he is a little fellow and it was such a big blast there must have been others."

"Do you have proof?"

"It's obvious. I pray to God that your son isn't involved."

"Why should he be involved?" Alex tried to look innocent and felt that made him appear even more guilty.

"Your son has been critical of many things."

"James returned to the football team."

"Oh, we know."

"You mean you have kept him under surveillance?"

"Now Alex," Graves said indulgently, "You don't think we would take any chances. We have to be careful that people don't take advantage of us."

"We? Who are We?"

Graves shrugged, then said, "Aren't you interested in winning?"

"It depends on what you are winning. Since you've had my son under surveillance, you must know that he wasn't involved in the bombing."

"It's not surveillance, it's just being aware of things. As it is, there will be hell to pay. We missed the one we caught."

"And I'm your hostage."

"Alex, you're a friend. The President greatly respects your opinions. I digest them for him often. You did speak to your son, didn't you?"

"So you've tapped my phone, too."

"Of course not! But after our last talk he did return to the team."

"Yes."

"What did he say to you then?"

Alex didn't want to answer, this was private and personal, but Graves looked so anxious he felt sorry for him—and he could hear old Iron Face chiding him, "That's the trouble with you, you're always feeling sorry for people"—and Alex replied, "James said he had a lot of plays to study, that Coach Borborg wants to please the President."

"We knew you would do your duty. That was one of the reasons the President decided to see *The Game*." Then suddenly, Graves frowned.

"What's wrong now?"

"To greet the President by blowing up a building? Such bad manners!"

"Perhaps it was done to frighten him. To keep him away."
Graves declared, "The President cannot afford to be
frightened."

But the aide had to visit the stadium before the crowd, to
check on the final preparations for the arrival of the President. He asked Alex to come with him to observe how
thorough he could be, although Alex felt Graves had other
reasons, that he wanted to impress him, and perhaps, to intimidate him. "It is my responsibility to see to it that every
precaution is taken to create a safe and sanitary situation,"
he explained. "After all, it was my idea that the President
attend *The Game*. With the bombing, we have to be extra
careful."

They were the only ones there, except for The Examiners,
as Graves called them. "Crack troops in our war against sub-
version," he said.

Alex noticed that The Examiners were in uniform. All of
them wore somber dark gray corporate suits with narrow
lapels and wide trousers. They were exactly alike with their
short sideburns, high hairline, and crew cut haircuts. Every
hair on their head was straight, whoever might have had
curly hair as a boy, had had it straightened, and now not a
hair stuck out in back or anywhere. They looked like over-
age and over-weight ex-football players, iron men going
slightly to rust, who were proud that they had made a living
belting people around, particularly opposing quarterbacks,
and they had the same expression on their heavy, square
faces—accusation.

They were everywhere and in great numbers. Alex was
startled; this was so different than when he had played.
Each inch of the playing field and the viewing area was
being examined with the utmost care. When the detonation
squad found sod on the field that had been cut up by
practice cleats—anyone who had played football should see
that, he longed to shout at them, but sensing that would be
unwelcome, he kept his mouth shut—The Examiners investigated those sections of the turf with special interest and the
latest in detonation equipment. Through the opening at
the end of the stadium he could discern tanks hidden in the

thick shrubbery outside, where they were supposed to be unseen, yet to remind potential malcontents of their presence, and to be close enough to the stadium to reach it quickly if necessary. Helicopters circled overhead and when Alex wondered why, Graves confided, "They have photograph equipment powerful enough to detect the whiskers on a 'mouse."

While Graves was busy giving orders a restless Alex climbed to the top of the stadium, to the last row, a favorite spot, where he enjoyed the splendid panoramic view, and he was ordered to move by The Examiners who rimmed the top row for the entire circumference of the stadium.

Thinking they were kidding, Alex went to sit down and the burly, middle-aged Examiner snarled, "Cool it! Don't sit! Or you'll end up on your back!"

Angry, Alex said, "Is it a crime to sit where I choose?"

The Examiner called over two of his colleagues and snapped, "We got a joker here. Let's move him, boys!"

"I'm sitting in the presidential section, with the President," said Alex, and showed them his ticket to prove it. "I'm with Graham Graves."

"Orders are orders," the three Examiners said with one voice. "No one sits here but us."

They were carrying billy clubs and pistols and Alex moved downstairs to his proper seat. But Graves was engaged elsewhere and Alex, still irritated and restless, decided to venture outside the stadium and to stroll about. He was curious about the bombing—had it really been very close? he wondered—and how had the students reacted?

The ticket ushers were as burly as The Examiners at the top of the stadium and they regarded him with the same chilly gaze. He was told that if he went out of the stadium he would not be allowed to return.

"Why not?" he asked, curious as well as irritated.

"Security."

Spectators were starting to arrive and everything they carried was examined, from ubiquitous paper bags with beer and hamburgers to hips that bulged with whiskey flasks. To Alex's surprise, no one questioned this but accepted it as part of the price of the game.

Upset and tense, Alex had to urinate—it was inevitable when he became tense and whenever he had played—and as he entered the toilet he was followed. For an instant he thought he was going to be accosted. But when he stepped before a urinal the heavily built man went to the wash basin where Alex could be observed from the wall mirror.

Even more upset, Alex was unable to urinate, for the man didn't stop watching him until he returned to his seat. He thought angrily, wasn't there anywhere one could have privacy? Wasn't anything sacred?

It was too late to try to be part of the crowd—the President was due at any moment and it would be discourteous not to be present—so Alex tried to ignore his discomfort. And when he mentioned the incident to Graves, the latter laughed and said, "Some Examiners are more zealous and conscientious than others. You shouldn't be self-conscious about it."

The President was not in the least self-conscious. Victor Winner took great pains to see to it that his picture was taken with Alexander Grant.

He informed the press, "The widely read columnist and distinguished All-American football player. And the only quarterback to win *The Game* three times."

But Alex wished he could go to the toilet. Examiners were everywhere, but especially about the President, and surely they ought to realize now that he was reliable. The college bands were playing, "Hail to the Chief," and everyone had to stand and that increased his need to go.

He cursed under his breath and the President, who was standing next to him in case any more pictures were taken, thought Alex was singing and complimented him on his patriotism.

"Yes, sir," he mumbled. "I wonder if I could be excused?"

"You will miss the kick-off!" The President was shocked.

Besides, Alex couldn't budge. The Vice-President had moved to the other side of him, so that he, Spleeno Bludgeon, like Victor Winner, could share the company of this distinguished football player. Between the brawny, overweight body of Spleeno Bludgeon and the long, pointed elbows and knees of Victor Winner, Alex felt pinned in like a sardine.

He tried to smile and relax, but as the teams lined up for the kick-off his tension increased and so did his desire to urinate.

He wondered if others had such problems, even Presidents? James, standing on the sideline listening to Coach Borborg's final exhortations, did appear to have his feet planted firmly on the ground. But the day, which had been cold but sunny, grew gray and gloomy. While Alex had been seeking to ease his discomfort it had become overcast. A gusty wind was blowing in from the north and it would be tough to pass, Alex thought apprehensively, and James was too small and slow to run successfully.

Staring out of the open end of the stadium Alex saw the park just beyond the parking lot, but it did not give him the lift it used to. The leaves of autumn were gone and the spiky branches of the trees were bleak. There was a dense, stifling layer of smog over the parking lot and it reminded Alex that the university planned to bulldoze the park so they would have space for the autos that came to the games.

Now the air was so oppressive and sickening that Alex could not tell how much of it was due to smog or the coming of winter, but his lungs filled with exhaust gas, for latecomers were still arriving, and as he coughed, Spleeno Bludgeon whispered to him, "There was a terrible traffic jam, I could see it as I flew in on my helicopter. You would think a university as famous as this one would be more efficient."

"They intend to be, Mr. Vice-President," Alex answered. "By next season they expect to level the park into a parking lot."

"Good. Don't you find the kick-off an unforgettable moment?"

Alex nodded, but now the weather had a tombish chill and he would have preferred to be sitting close to a warm fire. Only as the start of the game came closer and closer, the President and Vice-President grew more and more excited and as they pressed forward and toward each other Alex's seat got smaller and smaller. Yet he was afraid to

break in on them, they were so engulfed with emotion. Both
the President and the Vice-President were waiting for the
kick-off with such rapt attention, as was Graves, sitting on
the other side of the President, in the other place of honor,
Number One aide for the moment, while Shipmen
had been relegated to Number Two, on the right of the Vice-
President.

Shipmen looked irritated by the present pecking order
and Alex wondered if he would hold that against him, too.
Then Alex, to improve his own state of mind, marvelled out
loud that the President could sit in such cold weather without a coat, it must create a virile impression on the millions
watching the picture, and Spleeno Bludgeon whispered en-
viously, "He is wearing his thermal underwear and he has
a heater hidden under his seat." Spleeno Bludgeon looked
like an overstuffed teddy bear in his huge coat and even as
he applauded the refereee when the official placed the football for the kick-off, his face was a wan gray hue, his eyes
watered, his nose ran, and he appeared about to weep with
emotion.

Alex thought, It was in stadiums like this one that people
invested their dreams and he wondered uneasily if the investment was sound. To judge from the expressions on the
faces of the President and the Vice-President it were as if
something magnificent was about to happen.

Then suddenly, abruptly, the referee held up his hand for
a time out.

"But the game hasn't begun," Spleeno Bludgeon
grumbled.

Alex said, "It must be for the commercial, sir. For the
picture."

"No!" cried the President, "It's a disturbance in the
stands." He pointed to the bleachers behind the goal posts
where a commotion had erupted. "Graves, will we need
tanks? Think of my image! Are we safe?"

"I'm sure you are," said Graves, but Shipmen looked
pleased at Graves's discomfiture. "Sir, The Examiners will
take care of it, whatever it is."

Shipmen said, "Sir, I warned you it could be unwise to
attend this game. The university has a reputation for

treachery. I heard rumors there could be a booby trap in the bleachers. You know what happened last night."

"An isolated incident, sir," said Graves. "The students are delighted that you have honored them with your presence. You saw how they all stood when the bands played 'Hail to The Chief.'"

"Perhaps, Mr. President," Alex ventured, "the students are fighting because they don't like their seats." He didn't add what everybody knew, that the students had been moved from their usual seats in midfield to cheap seats behind the goal posts to make room for the President. "Or possibly, they are just drunk from singing the school's fight song."

The fighting subsided as The Examiners reached the commotion and the President said, "You could be right, Alex, and you ought to know. Graves, we mustn't be over-structured, too many Examiners could give an unfortunate impression. Couldn't they be less conspicuous?"

"Sir, that is why I had them dress so respectably. And everyone is seated again."

Those that weren't, Alex noticed, were hustled out of the stadium.

Victor Winner grumbled, "Very rarely do I get a chance to relax. Am I not entitled to some pleasure? Am I not allowed any privacy?"

No one replied and he lapsed into the reverie he was indulging in when the fighting had exploded. In it he saw himself as the quarterback of the year, scrambling, running, passing, winning, a dynamic figure throwing a football into tomorrow, with the fastest release, quicker than the best two gun sheriff, capable of hitting a finger-tip at fifty yards, his nerves as sharp as any razor commercial, and always the leader. It was much better than having to sleep with a board under his mattress, as he had to do now; or to be unable to sleep at all because his muscles ached, which was often; and his fingers were so arthritic he could hardly hold anything, he couldn't even throw a brick through a church window.

Spleeno Bludgeon sensed the President's dreams; he had his, too: the vision of being a great linebacker was enough to keep him alive. The thought of slamming into people

thrilled him. That was what football was all about, he reflected triumphantly, hitting, punishing, knocking quarterbacks on their ass, except the President, the President was
*his* quarterback.

As The Examiners emptied the section of the bleachers
where the battle had happened and examined it for booby
traps and the teams retired to their locker rooms to regain
their proper combat frenzy, Alex decided it might be an
opportune moment to obtain the Vice-President's views on
the Pacification Program, he had such a beatific look on his face.

"Sir, you've just returned from the Territory. Do you
think there is any chance that the fighting will end soon?"

"The boys love football. They all wanted to know who
was winning."

"Sir, that isn't what I meant. I read in the papers that . . ."

"You mustn't believe what you read in the papers."

"I mustn't believe their casualty figures, sir?"

"A columnist who does could find it counter-productive."

"But the casualties are continuing, aren't they, sir?"

"People get hurt playing football. Didn't you?"

"No."

"You were lucky."

Shipmen cut in, "If you want to stay lucky I would concentrate on peaceful subjects. Like you did this week. The
President is pleased with your recent columns."

"He's read them?"

"I read them to him. The parts I thought would interest
him."

"Roger is right," said Spleeno Bludgeon. "The President
is Number One. I just run interference for him. I'm Number
Two."

"I thought . . ."

The President, who had been discussing the merits of the
two teams with Graves, interrupted Alex, "We have all the
facts. We know best."

Alex replied, "That is why, sir, I ask questions. In the
hope that your answers will clarify the Pacification Program."

The President said, "We're only trying to protect ourselves."

"Protective retaliation," added Spleeno Bludgeon. "Like football. When you're hit, you hit back. And we have reduced casualties so now they range from moderate to light. It is becoming a very sanitary program. Soon we expect to pacify without any casualties of our own."

Shipmen said, "Mr. President, I've always said it was a mistake to make our casualty figure public, that they would be misunderstood. Look at the time Alex Grant has wasted misinterpreting them."

There was a tremendous roar from the crowd as the teams returned from their dressing rooms and the President said, "Alex, we're looking forward to you being part of our team. I wish I had a son out there. You must be a proud father. To have him be the quarterback yet!"

But Alex was thinking worriedly, Could James take the punishment, always more ferocious in *The Game*, which was played with fanaticism? Could his son withstand the charging linesmen who put Vaseline on their fingers so they could rub it in the quarterbacks' eyes and blind him and possibly damage his eyes permanently? Or the instant after James had thrown the football and the play was whistled dead the bastard who took a cheap shot at him from behind and the quarterback got up with double vision and a throbbing headache. The punishers who loved to pound quarterbacks into the ground. Who did it with a savage satisfaction. And James, as the quarterback, couldn't do a thing about it, the worst frustration of all. Could his son play when he was woozy, had trouble seeing and there was no escape from the thousand pounds of pain that was hurtling down upon him?

The President interrupted Alex's reflection by handing him the morning paper and saying, "Graves was reading me an article on the sports page about your son. They think he has an excellent chance of emulating his father. It is fine publicity, Alex. Didn't you read about it?"

"Not yet, sir. I was busy this morning."

"Take a quick look. There is still a moment before the kick-off."

"Thank you, sir," But Alex's need to urinate distracted him and he missed the sports page and mistakenly turned to

Page Fifty. There, on the last page, were the casualty figures, boxed in between the weather, the shipping news, and two advertisements for contraceptives and cash registers. As if hypnotized, Alex found himself counting the dead.

The President nudged him, said, "You're going to miss the kick-off!"

"Sir, my son isn't on that team."

"And they did lose the toss. His side is kicking off."

Spleeno Bludgeon said, "It is a beautiful time," and started to sing, 'Happy Days Are Here Again'.

The President confided to Alex, "I needed an offensive line coach and Spleeno needed a future and he does learn fast. You're not listening!"

"I'm sorry, sir. I was reading the paper you gave me."

"Oh, about your son. That's excusable. Here they go!"

Everybody stood up as the kick-off arched high in the air, seemed to hang for an instant like a bird in flight, then suddenly dropped toward the ground and into the arms of a receiver. The President exclaimed, "What a lovely kick! Excellent hang time!" The high kick gave the tacklers an extra second to get downfield and the receiver had time only to move a few steps when he was overwhelmed by tacklers. The President shouted to Alex, "It is so physical and emotional!" and the Vice-President was yelling, "Kill him! Kill him! What a hit! That's knocking him on his ass!" Spleeno Bludgeon was slobbering like a linebacker Alex remembered: every time the linebacker tackled him, the linebacker punched and bit him. The halfback who had received the kick-off lay prone, injured, and to the President and Vice-President's disgust there was another time out and the game had barely begun.

Alex's eyes strayed to the casualty figures he had been counting.

Victor Winner said, "That's a great write-up about your son. He can't let us down now. Coach Borborg invited me to sit on the bench, but while I would love to do so, I thought it might disturb the players. But if he wins, I will phone him later, and I will call your son, too, Alex."

"Thank you, sir." He thought, Forty-eight died in the

Territory last week. And he could have missed it. The President must have. The President was applauding the injured player who was being carried off the field. Forty-eight individuals whose dying laid a clammy hand on wives girl friends mothers fathers sisters brothers children friends. On the last page where few would see it. Yet he was sitting between the President and the Vice-President.

"Tell them!" he heard old Iron Face saying. But Victor Winner was staring at him as if he were crazy—how could he be reading a paper, even about his son—when the teams were lining up to resume play.

Spleeno Bludgeon was shouting, "Stick it down their throats, that's what this game is all about, hitting, if you can't take it, don't play—what a shot! You can count the bodies! Six guys hit the ball carrier!"

Alex sank back in his seat, feeling worn out, thinking, Maybe the President is right, maybe people don't want the Territory to be mentioned anymore, they are tired of casualty figures, the news is only as important as people make it, and he must play the king's jester, he must not let one grinning skull mock his own indifference—if he could only close his eyes and make the dead go away.

"They've lost the ball!" he heard Graves cry exultantly. "Now we will have a chance to show them! Alex, your son is starting!"

He opened his eyes and saw James trot out on the field with the rest of the team for their first offensive series. The ball was on the forty-yard line and the President said, "Excellent field position," and the Vice-President added, "The other side made a terrible kick."

Alex's heart was pounding as he wondered if his son's was, yet suddenly he blurted out to the President, "The casualty figures, sir."

"They're low this week. Very encouraging. Does your son like to pass on first down? The enemy linebackers are playing very close."

"Yes," said Alex. He was surprised that the huddle was taking such a long time. James must be planning something special, he thought, probably a pass on first down, hoping to catch the opposition off-balance. Just as Alex expected the referee to penalize James for taking too much time, the huddle ended, the team marched up to their offensive formation with the military cadence of which Coach Borborg was so proud, and there was a violent gasp from the crowd. James was naked. Alex rubbed his eyes, but the apparition didn't vanish. His son was naked. James was wearing nothing but a smug expression.

The President cried, "We have such bad luck!"

The Vice-President yelled, "It's psychological warfare. Arrest him!"

But was nakedness illegal, Alex asked himself. In his excitement he forgot that he had to urinate. He could feel his heart pounding furiously.

James stood behind the center—his uniform a neat pile behind him—while everybody watched, stricken with amazement and unable to move. He took the football from the center, held up his fingers in the V sign for peace, waved a large banner with the word *Peace* on it, and the President complained, "I can't see, Spleeno is blocking my view."

The President was standing on tip-toe, as was the Vice-President, and all Alex could say was, "We are more or less alike."

Spleeno Bludgeon retorted, "What is your son so angry about? We had only forty-eight dead last week and they had one thousand and two."

Alex was silent. Although it was bitterly cold he was sweating, yet James hadn't moved. The game had come to a complete halt. Then Coach Borborg and an assistant coach ran out on the field and the head coach tried to kick James in the groin, to destroy what he considered the offending parts, but James took out the two coaches with a superb block and Spleeno Bludgeon exclaimed, "What a great block! He wiped out two guys! Shook them to their toes! Why doesn't he stick to football?"

The President shoved the Vice-President out of his way so he could see better and shouted, "Spleeno, it is no time to run interference."

The other team went to tackle James and he evaded them, held the football high over his head with one hand and the peace flag with the other, and ran the length of the football field, avoiding one would-be tackler after another, as if he was scoring the winning touchdown.

Then, as many in the crowd, especially in the student section, cheered James, he ran around the track that circled the field. Passing the presidential stand, he waved his peace banner extra hard, but when his pursuers neared his speed increased. However, at the portion of the track behind the goal posts where most of the students were he halted. Here the cheering was loudest. The college bands began to play their school fight songs in a frantic effort to distract the students from what James was doing, but other students started to disrobe and joined him, blocking off James from the opposing team, and peace signs appeared in many parts of the stadium and the cheering increased.

Examiners, distraught by what was happening, rushed to capture James, but he dodged them with an open field skill Alex had not thought his son possessed, and rushed to the microphone behind his team's bench.

He shouted into it, "No more Pacification! No more killing! No more deaths! I demand Peace. No number must be . . ."

Examiners threw football blankets over James, muffling and covering him, and carried him, kicking and struggling, off the field.

The President mumbled, "How could he do this to me! He's a savage!"

"It's unnatural," added the Vice-President. "And he runs so well. I'd give him a punch in the nose. That would teach him."

Graves glared at Alex as if he had mortally wounded him, while Shipmen had a malicious, knowing grin on his face, saying, I told you so.

Many spectators were swarming over the field and more of them were disrobing and every time an Examiner stopped them others started.

The President declared, "It is an academic disgrace. I have never been so embarrassed in my life. Alex Grant, how could you do this to me?"

"Sir," stammered Alex, "I had no idea this was going to happen."

Other students began to tear down the goal posts and Alex noticed they came from both schools, that they were doing it with great zest, and now there seemed to be as many students on the field as in the stands.

The President cried, "They're halting the game! Ruining it!"

Shipmen asked, "Should I call in the tanks? They'll clear the field."

The President hesitated, then said, "No, it would give a bad impression. Graves, you assured me that nothing could go wrong. How can I ever trust you again?"

Graves said, "Sir, it must have something to do with the bombing."

"No doubt," said the President. "Birds of a feather."

"Of course," agreed the Vice-President. "They did blow up football equipment."

The goal posts came down and The Examiners ran out of blankets to cover the naked students, and now non-students were joining in, and the referee announced over the loud-speaker system, "The game is being cancelled due to circumstances beyond our control."

Spleeno Bludgeon cried, "The game cancelled? It's a national disaster." He turned on Alex, shouted, "How could you do this to us?"

"I didn't do anything," Alex said woefully.

"Maybe that's the trouble," said Shipmen.

"I wrote columns about autumn and Mozart."

"Why didn't you teach your son to feel the same way? He must be insane. Or part of a conspiracy."

"What do you mean?" Alex wished he could talk to James and find out what had really happened, but his way was blocked by Examiners.

"The bombing last night. This nakedness now. It doesn't seem like a coincidence to me," Shipmen announced triumphantly.

"You could be right, Roger," said the President. "Investigate. We will not endorse such scandalous behavior with our presence. I must leave as soon as possible. No one must think that I approve of nakedness." He motioned for his guards to form a protective wall around him.

By now many of the students had undressed and were doing a snake dance nakedly across the field to celebrate a victory, their victory. Any victory, thought Alex, that would bring peace and embarrass their elders.

At the President's command a solid line of Examiners blocked him from public view and hid the offending students from his gaze. Yet reporters refused to take the hint and approached him and as several shouted questions at him, he shouted back, "I have no intention of giving any statements. We moved into the new Territory to get out of the old."

Everyone in the presidential party acted as if James had betrayed his country and Alex protested, "I'm sure it was just a boyish prank."

"He insulted the President," said the Vice-President. "If he were in the army, he would be court-martialled."

The President said to Graves, "Why didn't Intelligence warn you?"

"I didn't expect such an escalation."

"God knows what this country is coming to? So much nakedness!"

Alex suggested, "Perhaps it was James's way of asking about Pacification?"

"What about Pacification?" The President bristled irately.

"James wants to know when it will end, sir."

"You will see."

"When, sir?"

"Our game plan is going according to schedule. Grant, I will be as forgiving and understanding as possible, but if you don't get your son to apologize I cannot consider you our friend." Assured by The Examiners that it was safe to depart, that no naked students would bar his way now, the President left, very irately, the Vice-President close behind him.

Graves added, "I thought you had integrity, at least most of the time, but now I don't know what to think." He hurried after the President.

Shipmen waited until he and Alex were alone. Once the President was gone no one tried to halt the naked snake dance and when the aide was sure he would not be heard, he said to Alex, "We are running out of time."

Alex asked, even more confused than before, "What can I do?"

"If you can't get your son to apologize, you must denounce him."

"The President didn't suggest that."

"Your son denounced us. And the sooner you correct what your son has done the better, before he says or does anything even worse."

"Where do you think they took him?"

"To the locker room, probably. In this business you are either loyal or you are out. We need team players, not individualists."

Alex followed Shipmen obediently, but he walked only a few feet when he was stopped by an elderly, white-haired woman who cried, "I have to talk to you!" He braced himself for a verbal assault and she added, "I must touch the man who touched the President." She grabbed Alex's hand and fondled it passionately. "I adore the President," she gooed. "He is so manly. He would never allow himself to be seen naked."

By the time Alex reached the walk under the stadium he lost sight of Shipmen. He didn't know what to do; he couldn't condemn his own son and make a public execution out of this rite, yet if he were silent the consequences could be worse. 'And as his tension increased, his need to urinate became overwhelming. Scalded with pain, he thought his childhood days when he was a bed-wetter had returned and the idea of pissing in his pants was too dreadful to endure. Shivering with a sudden chill, in his agony he could find only one refuge, the woman's lavatory. He blessed the circumstances that no one was in it and as he relieved himself, he thought, never had he experienced such an exquisite sensation.

He stepped out of the woman's lavatory, feeling better prepared to face his dilemma, and Shipmen greeted him. Alex blanched. Two Examiners were with Shipmen, but no one mentioned where he had been.

Instead, Shipmen said, "I didn't want to lose you."

"What happened?"

"Your son was taken to the university hospital."

"Was he hurt?"

"It is for psychiatric examination."

"There is nothing wrong with him."

"After what he did? He is also under arrest."

"What's the charge?"

"It hasn't been decided yet. It is a new situation and the authorities are studying the statute books."

"You mean, you don't know."

"I hope, for your sake, your son isn't tied in with The Demolisher."

"That's absurd."

"Nothing is absurd these days."

"When can I see James?"

"That is up to the hospital and the authorities."

"I will go see him now."

"We will go with you," said Shipmen, and the presidential aide and the two Examiners stepped alongside of Alex before he could elude them.

Feeling guilty, he mumbled, "I should have gone to the toilet earlier, but I didn't want to be discourteous to the President"—and he couldn't tell whether he was making sense to them—"so, I had to use what was available, and there was nobody inside but me," he ended lamely.

As the four of them stepped into the daylight outside of the stadium Alex noticed The Examiners carried miniature cameras around their necks and he was certain from the smug expression on Shipmen's face that they had taken pictures of him leaving the woman's lavatory.

The Demolisher was furious when he heard what had happened at *The Game*. He thought angrily, the quarterback is trying to get the headlines—just like a quarterback!—and taking them away from me. And when The Demolisher learned from his bed in the university hospital that he was next door to the quarterback, and they were having the same examination and there was talk that they were part of the same conspiracy, he became one of the angriest patients the university hospital had ever treated. As his nurse sought to soothe him, assuring him, "You are here for your own protection, we want to make sure you were not hurt by the explosion," it made his blood boil. He could have killed her. There was nothing wrong with him, and the fucking quarterback should have kept his hands out of his play. He lay in his beautifully clean white hospital bed, the first clean bed he had slept in for weeks, surrounded by the best in medical equipment, which he never could have afforded if he had fallen ill, and he thought irately, if I had my way, I would abolish football altogether, I would blow up the whole fucking stadium.

By the time Alex reached the university hospital, there was an official charge against his son. It was: "Unreasonably alarming the public by appearing in the nude." He heard also, that there might be other charges against James.

# Sid Virgin

Sid Virgin it's James Grant your quarterback
What plays are you making now
playing End in Football Heaven
The team missed you at the university

Sid *The Game* is not
your game anymore
You played your last one in the Territory
It was called the Pacification Program
You lost

But you were a winner after all
Now you can play for each dead
President
while we had only one President at *The Game*
But we would rather have had you
My regards to President Number One

Sid we owe you an apology
We owe you a game
A life
Small things like that
My regards to President Number Two

When all the Presidents come to apologize
They owe you something
like your personal history versus
the history of this country taught here
at the university
My regards to President Number Twenty-Two

Sid when they knock on your door
tell them from me
they missed the point when they were President
They should have listened to you
My regards
to President Number Two Hundred and Twenty-Two

Sid I wanted you to play End with me
Now I'll never play football again
I told the President we killed your game
I'll never forget you
Can you remember the living
Forgive me for asking
It's James Grant your quarterback


STYMEAN KARLEN

# Sid Virgin

The last time James had been in the university hospital had been to visit Sid Virgin. Now however, as if he were a dangerous explosive about to go off, he was rushed into emergency by four Examiners. And when it was decided that he would not explode, or explode anything else, he was hustled into the accident ward. But he kept thinking of Sid and remembering what had happened when The Examiners had seized him.

"You are in our custody for your own good," The Examiners assured James as they dragged him off the field and into his team's locker room, knocking the breath out of his body and almost suffocating him with the blankets they threw over him. "We are protecting you. You need an immediate examination. For security. And your own safety."

He heard loud cheering and he asked, "Has the game resumed anyhow?"

One of The Examiners said sadly, "No. The cheering is for the goal posts. They've just come down. We'll never hear the end of this."

"What about the President?"

"None of your fucking business. He'll manage without you."

What about Alex? Didn't his father give a damn after all? Was Alex still going to support the Pacification Program? Before James could ask any questions, he was told to dress and when he refused The Examiners dressed him and hurried him out of the stadium and into a car that far exceeded the speed limit as they drove him to the university hospital.

The accident ward was empty except for an interne, not much older than James, a young, pretty nurse, about the same age as James, and the four Examiners. Now they ordered him to undress and when he refused, saying, "The right to be naked is a personal right," they forcibly stripped him.

James was embarrassed. The nurse was the kind of a girl he dated and he felt exposed. His penis protruded like the handle of a hair brush, prickly and defiant, as if to generate another explosion and there was nothing he could do about it. He couldn't touch his penis; that would be mis-interpreted. Or psychic it into being a wriggly worm. His penis always stood up when he was aroused.

The interne, exhausted from working over-long shifts, didn't listen to The Examiners' explanations. The instant he heard the word "quarterback," he examined James as a piece of meat to be processed. Finished, he reported, "Knees okay. Broken bones—none. Fractures—none. No chills, back or respiratory problems, or any symptoms of bodily damage."

James asked, "Now can I get out of here?"

"Not so quick," said an Examiner. "Your examination has just begun."

James was clothed in a hospital gown and led into a beautiful private room. A showcase, he thought, to display the university's beneficence to an erring son, and far better than the room where he had visited Sid. When Sid had been diagnosed as a poor football risk, his friend had been put in the accident ward, surrounded with auto casualties, and the most casual attention. But Sid hadn't protested; he had accepted this situation.

Before James could ask any more questions, he was shoved into bed. He tried to get out of it, but The Examiners wouldn't allow that, although they did permit him to sit up against the backrest so he could be examined

most efficiently. Then three doctors marched into the room
in single file and The Examiners stated portentously, "The
university's medical examining board, which we have con-
vened for this emergency."

The Examiners stationed themselves outside the room so
no one else could enter while the three doctors introduced
themselves.

The leader was lean, handsome, and youthful in spite of
his closely cropped gray hair, and he announced that he was
the military doctor assigned to the hospital to examine
Pacification cases. He was followed by a short, stout middle-
aged man, who introduced himself as the staff psychiatrist.
The last doctor was solemn, elderly and he whispered
humbly that he was a general practitioner whose duty was to
verify the findings of the internes, who could be unreliable.

James mentally catalogued them as M.P., P.P., and G.P.,
and asked, "Why am I in bed? I'm not sick."

"That is for us to decide," M.P. said sharply. "Boy, what
do you have against this great and traditional sport,
football?"

"Sid Virgin."

"It was the President who was insulted. What prompted
you to risk your career with this shocking display of exhibitionism?"

"Sid Virgin."

"Very odd. You ask him factual questions and he
continues to indulge himself in fantasy. No wonder he did
what he did."

P.P. cut in, "Perhaps we are being a trifle hasty." His
voice became soft and soothing as he asked, "Son, who is
Sid Virgin?"

"My buddy on the football team. He was killed in the
Territory."

"But what has that to do with parading naked?"

"I was protesting to the President."

"Why?"

"He killed him."

Even G.P., who was checking the interne's findings for
likely errors, looked shocked, while M.P. declared, "The
boy is sick."

"I don't mean with his own hands. But, in effect, yes."

"There is no such thing," stated M.P. "Either you kill or you don't. And the President hasn't killed anybody."

"He supports the Pacification Program."

"So?" M.P. regarded James as if he were an idiot.

"The Pacification Program killed Sid. And many others. And the President is responsible."

"The President is responsible for the safety of our country. Even a fool knows that. He has many people to consider."

"Sir, the important number is one."

"That's absurd." M.P. was indignant. "He would need a computer to keep track of everybody. He would not have time for anything else."

But James knew that he must listen to his own heartbeat. He said, "The President could try. I would."

"Is that why the building next to the stadium was destroyed?"

G.P. said, "The Demolisher did it. He admitted it."

M.P. said, "The timing can't be ignored. There must be a connection."

"I didn't even know that the storerooms were blown up," said James. "Coach Borborg kept the team in seclusion the last twenty-four hours, so we would think of nothing but *The Game*. And I've told you why I protested."

"Nakedly!" M.P. turned to the others. "There is an obvious obscene tie-in with the demolisher. You can see it in his eyes."

The object in James's eyes was Sid Virgin. Sid was saying to him, *Lay off, kid, they can't hear you, the guns are too loud, I've tried to speak to the dead Presidents and even they won't listen to me. They are so busy justifying themselves to history, they refuse to listen to my history.* James couldn't repeat Sid's comments to the doctors; they would certify him as insane. He asked, "Why am I in bed? The interne said I was okay."

G.P. stated, "Your body appears to be."

"After he destroyed *The Game*?" exclaimed M.P. "He must be sick! Then, blaming the President! How could he? How dare he?"

James said, "I blamed him for Sid Virgin."

"You are obsessed. Obscene. Why did you conspire with The Demolisher?"

"I told you I never heard of him."

"He is in the next room," M.P. said triumphantly. "Waiting for us."

"Willingly?" James asked. He noticed that M.P. was also a colonel.

"That is not the point. There is really no difference between you. What each of you did, in effect, served the same purpose. As far as the result is concerned, you are accomplices. And, I believe, actually are."

P.P., who was watching this exchange with great interest, said, "Sir, we must be fair. This boy's involvement with The Demolisher has not been proven as yet." The psychiatrist was thinking. There was no problem in organizing and performing this examination, guilt was evident, the difficulty was to diagnose the patient's motives. This boy must have been deprived somewhere in his life, yet he had a penis of striking and visible proportions; P.P. could see it protruding under the hospital gown as the patient became angrier and more aroused. *Penis is destiny*, P.P. believed, and his had become tiny and shriveled, although he was not yet fifty. He asked, his voice husky with sincerity, "Son, why did you indulge yourself?"

James longed to retort, I am not your son, but that would be held against him and he said, "It was not indulgence. I thought about protesting for months, but I wanted to do it when it would be most effective."

"When your father would be there? When you could compete with him?"

"Where is my father now? Is no one going to defend me?"

"We are Son, what really prompted you to run naked before thousands of people. One doesn't do this on a whim. What sexual reasons?"

"I told you. For Sid Virgin. To speak out against Pacification."

M.P. said, "By yourself? I don't believe you. Who was behind you?"

"I did it by myself. But many of the students feel the way

I do. That is why they undressed, too, once I did. To show their support."

P.P. said, "They did it to display their penises."

"Indecently!" declared M.P. He was so irate he was developing a nervous twitch. "We don't worry about such virility in the Pacification Program."

"None the less," said P.P., "we must realize it was no accident that our patient exhibited the most dominant expression of his maleness. It is possible that he was revealing a psychic disability. That is why we have to be dispassionate. How friendly were you and this Sid Virgin?"

James was silent.

"I do want to help you." P.P.'s voice grew even more soothing.

*See. kid,* James heard Sid whispering. *You can't win, you're wasting your time, they won't listen to you either. They got to deodorize you, too.*

Suddenly then, it was G.P. who was agitated. He had been examining the bed while the other two doctors were questioning James, and he blurted out, "We've got him in the wrong room. This bed is for accident cases and the sheet is too short! How could they have been so stupid?"

M.P. said, "It was done so he would be next to The Demolisher."

P.P. said, "Besides, we don't have time to change his room. We have to formulate a diagnosis before it is too late."

M.P. agreed and the doctors withdrew into a corner for consultation. P.P. stressed that the patient had an obsessive-compulsive personality, plus a persecution complex. M.P. stated that the boy's criticism of the President's Pacification Program made him potentially dangerous, a security risk. And G.P. repeated that there was nothing wrong with him physically. But all of them felt that James's preoccupation with Sid Virgin was an infantile fantasy, and thus, he was not to be trusted.

M.P. informed James, "We have decided you are no longer capable of performing your duties as quarterback."

"I am officially being dropped from the team?"

"Yes," M.P. said portentously.

"But I've quit already."

"That is for us to decide. You have revealed an emotional instability, indulging in a general degradation of students and spectators at *The Game*."

"Is that all?"

"Furthermore, you have abused public confidence."

"What is the charge?"

P.P. said, "Unreasonably alarming the public by appearing in the nude."

M.P. said, "Although further charges may be preferred."

"When?" asked James.

"If your atrocious behavior continues," said M.P.

James was silent again, thinking sadly, *Sid, I tried, I did really. What do I have to do now to convince them*? But Sid didn't answer.

P.P. asked gently, "Son, what is troubling you now?"

"It doesn't matter."

"But it does. You have been self-indulgent but we do want to help you."

"Is my father outside?"

G.P. went to the door, looked out, and said, "Not yet."

"I didn't expect him to be here. I don't want to see him."

The Demolisher refused to answer any of the doctors' questions. Each time M.P. tried to connect him with the quarterback next door, he shouted, "I did it myself, don't give me a bad rap!" He ignored P.P.'s psychiatric queries and when G.P. checked his physical condition, for that had been neglected, he got stomach acid from his rage, begged for some gum to chew, and he was shocked by the quarterback's nudity. He yelled, "I ain't a weirdo, I would never appear naked, that's dirty, don't you associate me with him, the fucking quarterback!" M.P. insisted, "You are sure you don't know him at all?" and he screamed. "I don't know anything about him! I'm The Demolisher! I hate quarterbacks! Big shits! Stealing all the publicity! Anybody can throw a football but it takes guts to throw a bomb. I did it by myself, all by myself, you got the evidence, I did it in self-defense." And when the doctors started out of his room without acknowledging this, he shouted in a violent rage,

"Won't nobody listen to me? Won't nobody ever listen to me? Fucking doctors! They ain't any better than quarterbacks. I bet they listened to him." The nurse sought to console him after the doctors were gone, saying, "You were lucky, young man, you're unhurt, nothing vital was damaged," and he retorted angrily, "The next time I blow anything up the whole fucking world will hear it!"

Alex saw the doctors emerging from a hospital room and before Shipmen or any of The Examiners could halt him, he asked them, "How is James Grant? I'm his father. Is anything wrong with him?"

P.P. declared, "Your son has penis problems."

M.P. added, "And no self-control. His exhibitionism could very well be a form of masturbation."

G.P. concluded, "But we have given him the best medical attention."

Shipmen interrupted, "What about The Demolisher? It was his room that you were leaving. Have you found any tie-in between these two protesters?"

"The Demolisher confessed nothing," M.P. said regretfully, "except that he did blow up the storerooms. But I'm sure there is complicity."

"Do you have any proof?" Alex asked anxiously.

M.P. regarded him scornfully, as if Alex was naive, but he didn't reply.

"Anyway," Shipmen said brusquely, "proof can come later. Thank you, gentlemen. I will make whatever statements are necessary."

Alex said hurriedly, "What about my son? When can I see him?"

M.P. said, "He doesn't want to see you."

At Shipmen's signal the doctors left before any more questions could be asked.

"I must see James," said Alex. "He is upset, not himself."

"I will arrange that now," said Shipmen, unexpectedly gracious.

"Thank you," said Alex. "I will do what I can. Within reason."

"Of course," said Shipmen. "You are a sensible, reasonable man."

Shipmen spoke to The Examiners who were guarding James's room and indicated that Alex could enter. But as Alex hurried in to see his son, he remembered Shipmen's parting words: "I don't have anything against your son personally, but he is obviously involved in a conspiracy with The Demolisher, for they had a common purpose—to discredit the President."

Shipmen, pleased with the way he was handling this emergency, stationed himself in a nearby conference room to await The Examiners' report on The Demolisher, whom they were questioning themselves now. They were doing this on his orders; he was dissatisfied with the doctors' failure to elicit any important information, especially evidence that would lead to complicity between the quarterback and The Demolisher.

He was proud of his skill as an investigator. It was what he lived for. He was positive Grant would persuade his son to apologize, or if the quarterback refused, the columnist would issue a statement denouncing his son's behavior. He allowed himself a small smile of gratification, and the luxury of reflection. Matters were progressing as he wished now; it might even turn out this attack on the President could be maneuvered to his own advantage; that idea gave him special pleasure, as if he had thrown the winning pass with five seconds to play.

He even felt a little self-indulgent, a mood he seldom permitted himself, and something he never did when anyone else was around.

Shipmen was a very private man; he never let anyone know what he was thinking or feeling. He had a morbid fear of having his privacy invaded, or investigated. It gave him a tremendous advantage to know more about the other person than the other person knew about him. This was why he had never married, or had children, or why, as far as females were concerned, he was monastic. He was determined that no female, wife, love, mistress, or child, or anybody else, was going to spoil his career. He had seen it happen too often to others. Nobody was ever going to find him in such a predicament. Investigating took all his time and concentration. He couldn't afford to care for other people.

His reflections reminded him of the one time he had almost slipped. He did have one sister, a fact he had been unable to control, to his regret, and she had a son, which had happened also without his permission. When her husband died as the boy was about to enter the university and there was no money, Shipmen—in a moment of soft-heartedness, as he called it—offered to pay his nephew's tuition. Then a dreadful thing happened. Although it had occurred two years ago, it were as if it had taken place yesterday, the pain of the memory was so vivid. He would never forget it, even now, when he felt just one step away from his goal, to be the President's Number One aide.

He was in an immaculate, antiseptic hospital room identical to the one the quarterback was in, concentrating on recovering from an operation for hemorrhoids, and wishing he didn't feel so damned uncomfortable. His hemorrhoids were irritating, and somehow shameful, and he kept the nature of his operation secret from everyone.

When Graves asked, "What is wrong, Roger?" for he was in the university hospital on Graves's recommendation, he answered, "It is a bad knee, from too much touch football, it is a favorite ailment among quarterbacks." After Graves seemed to believe him, Shipmen told the President the same story and his boss regarded him admiringly, as if he were a war casualty and wished him a speedy recovery.

Yet when his nephew dropped in to ask how he was and what was wrong, Shipmen blushed. Then he was shocked. His nephew had allowed his hair to grow to his shoulders; he wore a heavy beard, blue dungarees and a T-shirt. Shipmen felt betrayed; his nephew had become a hippy, dirty; it was the fault of the university; if the President learned that he was putting a hippy through school his boss would never trust him.

"God damn it!" he exclaimed. "You look like a trouble maker!" What obscenity would come next? It was very embarrassing.

"I'm sorry, I didn't know you would over-react so." Harold had never seen his uncle lose his temper. Most of the time he was stone-faced.

"Over-react? Harold, couldn't you wear a clean shirt?"

"I thought I had the right to wear what I please."

"Within reason," said Shipmen, but he thought, he would never be able to trust his nephew any more. Yet he should have been prepared for this, he realized, Harold read too much and was always asking questions. It was his own stupid fault for helping him, for caring. Such a shame—this waste of tuition. It was quite annoying. "You look so dirty."

"I didn't mean to cause you any trouble," Harold stammered as his uncle winced from pain and he backed out of the hospital room.

Shipmen was depressed for a long time. He caught a terrible cold which almost became pneumonia and he had to stay in bed another week.

He only started to recover when his nephew informed him, "I'm quitting the university."

The twenty-year-old Harold stood awkwardly at the foot of his uncle's bed, having returned to the hospital a week later with the intention of apologizing, at his mother's instigation, but suddenly he couldn't compromise when his uncle frowned at his appearance, and so, while he was afraid of him, he had to blurt out, "Thanks for your help, but I don't want to be an accountant, I want to write and the school isn't relevant."

Shipmen was relieved. Then, realizing that Harold felt guilty—which was fitting, after all his nephew had not lived up to his obligations—he shouted "You're walking out on me! After what I have done for you! I don't want to have anything more to do with you!" Shipmen turned his back on his nephew and his nurse had to usher out an embarrassed Harold.

From then on, Shipmen knew he could not be a perfect investigator and care. He returned to his original premise: no one was innocent of wrong-doing and if he investigated them efficiently he would always find something of which they were guilty. Now he spent his free evenings studying the intelligence files on potential dissenters. He could absorb the facts in a dossier almost as quickly as a computer. Once, when he revealed this talent to the President, his boss said, "Roger, you have the mind of a weapons analyst." It was a compliment he treasured. He could ferret out the flaws of an opponent more effectively than anyone the President depended on. He yearned for chances to prove his skill, and he created the opportunity when it did not present itself.

If he were in Graves's situation, he told himself smugly, he would never have advised the President to attend *The Game*. The university allowed too much dissent to be reliable. But he had not tried to halt the visit, and that was smart, he thought. Now the President was angry at Graves, as he had hoped. Graves was guilty of failure, the worst sin of all. Victor Winner said there was no place in his organization for failure, or any act that resulted in embarrassment to him. One more mistake by Graves and he would end up answering mail, which was mostly junk and complaints. Graves had committed a grave error trusting Grant. But he wouldn't. He wouldn't even allow the columnist to get him parking space.

His reverie was interrupted by an Examiner with important news.

"Sir," said The Examiner, "The Demolisher must have been Army trained."

"Are you sure?" asked Shipmen. "There must be no mistakes here."

"Yes. The method he used is the same as is used in the Territory."

"Did you find some unused material?"

"One stick of dynamite, which he tried to hide on his person. But he didn't realize that we would give him a rectal examination, too."

"What does he talk about?"

"Quarterbacks. How much he hates quarterbacks."

"That must be a cover up. Any indication that females were involved?"

"Not so far. He sounds to me like he craves attention."

"What do our undercover agents on the campus report?"

"It is hard to say. They have been watching Grant for some time, but we have no evidence, yet, that anyone else was involved with him."

"Then we must find some. Was The Demolisher a student, too?"

"We don't know his name and the university doesn't fingerprint students, although we asked them to. If they had, it would be easy to find out."

Shipmen sighed, "It is not a perfect world. We mustn't be too unhappy about what has happened. When the columnist is finished with his son, tell him to phone me. I have to report to the President, he will want to know what I discovered."

"I'll question The Demolisher again. At once. Until he talks."

Shipmen nodded approvingly, but he didn't tell The Examiner what he was sure of already, that he had information that should silence the columnist's criticism, that Grant was vulnerable to compromise. He strode out of the hospital and into a waiting helicopter, feeling strong and purposeful, and thus, very masculine, although he was proud of his continence and chastity. And when he was in his helicopter he didn't go to the President first, but stopped off at his offices. He wanted to check with his computers. Shipmen had two computers in his offices, one to check on his facts and one to check on the first computer.

The Examiner strode up and down The Demolisher's room until he was exhausted, but the answers to his questions were always the same. He repeatedly suggested that the least the young man could do was talk to the quarterback, after all, they did have much in common, they had both protested to the President, and The Demolisher retorted, "I don't associate with such weirdos, the nudo, he's immoral, I'm choosey."

James didn't want to talk to his father.

Alex stood by the hospital bed and his son turned his back on him.

"I came as soon as I could," said Alex.

"You should have come sooner."

"I was detained by the authorities."

"So was I. Oh, why don't you go away."

"Do you really want me to, James?"

His son didn't answer.

"Are you comfortable?"

"I'd be more comfortable out of here."

"I'll see what I can do."

"Please, don't bother. I'll manage." But James turned around in his large hospital bed so that he was facing his father, and Alex was relieved to see that his son looked unhurt. His color was higher than usual, from excitement probably, thought Alex, and his fists were tightly clenched, as if determined never to throw a football again, yet some of his tautness vanished when he said, "I did shake them up, didn't I?"

"Yes." Alex surveyed the hospital room. He was shocked to discover that the windows were locked and there were bars on them, but everything else appeared normal. The room was spacious, large enough for several beds. There were oranges on a little table by the side of James, a television in the corner, several chairs, and magazines and newspapers in a rack. However, all of this was untouched, for James still lay in bed, as if that was a protest, too.

"I know you don't approve. But don't try to criticize me."

"I want to help you."

"Like they did? The only reason they put me in this fine room is to demonstrate to the public how kindly they treat their prisoners of war. And so I can be coupled with The Demolisher next door. Poor bastard. To do such a stupid thing. Blow up the football storeroom. That will only make them angrier and he could have hurt somebody."

"Then you didn't know him?" Alex felt better suddenly.

"Did you think I did?"

"The timing was suspicious."

"I did it for Sid Virgin. I'm tired of being a nice guy. If being a nice guy isn't doing anything, like you, I don't want to be nice. Nice stinks. If you were not going to commit yourself, I had to. Or they just kill you off. Like Sid Virgin."

"But the method you used? Was that really necessary?"

"I warned you. And today, you have to scream for a whisper to be heard."

Alex asked, "May I sit down?"

"Nobody is stopping you."

"Or asking me."

"Did I ask you to be born?"

"What has that have to do with what we are discussing?"

"If you give somebody life, you ought to give them something to live for! What has it been this week, sixty dead, or only thirty. Only thirty! They've cut it in half. Not bad! What did the President say?"

"He was embarrassed."

"Was that all?"

"He was also very angry."

"Isn't he going to do anything? Doesn't he realize how we feel?"

"He knows how *you* feel."

"Many of the students followed my example."

"Yes. I've never seen goal posts come down so quickly."

"Their reaction was more than that, Alexander, and you know it."

Much more, thought Alex, wondering how he could prevent his son from being destroyed, or himself. It wouldn't do any good to say anything now, it would just make James mad. And yet Shipmen was waiting, too.

"Like I said, I did it for Sid Virgin, too."

"I'm sure he appreciated it."

"Don't be sarcastic, Alexander."

"I'm not. I've known some Sid Virgins in my time, also."

"There was only one Sid Virgin. He was like nobody else." How dare Alexander take that away from him, and the idea infuriated James.

"So was mine. I lost him in my war. The war to end war."

"That is the excuse they give us now."

"Wars are usually fought to end wars. Instead, they generally breed them."

"Why don't you write that in your column?"

"I will."

"When? After the next war?"

"I don't know."

*See, Sid, my old man is no better than the rest. They have processed him, also, into their status system.*

*What else could I say, Alex confided to old Iron Face. Anyway, James isn't listening to me now, he is very distracted. And Shipmen expects the impossible, but so does my son.*

Thus, they sat, James in his hospital bed and Alex in his hospital chair, the gulf between them as wide as an ocean, each preoccupied with their silent thoughts, for a time that neither of them could measure.

*Sid, what can I say now? My old man doesn't hear me either.*

*Kid, they are all the same, they think if they go to church on Sunday anything they do on Monday will be okay.*

*But my old man doesn't go to church. I don't think. He never took me. On Sunday, we always went to the football game.*

*Forget it, kid, it's no use, it doesn't matter, nothing does.*

That was more than James could endure and he cried out in his misery.

"What's wrong?" asked Alex, shaken out of his own reflections.

"Nothing! Nothing!" shouted James. How he hated that word! Didn't Alexander know enough to leave him alone. He closed his eyes, to shut out his father and all the other killers, but Sid was gone. And no matter what he thought, what he said, even as he pleaded, *Sid, I didn't mean to offend you, listen to me, please,* there was no answer.

Alex was grateful he could visualize old Iron Face and talk to her. But sometimes, he thought disgustedly, she was no better than a shrewish housewife. He repeatedly asked her, *What should I do?* and she repeatedly replied, *Do don't. Will won't. Hill kill. No one blames you for what he does don't will won't. Saturate your readers with excuses and they will won't believe you. Do you don't you blame the*

*weather man for rain and snow how many helicopters and*
*computers do you own?*

"Good afternoon, James," interrupted a new nurse, who
had just entered. She was middle-aged, plain-looking, and
cheerful, as she asked, "Everything going all right? Is there
anything I can get you?"

"You can get me out of here!" James snapped.

"I'm afraid I can't, yet. The university's medical board
hasn't issued its final report. What would you like to eat?"

"If I'm healthy enough to eat anything, I'm healthy
enough to get out."

Alex said, "I think so, too."

The nurse said brightly, "I'll bring a menu, then you can
choose for yourself. I hear you may need another examination. Or inspection."

James was grateful she was older; at least he wouldn't feel
so uncomfortable naked before her. Then she was gone in
search of a menu.

Alex said, "You could get out of here if you gave in a bit."

"How?"

"The President suggested that an apology would be
helpful."

"Do you want me to apologize, Alexander?" James's eyes
gleamed.

Alex hesitated, then admitted, "It would be easier."

"And the convenient, and correct thing to do?"

Alex shrugged.

"Then I would get out? Immediately? Before the end of
the day?"

"Probably."

"I will," James said suddenly, decisively, "If . . . ?"

Now what, thought Alex, but he asked, "What are your
conditions?" Sometimes, James didn't sound much different
than Shipmen.

"If the President apologizes to Sid Virgin."

"You know that is impossible."

"What are you supposed to do if I don't apologize?
Denounce me?"

"That's about it."

"Will you?"

Alex walked over to the window that overlooked the handsome lawn, so perfectly cultivated he wondered if anyone ever walked upon it. Then he turned to James, who had gotten out of bed and was standing in his bare feet and hospital gown on the polished tile floor, and who was unconsciously starting to curl his already curly hair with his right hand. His football throwing hand, reflected Alex. Was James as tense and as uncertain as he was? He doubted that; James appeared so positive.

"Or will you write a soothing essay about the necessity of seeing both sides of the question?"

"I'm going to try to get you out of here. As soon as possible." Suddenly Alex had to smile. He was remembering the expression on the President's face when his son had run around the track.

"What's so funny?"

"The President's reaction when you stripped and ran."

"I had to do it, Alexander," James burst out. "I felt so frustrated and hopeless. I tried to petition him to halt the Pacification Program. Other students tried, too, but nobody listened, not even you, and I could not think of any other way to protest. You do understand, don't you?"

"I think so."

"You will support me then?"

"Will? Won't? Your protest won't end the Pacification Program."

An Examiner entered with the nurse, who had found a menu, and he announced, "Grant, I just had a call from Shipmen. He wants to know if you have anything to report."

Before Alex could reply, James shouted, "Tell your friend, Alexander, that I am glad I did it and that I will do it again if I ever get the chance." Then everybody was converging on James but he couldn't see anything but the shadows in Sid's eyes and he rushed into the bathroom for relief, only to be followed by The Examiner. And just as abruptly as James had run into the bathroom he ran out, yelling, "Do you have to watch me even when I go to the toilet? We have doors on bathrooms so we can have privacy. Privacy is a very private thing."

"I was only doing my duty," said The Examiner. "Don't you want to talk to The Demolisher next door?"

"I don't want to talk to anybody." James turned his back on Alex, The Examiner, and the nurse, and ignored them until they all left the room, saying to himself, *Sid, what do they need to listen? An earthquake?*

# *Take a Nail and a Hammer*

Take a nail and a hammer
Or better, a hammer and a nail
and hammer hammer
down the floor
Attach the wall or better
Wall the attach and hammer hammer it in
Put up the roof and the ceiling
and hammer hammer up
Put down the hammer
and take up the glass
Put the glass in the window or better
The window in the glass
Put the door on the doorknob
Or better, the doorknob on the door
Put the hole in the keyhole
The keyhole where the flaw is
Then pick up the hammer
and hammer hammer
until you strike down
all that you hammered hammered up


Stymean Karlen

# Take a Nail and a Hammer

The fog plastered itself against the windows of Shipmen's office and shut out the world. But he did not mind the gloom outside, events were progressing as he expected and Graves should be in trouble by now, and he was about to consult his computers. There was no fog in his mind and *Hush* and *Hush-Hush* should dissipate whatever gloom remained because of the cancellation of *The Game*. Thanks to his investigations the future should develop as he anticipated.

Anyone who entered his suite had to realize he was vital to the President. His six rooms were spacious enough for a regiment to pass in review. His front office, which he used for obvious business, was dominated by a king-size desk for his own needs; there were also two small desks for his secretaries. Behind this office was a marble bathroom, a kitchen with every modern appliance he could think of, and a huge living room where he could nap and dine in when necessary. He had chosen the sofa himself, to be sure it was of the best quality, with a special backboard for his weak back, and he had added executive walnut panelling to verify that he was a man of consequence.

But his most prized possessions were his computers and conference rooms. The government had spent thousands of dollars to spy-proof his security room so that no one would be able to overhear his conversations. This was where he compiled his confidential reports, there was an alarm system

with chemical sensors to discern the presence of humans by
their smell, and a seismic intrusion device, which Shipmen
called *S I D*, that detected any vibration for many yards and
which was especially effective in exposing another surveillance instrument. Even so, before he had moved into his
spy-proof conference room he had every inch of it and all of
his rooms examined for hidden surveillance devices. Every
week he had his office checked; he guarded his words as if
the very air had ears; and to protect himself fully he had
dossiers on everybody in the government, but particularly
on Graves, Spleeno Bludgeon, and Victor Winner—a fact
no one knew but himself.

However, he was proudest of his computers. As he
hurried to consult *Hush* and *Hush-Hush* he was elated.
They contained vast banks of data information and they
were very good figurers. Shipmen always had to have a
figurer; he believed that his own brain was a good figurer,
but *Hush* and *Hush-Hush* were better. To keep them happy
he had placed a flag beside each of them, and he had
installed air conditioning, for they were touchy creatures
who could not endure being over-heated, since they
operated by temperature. In addition, he had just shaved
again—he had shaved once already today, but he had five
o'clock shadow and the irritating need to shave twice a
day—and he was always sure that he was clean shaven when
he programmed *Hush* and *Hush-Hush*. His fingertails were
impeccable and his body was deodorized. His coat was on
out of respect to his computers—he despised people who
were untidy—and he expected *Hush* and *Hush-Hush* to
react as he did. They were his *Analysis Security
System—A S S*—and they were as close to being foolproof
as he could construct. *A S S* was, in his view, the eye that
kept watch on the country.

*A S S* was also his secret computerized file on all those in
the country who were under suspicion of being against the
Pacification Program, the body count, and the President.
This data bank contained over two million names and
dossiers on each name, and he divided the suspects into
groups, with a different color card for every group.

Red cards were attached to the first group: those he con-

sidered the *Subversives*. Black cards were on the second
group: the *Doubtfuls*. Green was for the next: the *Riskys*;
blue was used for the last group of suspects: the *Potentials*.
Shipmen was not surprised by the large number of names
on his list. He knew that everyone in *A S S* were of
questionable citizenship. He assumed that at least ninety-
nine per cent were guilty of something; the other one per
cent he allowed as a margin for error.

He programmed both *Hush* and *Hush-Hush* to verify his
figures and he was pleased that they coincided. Each computer showed 313,313 *Subversives*, and 477,771 *Doubtfuls*.
The sameness of their answers impressed Shipmen and
added to his confidence in their accuracy. Now he was
positive they would tell him what he wanted to know, that
the quarterback and the Demolisher were in collusion. He
had dossiers on Alex and James in his *Doubtfuls*, and so he
ignored all his other files.

Yet while the room was cool he began to sweat profusely.
He found himself crying, "Hurry up! The columnist is going
to phone me at any moment and I need more evidence!" But
the replies that came from his computers were still confusing and baffling.

The only thing he could find in his dossier on Alex that
he could use against him was the petition to put the
Communist Party on the ballot the columnist had signed
many years ago, and that might not be as effective as he
desired, since the Communists had been a legal party at the
time. Moreover, the columnist had an excellent war record
so it would be difficult to accuse Alex of being a traitor or
unpatriotic.

"But there must be something else!" he shouted at his
computers. "What about his sex life?" He banged on *Hush-
Hush* indignantly and it replied, "Alex Grant was married
three times."

"Is that all?"

"He seems to get pleasure out of sex."

"How about his son? James Grant?"

"He dates girls but our agents haven't found anything else
out."

"Then we will have to create some evidence. Can you?"

*Hush-Hush* was silent.

Perhaps it was a loose wire and he turned to *Hush* and asked for the Grants' credit rating and the answer was, "Good. No outstanding debts."

"What about their friends?"

"A few *Riskys* and *Potentials* but no *Subversives* or *Doubtfuls.*

Shipmen almost kicked his computers in his vexation—were they going to be useless after all? If he couldn't do better than this, the President would demand his resignation. His computers contained enough information in their data banks to fill a thousand volumes and they couldn't come up with anything on the Grants but the petition. It made him very angry. He shut off *Hush* and *Hush-Hush* and hurried into his front office and telephoned the university hospital to find out what their medical computer had learned.

M.P. answered, "That examination is just starting. It was delayed by the columnist's visit with his son. I will report to you as soon as it is over. Where should I call you?"

"At my office." He gave M.P. the number that was in the telephone book and hung up. By now Shipmen was so absorbed in his investigation he had lost track of .the time. There must be sewage in the Grants' lives, he assured himself, there was in everybody's. And he must prove to the President that he knew what he was doing. He strode vigorously to the window and stared out, but his virility failed to penetrate the fog and the darkness, for the world beyond his window remained obscure and he felt cut off from the sources of his power. Then suddenly, his spirits lifted, for his telephone was ringing and it was Alex Grant, as he hoped.

The urgency in Grant's voice was hopeful, too, for the columnist was saying, "I must see you at once."

But while this was what Shipmen desired, he sounded reluctant as he replied, "I have appointments with the President and Graves."

"I won't be long. Can't you squeeze me in somehow?"

"The President has to discuss what happened this afternoon." Shipmen made it sound like it was a national emergency. "After all, he was the one who was insulted. And Graves, too."

"Give me five minutes."

"Five minutes? Even that would be very difficult."

"That's all we should need."

"I thought you would still be at the university hospital."

"I'm at my office. I hitched a ride in Graves's helicopter."

"With his permission? After what happened at *The Game*?"

"He went ahead with the President. And since I was Graves's guest coming up for *The Game*, nobody questioned my returning in his helicopter."

Shipmen thought, We will have to tighten up security, but he said, "What is your rush now?"

"I'm concerned about my son."

"Grant, you will have to be more specific than that."

"I will be. Can I come to see you now? Immediately?"

"Do you know where my office is?" Shipmen had to struggle to keep from gloating, Grant sounded so eager to speak to him.

"Yes."

"I can give you only five minutes. As it is, I'm squeezing you in between the President and Graves, so there will be no time for discussion."

After Shipmen hung up he checked all his surveillance weapons, but particularly his chemical sensors and his seismic intrusion device. He was curious about Grant's smell, he believed it could be very revealing, and *S I D*—which was as vital to him as his analysis security system—would protect him against any surveillance instruments Grant might be carrying. When he turned on his hidden tape-recorder he allowed himself a small smile of satisfaction. He knew that he and *Hush* and *Hush-Hush* were a national resource. And all his systems were go!

M.P. was delighted Shipmen ordered the university's medical examining board to be reconvened to re-examine James Grant and The Demolisher with his computer. The lean, handsome military doctor was proud of the university's medical computer and the laboratory attached to it.

It was one of the most powerful computers in the world, and for M.P. it was *his* computer, *his* hardware, *his* favorite hardware, a superflush. He liked to say, "It gets the shit out of everything," and he called it *The Crapper*. It was worth two Nobel prizes in medicine. How he loved this computer!

P.P. didn't share M.P.'s views; the plump, middle-aged staff psychiatrist was disturbed that *The Crapper* had puritan hangups, for it didn't condone masturbation, penis envy, and other normal neuroses. Moreover, P.P. had arrived at his diagnosis.

G.P. didn't understand *The Crapper*; he was old-fashioned; for flushing purposes he preferred enemas. And the elderly doctor was tired.

But neither G.P. nor P.P. trusted M.P., and they didn't want him to get ahead of them. They joined M.P. by the side of the medical computer while James and The Demolisher were brought into the laboratory next door.

Then the three doctors peeked through hidden peep-holes in the wall as a secret tape-recorder was started, and they waited expectantly for the two young men to greet each other. Instead, James and The Demolisher stared at each other blankly.

Examiners were stationed outside of the laboratory, a nurse was with each young man, who was dressed in a hospital gown. Everything was ready, M.P. thought angrily, and nothing was happening.

The Demolisher growled, "I told you that I didn't want any visitors!"

James asked, "Who is he?"

His young, pretty nurse answered, "They say you know him."

"I never saw him in my life," said James.

"Neither did I!" shouted The Demolisher, determined that no one was going to outdo him. "What am I doing here?"

His nurse, who was much older than the one attending James, replied, "We have some tests we want to take?"

"Medical?" The Demolisher asked suspiciously.

"Yes, yes," said his nurse. She pointed to the huge machine which looked like an iron lung and added, "If you will lie in this compartment and relax, we will program your brain."

"My brain?" The Demolisher looked indignant while James grinned.

"Yes," said his elderly nurse, pleased that she had been given such a vital assignment. In circumstances such as these she felt like a missionary, sent to the laboratory to convert the heathen. "We are going to estimate the weight of your brain, so you can develop better brain control."

"Shit!" cried The Demolisher, "You don't have to weigh dynamite to find out how far it will blow." He refused to lie in the machine.

James asked his nurse, "What is the real reason we are here?"

"To be examined."

"But I have been examined."

"That is where you are wrong. The doctors were just talking to you, but this machine is scientific, now it will find out . . ."

James interrupted, "What is wrong with me?"

"If anything is wrong with you," his nurse said hurriedly.

"Did my father order this new examination?"

"No."

"Is it because I protested?"

His nurse didn't answer.

"I already told them why I protested."

"Running nakedly around the stadium, waving a football, out of control!" exclaimed the other nurse. "For heaven's sake, I never heard of anything so awful. It's the fault of all the sex education they give these days!"

The Demolisher stared at the compact young man with the lean, angular face and brown eyes and hair and suddenly he yelled, "It's the quarterback!"

"He was," said the older nurse. "Perverted young man."

"We mustn't be too harsh," said the younger nurse. The quarterback was well built and attractive, not like this blond shrimp who shouted so much. "He said he had a reason. Not like this demolisher."

"I had a reason!" screamed The Demolisher. "You'd

never catch me naked! Fucking fool! How did he ever make the team?"

James said, "I was lucky."

"If I had made the team, I would have played."

"Why did you blow up the storeroom?"

"None of your god-damned business!"

"Was it a protest, too?"

"Fuck you! I don't go for such kid's stuff. I'm a demolition expert. In training camp, in the Territory, in the field, even in the bush, and at all the firebases, I was Number One, I was the best. There's nobody better trained. But political—do you think I'm a prick like you? Not on your life!" The Demolisher stood in the middle of the laboratory, thinking, they want to experiment on me, but I've already experimented, I've played with dynamite and I like it fine. How can they expect me to walk away from my precious sticks when it has become my finest talent!

James looked at the slight, very short, blond-haired boy and wondered what had put him in such a rage. The Demolisher was just about twenty-one; he could have been a classmate; yet it was as if only anger was keeping this boy alive. But he had no reason to hate him. James said, "Why are you so mad at me? I'm not your enemy."

Everybody was, The Demolisher said to himself, but he merely glared at the quarterback and didn't reply.

"What about the examination?" asked the older nurse. "Isn't anybody going to take it? Are you both afraid?"

James said, "It is an invasion of privacy."

"Nonsense. Unless you have something to hide."

Annoyed, James retorted, "I have nothing to hide. As I said before."

But as he stepped toward the compartment in which he was supposed to lie, The Demolisher shoved him aside and cried, "He ain't gonna get ahead of me! I may have flunked my chemistry course but I sure succeeded as a demolisher. And don't get yourself in a vaginal uproar, nurse, you can give me your brain programming, the world is in a mess anyhow, you can't mess me up worse. Not anymore. Fucking quarterbacks! Everybody wants to play that position! Even Presidents!"

The Demolisher laid down in the laboratory machine that was connected to the medical computer, after his nurse gave him sedatives to quiet him. M.P. programmed him; M.P. thought jubilantly, This will expose him, this will reveal his brain-wave rhythms, his tensions, his anxieties, his memories, his day-dreams. *The Crapper* will get rid of all his shit. *The Crapper* was a lovely, beautiful piece of hardware, and as M.P. waited for the result he was hopeful it would lead to a medical computer that would perform brain training. That would program the personality. Then he would be able to solve a lot of problems. It would be a great day, M.P. told himself, when he could construct brain training and control the brain itself; it would put an end to controversy.

He wondered if the other doctors were as excited as he was; they were listening intently. M.P. hurriedly attached his ear phones to record The Demolisher's brain.

His words were one long howl: "Pretty hairy in the Territory, you could get raped there, especially on the venereal detail. It was mind-blowing. The only way to get back to the world was not to ask any questions, keep your ass down, and just walk up to the enemy and hit him in the mouth. We got right down to reality. I'm not a hippy. They are full of that love crap, as if I owed it to them. I don't owe nobody nothing. Up-tight bastards! They march around with a peace symbol and expect you to march right behind them. Maniacs—that only gets you humiliated. They're crazies. I know what I'm doing exactly. I don't want to be with people I've hated since I've been seven. You ain't gonna kill me with your fucking slogans. That's what I'm doing, fucking you before you fuck me. Get it. I'm twenty-one, going on forty."

Then *The Crapper* halted, and M.P. felt helpless, a feeling he hated. The Demolisher had fallen asleep. He could see P.P. regarding him austerely, and even the usually humble G.P. had a touch of arrogance, as if he had failed. And all he could think of saying was, "Maybe it is a touch of indigestion."

"Maybe," P.P. said skeptically.

"Who has a touch of indigestion?" asked G.P. "I can cure that."

"That's nice to know," M.P. said sarcastically. He wasn't sure himself where the difficulty was. He had been a military doctor ever since he had graduated from medical school, it had seemed to be the most secure of careers, there was always somebody getting hurt in the military, but they hadn't prepared him for such emergencies. He gave the signal to take The Demolisher from the machine and that the quarterback should be examined, when the elderly nurse informed him that they had given the patient so many sedatives to quiet him that they had worked—finally.

The quarterback's brain waves were like two tape-recorders speaking to each other. James Grant talked continuously to someone named Sid Virgin and Sid Virgin kept answering him. But they said nothing much, M.P. thought regretfully, only how much they missed each other, needed each other, and were surrounded by strangers.

M.P.'s depression became, if anything, even worse than his feeling of helplessness, for now *The Crapper* was spewing out information indiscriminately, although both The Demolisher and the quarterback had been taken back to their rooms and nobody was lying in the compartment next door. And while neither P.P. nor G.P. commented on the failure of the brain programming to reveal anything new, each of them returned to their offices with a smug attitude. This added to M.P.'s determination to prove they were wrong, that the young men were co-conspirators, and that he must find evidence to vindicate himself.

"A problem was a problem was a problem," he said to himself, and suddenly, his pent-up feelings of frustration exploded and he kicked *The Crapper* and it replied, "Neither of the patients have athlete's foot, bad breath, scrofula, cancer, pericarditis, smallpox, leprosy, fever, high blood pressure, scabs, there is no trace of rickets or of a vitamin deficiency or cholera or catarrh, and their intestines are clean, they have been flushed recently, and their skulls indicate they are between eighteen and twenty-five, and the taller one is characterized by a large skull, a high square forehead, a wide nasal aperture and he may have a sinus condition. The little fellow has a voice like a bulldozer and he was very hard on my system."

M.P. shut off *The Crapper* with an angry bang and decided to blame P.P. and G.P. for not obtaining more information about the patients; they were doctors, too, they should have done better homework. But he knew this would not satisfy Shipmen.

Shipmen said to Alex, "As I told you, I have only a moment to spare." The more he rushed Alex, the more he would have him at a disadvantage.

Alex was uncomfortable, upset by Shipmen's brusqueness. He had just entered the offices of the chief investigator, yet he was not asked to sit down or to take off his hat and heavy overcoat. And he was startled by the hugeness of the front office; he felt overwhelmed by its size and the enormous desk which Shipmen sat behind threateningly.

"What have you decided to do? Quickly now?"

Alex longed to reply, Bla bla bla, meet the sheep, but he felt driven and he disliked that feeling. So he hesitated deliberately, wishing he could take off his overcoat, and thinking, we've got off on the wrong foot already and we haven't really started, he said, "That depends on you."

"You are the one who wanted this meeting. Who was so urgent about it. Are you ready to issue a statement apologizing to the President?"

"Are you going to release my son?"

"We don't have to."

"He is entitled to bail."

"After what he did?"

"The charges aren't that serious."

Shipmen glanced under his desk to verify that all of his systems were working. *S I D* indicated that Alex didn't have any surveillance devices on him, which added to his confidence, but his chemical sensors were vibrating strongly—Alex was sweating profusely now in his heavy overcoat—and this must be investigated. Shipmen said, proud of his sense of smell, "If you are so sure of your position, why are you nervous?"

"I'm not nervous."

"Then why are you sweating so? I can smell it over here."

"It's my overcoat."

But Shipmen merely shrugged and said, "My patience is wearing out."

"My column this Monday is a defense of football. Isn't that enough?"

"It's a start. But not enough. Time's up. Good day."

Alex couldn't endure Shipmen's patronization any longer and he said, "If you don't release my son, my next column will point out how you violated his constitutional rights."

"You used your constitutional rights to put the Communist Party on the ballot. That could alienate many of your readers. And your publisher."

"Perhaps."

"And you have been married three times."

"So?"

"It shows emotional instability. I know a man who lost the Presidency because he was divorced once."

"I was divorced twice."

"See." Shipmen's tone of triumph increased. "I doubt that any of your ex-wives will portray you in a favorable light."

"Two of them are dead."

"Oh!" Shipmen couldn't hide his feelings of frustration and he changed the subject. "I'm sure your son was involved with The Demolisher."

"That's not true. There is no proof."

"They both protested. At the same time. We will find proof."

"Do you have children?"

"Why?" Shipmen was annoyed; this was an unfair attack.

"It would help you understand what James did."

"I understand. He doesn't want his father until he gets in trouble and then he cries, 'Help!' No, I don't have any children, but I'm just as concerned as you are. As is the President. We're all his children. Now, if you will excuse me, the President is waiting to talk to me."

"Just one more moment."

"I can't keep the President waiting."

"If my columns are more moderate will you release my son?"

"We make the terms, not you. You are the one who is guilty, not us."

This was more than Alex could endure, and now, too, he had to prove to James that he could free him, that he did care for him. Disregarding the sweat pouring out of him, he stated, "If you don't release my son tonight on bail, I will denounce Pacification as well as the body count."

"You wouldn't dare."

"Try me."

Shipmen sought to stare him down, but Alex's gaze didn't waver. Then his telephone was ringing and he said, "It must be the President now," and he hurried to answer. He was greatly let down to hear M.P.'s voice.

M.P. said, "I have given both young men a thorough brain examination and I find that they are guilty of a disorder of human communications."

Shipmen wanted to shout, no one will worry about that, but he said, for the columnist could hear him, "Good! They knew each other."

"They didn't admit that, but I'm sure they do."

"That is what I thought." Shipmen assumed the air of respect he gave only the President. "What do you propose, sir?"

M.P. heard Shipmen's tone and thought, I am doing better than I expected. He said, "We must keep them under constant surveillance."

"At the hospital, sir?" Shipmen's attitude of deference increased as he noticed the columnist appeared to really believe he was speaking to the President. "Or would you suggest something else, sir?"

"I would let out the quarterback, on probation. I am sure he will lead us to his fellow-conspirators. He is bound to."

"Thank you, sir." Shipmen hung up, turned to Alex, who was waiting anxiously, and said, "The President wants to be merciful. If I release your son, on probation, you must be understanding, also."

"I'll try."

"That's not enough."

Alex thought, they want me to file my knife down until it is completely dull, but still he had no choice. He said, "If you want me to trust you, you will have to trust me. At least a little."

Shipmen didn't trust anybody, except himself, but he said, "We'll do what we can. And you will apologize for your son's behavior."

"As much as I can."

"Remember, if you betray me, you will regret it." Suddenly, remembering that he had caught the columnist coming out of the ladies' room at the stadium and he had film to prove it, he felt elated. He was proud that his Examiners were also electronic specialists. There was nothing to be afraid of now. "Give Marcia my regards."

"Are you watching us, too?"

"Alex, Marcia is my friend! I want the best for her!"

"What should I tell my son?"

"We will tell him. Through the university authorities."

After the columnist was gone, Shipmen examined his chemical sensors with special attention. As they indicated, Alex Grant's body wastes had flown so profusely the columnist must have been very afraid.

Shipmen recorded that on *Hush* and *Hush-Hush* and when they agreed with each other he was comforted. Fear meant guilt to the chief investigator and so he transferred this information to his analysis security system, and for a moment he thought of shifting his dossiers on Alex and James Grant from his *Doubtful* file to his *Subversive* file.

Then he decided to wait, until he possessed more substantial information. He was positive he would obtain it. He had everything programmed and *Hush* and *Hush-Hush* agreed with his seismic intrusion device and his chemical sensors on what course to take.

# Don't Talk to a Rock

Dont talk to a rock
as you would to a stone
The vocabulary of each differs
with its sensitivity

The rock has an alphabet that
determines it
But the stone's is spelled
by its thrower

STYMEAN KARLEN

# Don't Talk to a Rock

The next day the university announced that James Grant was being released from the hospital on probation, that he would be allowed to return to his classes, provided he behaved correctly from now on, but that he had been dropped from the football team.

When Alex heard the news, he hurriedly telephoned the hospital to speak to James, but he was told that James was gone.

M.P., who had become the medical supervisor on the case due to his special skill with *The Crapper*, informed Alex, "There is nothing to worry about. We are watching your son carefully."

"What about the charges?" asked Alex.

"They are pending. They will depend on how he behaves from now on."

"Did he ask for me before he left?"

"No."

"Do you know where he went?"

"He told his nurse he was returning to his dormitory and that he was resuming classes tomorrow. At least for the time being," he said.

"What about The Demolisher?"

"He is being put under further observation."

Alex thought, They ought to put the Pacification Program under further observation, but he said, "I'm sure there is no connection between him and my son."

"That is not proven yet. The Demolisher is so vengeful toward the university. I'm inclined to believe he was a student there once. We are checking that out now. But without fingerprints it is difficult."

"How does that connect him with my son?"

"They could have been in the same class, in the same . . ."

Latrine, Alex thought, but he said, "You don't have any evidence."

"Oh, yes we do." M.P. had recovered from his disappointment with the initial examinations and he was convinced more examinations of The Demolisher would reveal a link between the two boys. They had protested at the same time and at the same place and that in itself was almost enough to convict them. But this columnist, with his prying mind, would demand more proof. M.P. added, "My computer acted very suspiciously. But we will be fair about it, my computer and I. Before we convict anybody, we will be sure we have enough evidence."

"What kind of evidence?" asked Alex.

"Their brain skulls are somewhat the same, my computer verified this, which indicates they had somewhat the same kind of education." That should shake up Grant, M.P. thought gloatingly. "Good day." He hung up.

Alex was anxious now, for the military doctor sounded positive that he would obtain an eventual conviction of his son. He telephoned James at his dormitory to warn him to be careful, but there wasn't any answer.

Then Alex, realizing there was nothing more he could do, remembered he had an engagement with Marcia at her country retreat this Sunday evening and he telephoned her to confirm it. Still apprehensive and unsettled, he half-expected her not to answer, or to cancel their engagement, or, at the least, to scold him for what James had done. Instead, she didn't mention James or *The Game* but seemed eager to see him.

They bedded at once, as if Marcia needed sexual fulfillment as much as he did. When Alex asked, "What about Stan? Is there any chance he will interrupt us again?"

Marcia replied emphatically, "No! Stanley needed a rest, in warmer weather, so I gave him enough money to go south, to warmer weather, it only costs a few hundred dollars, and the poor boy has been overworking and he has a birthday coming soon, and he needs sun and fresh air." If anything, Marcia was even more responsive than before, and Alex was surprised and pleased by the intensity of her passion.

Yet even as she expressed the proper ecstasy, he sensed that a part of her was calculating the extent of his potency. She regarded his penis as if it were a giant pencil which possessed a logic of its own, and the power to reason. Marcia asked Alex, "Is Wally, as you call him, easily influenced?" And when Alex didn't reply, she persisted, "When my husband and I had intercourse, he could be thrown off easily if I began to talk. Is Wally?" Alex wished she would change the subject; Wally was quickly distracted and upset, with a sensitivity that once in a while threatened him with impotence. For a moment he wondered if she assumed he was sexually expendable, and then as she caressed Wally he decided he was being unduly suspicious.

But afterwards, as they reclined close to each other, Alex asked her, "What did you think about my son's behavior?"

"Stan said he did it to show off."

"Was Stan at *The Game*?"

"He said he was."

"Did your son disrobe?"

"No. He said everybody was doing it. What was the point."

"Have you spoken to Graves or Shipmen about *The Game*?"

Marcia hesitated, then said, "No. Should I have?"

"That's up to you."

"Why did you ask?"

"I just wondered."

"What are you going to write about next?"

"Tomorrow's column and Wednesday's are already written."

"After that? What direction are you going?"

"I don't know."

"I thought . . ." She caught hold of herself, and halted.

"... that I should apologize? Is that what Shipmen intimated?"

"It's natural for a father to apologize for such behavior from his son."

"Marcia, children no longer buy 'My country, right or wrong, My parents, drunk or sober.' They make up their own minds these days."

"You are still responsible for what he does."

"As you are for Stan?"

She frowned, then said, "That's not fair. Stan doesn't have a father. But at any event, I'm sure you will write something sensible."

Marcia's advice repeated itself like a hammer on Alex's head as he sat before old Iron Face the following morning and sought to write his next column. It might be easy to appease Marcia, but old Iron Face was a different matter. She was his conscience, he thought, if he had any; she was his justification for being, if there was any; but now he felt like a P.W.—a Prisoner of War, he typed out—but that was not the title for what he was thinking.

"Round and round we go," old Iron Face replied.

He gazed angrily at her as he started to type, "We must feel compassion for the President. He must consider many things. Reality tells us . . ."

A key stuck, then another, he skipped a letter, blurred the next, and suddenly he had to stop. Old Iron Face seemed to be regarding him with such loathing he could not continue. He decided to postpone the writing of this column until tomorrow. He would sleep soundly tonight and clear his mind of all thought of Pacification and Kill Zones and body counts and sons. And by tomorrow there should be a reaction to this morning's column, *Festive Frolic*, which could cue him for Friday's.

At noon, just as Alex was preparing to play tennis, there was a long-distance call from James. Before Alex could ask James how he was feeling, his son said accusingly, "You've betrayed me! *Festive Frolic* stinks! How can you be so crass?"

"I wrote it last week."

"That's no excuse. Alexander, you haven't got the guts to stand up for anything. How much did they bribe you to get me released?"

"Nothing."

"What did you promise to write now? More columns like *Festive Frolic*?"

"I haven't promised anything."

"Then how did you get me out?"

"I told them that if they didn't release you, I would denounce Pacification as well as the body count."

James started to laugh.

"What's funny?" Alex was indignant at James's skepticism, and angry.

"M.P. said, as he ordered my clothes returned to me, that I had better keep them on this time, or the consequences would be much more serious."

"Wouldn't you expect him to say just that?"

"I also expected him to say, as he did, that he would not be releasing me now, except that you were going to apologize."

"He couldn't allow himself to appear defeated."

"But did you say that you were going to apologize for me, Alexander?"

"I said you had reasons for doing what you did."

"I will believe that when I read that in your column."

Alex was silent.

James said scornfully, "It isn't enough that you pay my tuition."

Alex said quietly, "Are you going to stay in school?"

"Are you going to denounce the Pacification Program?"

James hung up before Alex could answer.

Then the telephone was ringing again and it was Shipmen, irritated that he hadn't been able to reach Alex sooner. The chief investigator said, "We have lived up to our side of the bargain, but you haven't."

Alex replied, "I didn't make any bargains. I said . . ."

"I know very well what you said," Shipmen interrupted crossly. "But it is what you intend that matters. *Festive*

*Frolic* was an improvement on some of your earlier columns, but it doesn't go far enough."

"I wrote it a week ago."

"That is your problem."

"Wednesday's column, too, was written last week."

"When are you going to discuss *The Game*?"

"Friday. I'm working on it now. I hope to complete it by tomorrow."

"The President is giving a news conference tonight. You should listen to it. He is going to discuss *The Game*, too."

"And give me a directive?"

"What you write is up to you. But you could be sensible."

Shipmen felt better, now that he had reminded the columnist of his obligations, and put him in his place and he was able to return to *Hush* and *Hush-Hush* with some of his old confidence in them, although he could not forget what had happened earlier in the day.

It was a shock to be summoned to a breakfast meeting with the President, and to find Graham Graves and Spleeno Bludgeon there, too. Shipmen was looking forward to the time he would be the sole confidant of the President, at least on security matters. Instead, although Graves was somber, as if he had received a severe scolding, the chief foreign policy adviser still sat next to the President.

Then Victor Winner said, "Roger, I'm putting Spleeno in charge of the Grant situation." When he saw Shipmen's dismay, he added, "Oh, you are still on it, too. But from now on, it will be the Vice-President who will discuss the affair publicly."

"What about yourself, sir?"

"I must be above personal feelings. But I will mention *The Game* during my news conference tonight, just to place it in the proper perspective,"

Spleeno asked, "Roger, does the columnist intend to apologize?"

"I think so, but it is possible that he won't."

"Have you thought of transferring him to your subversive file?"

"I'm gathering evidence for that now. Just in case . . ."

The President interrupted him. "That is up to you. I'm sure both of you will do the right thing."

But after Victor Winner was gone, with Graves still at his side, which added to Shipmen's disquiet, Spleeno said, "Personally, I am a devoted pacifist, but when a man bites me, I bite back. Do you have much on Grant?"

"Which one?"

"Either one. We still live in a world where fathers are responsible for their sons. Thank God! Roger, is your information reliable?"

"I think so, sir."

"You must be sure. We must have absolute information. We cannot let our leader down. I'm a realist. If we get caught in the Grants' cross fire, we must make people understand how untrustworthy they really are. And I, for one, don't trust them. Do you?"

"No, Mr. Vice-President."

"With that point of view, we should operate intelligently. You must force the columnist to commit himself. Soon. Remember, the President expects every member of his team to do his duty."

"Yes, sir."

But this discussion depressed Shipmen; he didn't trust Spleeno. If he succeeded Spleeno would take the credit; if he failed the Vice-President would blame him. Yet now, checking his file on Spleeno, his spirits improved. The Vice-President was thin-skinned and information planted in the press could inflame him to hasty action. And after all, he thought more happily, he had programmed *Hush* and *Hush-Hush* for guilt and he was a perfectionist.

By now Alex was in the wrong mood for tennis, although he kept his appointment with Eric Losell, a fellow columnist. They played every Monday and Alex's usually steady game was generally too much for the erratic Eric. Whenever it came to a key point Alex could outrun and outlast the stocky, heavy-set Eric, even though Losell was ten years younger and had a strong backhand and a fine first serve.

This afternoon however, Alex played badly, for his mind was focused on Shipmen, the President, and James. Each time he hit the ball out or into the net, which was often and not like his normal stroking, he cursed them for destroying his concentration and ruining his game. Yet finally, he had match point, after splitting two sets with Eric—the first set Eric had won from him in months, which secretly, he considered a disgrace—and he hit a strong forehand that forced Eric to lift a weak lob. He rushed up to the net to put the lob away and he saw the face of Shipmen instead of the ball, and he smashed it yards out of the court. Several points later the same situation occurred. It was match point again, and this time it was the face of the President that Alex saw instead of the ball and he missed it entirely.

He paused as he prepared to serve once more. He wondered woefully whether they were emasculating his tennis game, too. He double-faulted. Then, even more on edge, he double-faulted the game away.

If there was any way that Alex hated to lose—and he hated to lose any way—it was with double-faults. Disgusted with himself for allowing himself to be distracted, he wanted to smash his racquet, but that was impossible, it was steel. In his frustration he banged himself on his non-racquet hand with the metallic frame of his racquet and his knuckles bled so profusely he needed Band-aids to halt the bleeding.

Eric was willing to halt; he was even, which was a moral victory. He hadn't drawn with Alex in months,.and moreover, he was tired.

But Alex, who at this moment was hating everybody, but especially himself, insisted on continuing. To quit would add to his self-hatred.

Yet James wasn't any aid to his game either. Instead of concentrating on returning Eric's serve, which usually he did accurately, he continued to remember how James had hung up on him, and in his anger he made four consecutive errors and lost Eric's serve without a struggle.

Now, his concentration completely gone, Alex felt everything was conspiring against him: the sudden gusts of wind, growing in intensity and blowing into his face; the sun high overhead and directly in his eyes as he served; the scuffed grass court and the bad bounces, which, at this instant, seemed to be happening only to him; the net cord shots that all went against him; his aching knuckles, yet he had hit nobody but himself, which, in a way, was the worst irritation of all. He mumbled, "Tennis, a masochist's misery."

"What was that?" Eric answered. "What did you say?"

"Nothing." If he admitted he was talking to himself, Eric would regard him suspiciously, too, and probably end in a computer file as an enemy.

Eric was grinning, which added to Alex's anger. Did his opponent think he was crazy? Alex, in his anxiety and over-eagerness to win, overran the first point, underhit the second, which added to his self-contempt, drove the third over the backstop as the wind subsided suddenly, and lost the fourth point and the match when Eric pushed a freak shot off the handle of his racquet and the ball hit the net cord and squirted erratically just out of Alex's reach. Infuriated, he slammed his racquet down on the ground, but he made sure that he didn't hit himself, even as he disliked himself for such a display of bad temper.

Eric was surprised. This was not like Alex, who usually played calmly. "What's wrong?" he asked, as they strolled toward the shower.

Alex shrugged, grunted, "I just had a bad day."

"Is that why you are so upset?"

"I'm sorry. You played better. I shouldn't take that away from you."

"Thanks for the gesture, but you were off. You weren't concentrating, and generally, that is the strongest part of your game."

"It's this Pacification Program. It gets more bloody, not less."

"Naturally. It is a fact of life and you ought to live with it."

"Do you?"

Eric paused. He was good-looking, with thinning blond hair, rugged features, blue eyes surrounded by laugh lines, and usually debonair. But now he smiled cynically as he said, "Since man learned to walk, he has learned little else. Man didn't invent the wheel for progress, he stumbled upon

it by accident and first used it to kill other men. Fire was discovered to burn your enemy, not to heat yourself. War is a
game, our Super-Super game. And football is the home-
front expression of it. Your son is young, naive, he hasn't
learned yet you can't stop the killing. Man would be bored
without the killing. But you should have learned this, you've
lived through Hitler and Stalin and they probably registered
the biggest body counts on record. I'm surprised you
allowed that to ruin your tennis game."

"Are you going to listen to the President's news conference tonight?"

"I have to be there," Eric said disgustedly. "My news syndicate has planted a question with him, which I'm supposed
to ask—spontaneously."

"What is the question?"

"Does he believe in young people? Especially college
students?"

Victor Winner gazed directly into Eric Losell's blue eyes
when that question was asked. He knew this cynical
columnist believed in nothing, but Eric had many readers
and millions were watching, and he assumed his super-
sincere tone and said, "Indeed, Eric. They are going to be
the salvation of our great country. Especially college students."

Eric asked, "Sir, even those who run around football
fields naked?"

"I believe in freedom of expression. But, of course, it can
go too far. I do not support violence of any kind."

"Nobody was hurt, sir."

"Fortunately, sanity prevailed. And Alex Grant, the
columnist and the father of the boy who took the law into
his own hands, was as distressed by this exhibition as I was.
He assures me that it will not happen again."

Alex wanted to shout: Victor Winner, how dare you commit me without my permission! But no one would hear his
denial now except the television set which grinned at him
mockingly.

A reporter asked, "Is it true, Mr. President, that the Pacification Program is spreading, that we are invading a new
Territory?"

"Not invading. It is protective retaliation. An excursion."

"You mean, sir, to wind down the Pacification Program?"

"Exactly. We are going into the new Territory to get out of the old."

"But what about our casualties, sir? They are rising again."

"Temporarily, Jack. Our deep and sincere hope is to reduce them to an acceptable number."

"But, sir?" asked a second reporter. "Isn't even one casualty terrible?"

"That is always a sad thing to discuss, Ralph, this week, or any week for that matter. But we mustn't go to pieces. The ratio of enemy dead is still ten to one in our favor. Our command reports that since the start of Pacification there have been 717,555 enemy troops killed in the Territory, while our losses are much less, under a hundred thousand."

Killing is our business, Alex thought angrily, and business is fine.

Victor Winner added, "This is our *true count*."

Suddenly the stress on statistics struck Alex as ridiculous. Yet they were no laughing matter.

Ralph asked, "You mean, sir, *true count* is replacing the *body count*?"

"Yes," Victor Winner stated proudly. "We have developed it to clarify matters and to end confusion. And to expedite getting our men out."

"Sir, are you saying that we must get deeper into Pacification in order to end it more quickly and more safely?"

"Precisely."

But who has measured the blood?

Long after Alex stopped listening to the news conference, he repeated that question to himself. Then he wrote titles on old Iron Face.

"*True Count?*"

"*False Count?*"

"*Real Count!*"

"*Bullshit and Blackmail.*"

Old Iron Face did not resist him, but none of these titles seemed right for what he wanted to say. The President had blackened him in the eyes of his son, but he could not write that either. He felt lost in his speculations and he recalled his own war duty and how he and his detail had learned to become killers. The best damn killers in the world, his general had proclaimed. Their assignment had been concrete: no prisoners! Prisoners were an embarrassment, prisoners encumbered a detail, and in the jungle a detail had to be able to move unhampered by any excess baggage. Either you got them, or they got you. His C.O. had been quite explicit about this order. Then, to moor himself in some kind of endurable reality, Alex wrote down his street number city state country hemisphere planet universe, and just as suddenly, feeling desperate, he scribbled more titles in the hope one of them would suggest a theme for his next column.

"*What Time Is The World?*"

"*Where Is Place?*"

"*Hereafter Is Now!*"

But he had used that already. He knew he was not a religionist and yet in his despair he wrote: "*Lord, Make Me God for One Second to see Your Aim.*" Then realism became unlikeable and unbearable and he couldn't take anything seriously, and he saw all governments as silly children grasping for victories as they would for toys. The President had stated, "This is just another excursion, a *true count*," but no man had a capacity for infinite pain, thought Alex, and he felt even more dispirited.

Alex decided to go to bed, although it was much earlier than his usual retiring time. In his sleep he would forget the bunkers jammed with corpses, the ditches choked with bodies. He closed his eyes and tried to stop thinking of all the times he had been told the killing would end. In his sleep he would not see James naked, or himself, or his son's contempt. Gone would be the great weight upon him and the calculated-to-deceive verbiage and the casualties light to moderate when they were your own but acceptable, yet always heavy and swelling on the other side, and in his dreams he would restore all the casualties back to life. He closed his eyes but sleep did not come. He thought of tennis, which often put him to sleep, but he had played so badly it only made him feel worse. Mankilling was the name of the game, and he imagined himself swimming, which he loved, but he didn't love himself now, and who has measured the blood?

When Alex could not fall asleep after many hours of tossing, he typed the rest of the night. Old Iron Face was co-operative, as if for a change, she approved of what he was writing. He put his ideas down as they came, and by dawn he had written:

"The body count is an obscenity and Pacification must end now, before it ends us. We must speak for the young people who cannot speak for themselves and who act out of blind impulse from inherited unconscious memories and I SAY they have that right because it acts like a necessity in them. How can the human brain—unless it has been de-humanized into brainlessness—kill, especially when it is killing itself? We spend many hours on toilet training our children, when we should be training the parents. A child may wet his pants for years to get attention, but when he shouts that he doesn't want to be killed he is ignored. We act as if war is great fun, but the boys who are being shot at don't think so. Why should eighteen be the most dangerous age, the battlefront age, the conscription age, when it is, actually, the age of conception? We become very concerned now that we must not destroy our trees, our soil, our waters, but what about our children? Aren't they, too, part of our ecology? That is why James Grant behaved the way he did. Lady Godiva became a legend by using her nudity in defense of peace—as did James Grant."

This became Friday's column and Alex titled it, *Who Has Measured the Blood?* The rest of the week he played better tennis and he sketched out several more columns, but he wrote out none of them, waiting for the reaction to Friday's. He didn't call anybody and nobody called him.

Friday was a typical late autumn day, smelling of dead leaves, heavy smog, and automobile fumes. Alex expected many calls after *Who Has Measured the Blood*? but there was only silence.

The following day a photostat of the petition to put the Communist Party on the ballot that Alex had signed appeared on the front page of many of the leading newspapers as a vital national news item. Above the story, which was in a conspicuous place in most of the newspapers, was the headline: "*The Name Is Alexander Grant.*" The text, which sounded like a press release, stated: "This columnist is proud of his impartiality, but his signature on this red petition will cause many of his readers to wonder about his veracity and his patriotism."

Alex thought ruefully, Finally, he was on the front page.

Shipmen thought, Spleeno Bludgeon was too mild in his denunciation of this columnist. The Vice-President called him, "disreputable," but Shipmen transferred him from his *Doubtful* file to his *Subversive* file.

# The Yellow Bear had One Velvet Ear

The yellow bear had one velvet ear
The other was bear
He was looked at with fear
His own clan did mistrust him
He wondered
"If I am not all bear
what am I then"

An ant crept onto his nose
Looked into his eye
And it said
"I am from above
And I was there
when God touched your ear
Now you know, nothing is the same
under God's hand"
And it crept away to the above

The yellow bear cried with love
And he told his own clan
what the ant had claimed
about God the ear and His touch
And war was declared by those
who said it was sacrilegious
and would not believe him
It is still being fought
although it began ago ago

The yellow bear still has one
velvet ear
The other is bear
He is still looked at with fear
His own clan do mistrust him
He wonders
"If I am not all bear
what am I then"


STYMEAN KARLEN

# The Yellow Bear had One Velvet Ear

"Alex, why don't you take a vacation?"

Harold Hinton, publisher, man about town, tennis buff, stopped pacing the length of his hotel living room to offer this suggestion. Honest Harold, as he was known to his employees because of the candor of his opinions, had come to the capital for political reasons, but he had decided it would be useful to talk to Alex, too, and so he had summoned his columnist to his large, luxurious hotel suite this Sunday morning.

"Not that much is happening," added Harold.

Alex answered, "*Who Has Measured the Blood?* must have upset you."

"Of course not. But you can write better than that."

Alex frowned, and stood up to go, and Harold Hinton halted him.

"I should have let you sleep all morning. But since I was in town I thought it would be helpful to you to discuss your work. I'm sorry if I woke you too early, especially on a Sunday morning."

"You didn't wake me up, Harold." Alex had orders to call Harold by his first name, it was the publisher's way of being democratic. "Somebody else did, before you called." Marcia, he thought angrily, who had telephoned him to tell him that she could not see him tonight as arranged. She had said, "I have a splitting headache," and she had hung up before he could say a word. "What didn't you like about my last column?"

"Don't be offended," the publisher replied, "You are too competent to resent criticism." The chunky, middle-aged millionaire and newspaper tycoon, ten years younger than Alex, proud of his tennis game and his bright blue eyes and ruddy cheeks, also was proud that he was cultivated, sophisticated, that his syndicate was the most widely read in the country, and that he was tough. The syndicate had been founded by his grandfather and developed into its present prosperity by his father, but Harold felt he was a self-made man, for he had tried several new ideas. "Alex, why don't you take off a couple of weeks. Drive through the country. Before the leaves vanish. It would be quiet, scenic, comfortable. Learn what people are thinking. It will give you perspective. Some of the country is still beautiful. Your column will be here when you return. I will be the custodian for it until you get back."

"My last column really has upset you."

"Not in the least. But you are taking Pacification too seriously."

"I should have been more discreet?"

"There has been an immediate backlash to your last column. I have received many telegrams denouncing you. They claim you are tearing down the monuments to the dead. But that is not all. Six of our outlets refused to carry *Who Has Measured the Blood*? and when the item about the petition appeared four of them said they were dropping you."

"What did you think about Friday's column? Candidly?"

"I am no stranger to the dangers and difficulties of being impartial. My son is in the Territory right now."

"In the infantry?"

"As a correspondent. I understand your need to defend your son. That is natural. But too much personal involvement can destroy your credibility. Especially since that item about the petition appeared."

"Do you believe it?"

"It doesn't matter whether I believe it. Many readers do. The appearance of the petition on the heels of Friday's column has caused people to be suspicious of you. Why did you sign a Communist petition?"

"It was many years ago. Ages and ages ago."

"There must be a rational explanation." Harold's eyes lit up as he suggested, "You were fooled? You didn't know what you were signing?"

"I knew."

Harold looked startled as if he had not expected such a reply. He gazed at Alex with a worried expression, asked, "Were you a Communist?"

Alex laughed.

"What's funny?" Harold was annoyed; he hadn't said anything amusing.

"I was an individualist."

"That is no excuse. How did it happen?"

"I was tired, depressed, rebellious. And it involved a girl."

"You signed a petition because you were in love! How could you be so stupid!" Harold regarded Alex with scorn, and a trace of petulance.

"I didn't say that. But it didn't happen yesterday."

"What's the difference!" shouted Harold. "You did it. Didn't you?"

"Yes."

"Why?"

Alex hesitated, wondering whether he could trust Harold, and then he realized that if he wanted to keep his column he had no choice. The publisher was waiting expectantly. But he had to say, "If I tell you what happened, will you promise not to reveal it to anyone else?"

"Go ahead." Harold sat down. "But be brief. I have an appointment with an important politician and he will be here in a few minutes." When Alex continued to hesitate, he snapped, "You want me to have confidence in you, justify it. I'm listening," he added with a sense of righteousness. Harold Hinton knew he was superbly objective.

Yet the recollection did not come easily to Alex, although it had remained in his memory since it happened. He said slowly, "It occurred a long time ago. Just before *my* war began. I was a member of a little theater and they were rehearsing a play of mine, called, *My Brother, My Keeper,* and it was against war, a war I sensed was coming soon and violently. I had worked all day as a social worker and . . ."

"But you were a famous football player," Harold interrupted. "It was why you were introduced to me. Then we began to play tennis together. We won a lot of doubles."

"That was after the war—*my* war."

"Couldn't you have played football professionally?"

"I didn't want to play football. I wanted to be a playwright."

"A playwright? You never told me!"

"I didn't tell anybody, except the playwrights' group I belonged to at the little theater, there were ten of us in this group, and when they chose my play for their first production of the season, I was very excited. I saw myself as another Eugene O'Neill."

"But you said you were also a social worker. How did you ever fall into such a field?" The publisher could hardly restrain his contempt.

"It was the only job I could obtain, except possibly, in football. And I thought it might help my writing, bring me closer to life."

"Did it?"

"I learned that poverty was romantic only to the rich."

"Besides," Harold said hurriedly, "I don't have much time and what has that to do with signing a Communist petition?"

Alex corrected, "A petition to put the Communist Party on the ballot."

"What's the difference! Why did you sign it?"

When Alex resumed speaking his tone was mocking.

"I was worried about my play. *My Brother, My Keeper* was about two brothers fighting on opposite sides in a civil war and it concluded with one brother going over to the other side in an effort to halt this war. The little theater chose my play because they felt it expressed their side, the Left, although they were suspicious about some of my views, for I depicted the brother on the Right as a decent man, which was heresy.

"But they excused me on the grounds that I was naive and hoped to convert me to the True Faith, which was Communism. When however, I did not change the brother on the Right into a symbol of evil, I heard rumors that the committee of actors who ran the theater were dissatisfied. I knew these rumors were real, for other playwrights told me that my play lacked proportion, was self-indulgent, dated.

"None of this was going to halt me, however, I was young, energetic, optimistic, I was determined to succeed. At twenty-five I was positive I could solve any problems. And while I sensed that the theater was Communist-oriented, I was confident I could maintain my own ideas, since I was convinced that my belief in democracy was sound and good. Moreover, this little theater was the only one that would do my play.

"Yet, one night, after an exhausting and infuriating day at work—where I felt frustrated by my inability to really aid people on relief—when I arrived at the theater to find my play about to collapse some of my confidence evaporated. Then I was in a vile humor.

"As a social worker I had been forced by Agency rules to take away relief from two single men who had been caught working part-time. But I couldn't blame them, for it was impossible for a man to live on four dollars and eighty cents without stealing or cheating. Not only did the State destroy their pride, I thought unhappily, it forced them to lie, and yet was righteous in its punishment. But I had no choice. If I hadn't cancelled their relief, someone else would have.

"At least I sought to do it painlessly, which, of course, was impossible. I was bothered, too, about my girl friend. She resided in a seedy five-story rooming house and the front door was locked by twelve, and often earlier. The previous night the rehearsal had dragged and by the time I arrived at the rooming house, a few minutes before twelve, running most of the way, the front door was locked and I couldn't get in.

"It was awful. My girl friend was the most sexually responsive girl I knew, vital, aggressive, and a mixture of bitchery and tenderness, and when I went home unsatisfied I felt I would bust my britches.

"And now, as I saw the anxious expression on the director's face, I sensed it was going to be another long, painful night. What had I gotten into, I wondered. I had not written the play to suffer.

"Artie, who was small, wiry, a pugnacious, stubborn older man, who used his age to prove his superiority, informed me, 'The Committee wants the resolution changed. They say it is irresponsible. The way you wrote it, the audience is going to sympathize with the brother on the Right.'

"I said, trying to stall, 'I'll think it over.'

"'No,' said the director, 'Time is running out. We need the rewrite tomorrow.'

"'But I work all day!' I exclaimed, beginning to feel a noose tightening around my neck. 'I cannot write a new conclusion by then.'

"'You will have to,' said the director. 'Furthermore, the first scene needs more work, too. The first three lines are awkward. Ordinary.'

"After I rewrote these lines, I wondered why I had done so, for the actor read them in a droning, monotonous voice which bore no resemblance to my intention. But the director was pleased. Artie had established *his* point: he was running things, which was the basic issue.

"At eleven he was still rehearsing the same five-minute opening scene, as he had been doing for days. Artie adored detail; he was an admirer of Stanislavsky; he loved to tell how this genius had rehearsed picking up a glass of water for a week. But I felt miserable and angry. I could hardly stay awake. I had never expected my own writing to bore me. Play writing was becoming a form of masochism. Artie was going to rehearse this first scene forever, I thought despairingly, the whole play, which ran only half an hour, had been in rehearsal for weeks and there still hadn't been a complete run-through since the first reading.

"No wonder the Committee was dissatisfied, I told myself, and it added to my anger and my misery. The cast seemed to be sleepwalking, and the audience—chiefly other members of the playwrights' group, who were supposed to learn by watching—were half-asleep.

"My depression grew. There was no drama in my play. I had failed, I reflected bitterly, I should run for my life. Was I such a dreadful writer? I couldn't be that bad, I assured myself. They were flushing my play down the toilet. It was becoming unspeakable. And I would never see my girl friend tonight, which added to my despair.

"Thus, distracted and disgusted, I was irritated when another playwright, Ira, who was my best friend in the theater, nudged me with passion. He, too, was older, which he used to demonstrate that he was better informed than I was, and he was short, spare, and graying.

"I asked, 'What's wrong?' Did he want me to rewrite, too?

"He said, 'I have a nominating petition. Sign it, will you?'

"I asked, 'A nominating petition for what?'

"He said, 'To put a party on the ballot.'

"I said, 'Let's be specific. What party? Or is it a secret?'

"He said, 'Don't you believe in democracy? You are always bragging about how much democracy there is in this country.'

"'You mean this is a Communist petition?'

"Ira said emphatically, although his sallow features flushed, 'What is the difference! They are a legal party.'

"'But if I sign the petition that indicates I am a Communist. And I am not.'

"'It doesn't indicate anything of the kind. At the top of the petition it states clearly that to put a party on the ballot doesn't signify the signer is a member of that particular party, or has to be. Let's go to the back of the theater where you can see for yourself.'

"'What about rehearsal?'

"'You won't miss anything!'

"Ira grabbed me by the arm and pulled me to the rear of the theater, where I was able to read the nominating petition. He was right; what he told me was printed plainly at the top of the paper. But still I hesitated, for I was not a Communist.

"'Don't you always say they have a right to be on the ballot?'

"'Yes, if we are a democracy, and if they are a legal party.'

"'They are a legal party. You know that. And we are supposed to be a democracy.' But when I still hesitated, Ira sneered, 'You're a hypocrite, too, bragging about democracy, like so many others, but when it comes to practicing it, you're as cowardly as the rest. It's your football training.'

"I saw the three members of the Committee who ruled the playwrights halt my play. One of them had been against it always, the second had seesawed before giving his consent, and I cried out, 'What's wrong?'

"Artie answered, 'They want to review the ending.'

"'But you're rehearsing the beginning, not the ending.'

"'They say the beginning appears politically unreliable, too, now.'

"What had changed, I wondered. How could I convince them that my play should be done? This had become vital to me, even more so than before.

"Gus said, 'They could feel differently if you signed this petition. But you are afraid to see the party on the ballot? To take a chance?'

"I asked Artie, 'Will there be a rehearsal tomorrow evening?'

"Artie answered, 'It depends.'

"'On what?'

"'That is up to you.'

"Ira said, 'But the more you think about it, Alex, the more you won't do it. Like your play. You're easily intimidated.'

"Yes, I reflected, afraid to appear afraid. I glanced at my watch and saw that I could reach my girl friend before they locked the door, if I ran all the way, and I said, 'Give me the petition.' Ira looked triumphant as he handed me the petition and Artie smiled, and I wondered whether this was a conspiracy to determine where I stood, and yet if it got my play produced it might be worth signing. And feeling intimidated by the Committee, and eager to demonstrate that I was truly democratic, and infused with a need to protest, to shout out against the unfairness of the Welfare Agency and the State, and the damage which was being done to my play, and exacerbated by many irritations, and assured by the other signatures, several of whom I recognized as members of the theater, I signed the petition. I could rebel, too. I thought vengefully.

"Then I ran. I was glad I was in condition, for I ran all the way.

"I reached the rooming house just in time. As I tip-toed up the back stairs to my girl friend's room on the third floor the front door was locked. She was surprised to see me, although pleased, and prepared.

"She said, 'I thought you were going to stand me up again.'

"I said, 'I didn't want to. It wasn't my fault.'

"But first I had to sit down to regain my breath. Now however, she was willing to be patient. My girl friend was tall, buxom, with voluptuous breasts and buttocks, and the most skillful vagina I had entered. She was also a divorcee, with one young son, and a well-used diaphragm and an obsessive need for sexual gratification. Her physical desires were often exaggerated, unreasonable, but always passionate, with a bottomless supply of energy, and I loved the situation. I had met her in my Agency office, where she was a supervisor, but tonight she was playing a different role. She greeted me dressed in a severe black silk nightgown which stressed her sensuousness, but her usually smooth, handsome features and ivory skin were stretched and taut.

"She said, 'I don't think I could have endured another night without it. Why are you so late? What happened? What held you up, Alex?'

"I told her and when she heard that I had signed the petition, she was outraged and she cried out, 'They shouldn't have asked you! All members of the party were warned not to sign!'

"'But I'm not a member of the party,' I reminded her.

"'I forgot,' she said. 'You do belong to the theater.'

"'Does that make me a member? Oh, I know some of the company are, I can tell from their attitudes, but I didn't know it was compulsory.'

"'It isn't. But the majority of the members are. Otherwise, they wouldn't get anywhere in the theater.'

"'Are you positive that no members were supposed to sign the petition?'

"'Yes. Especially those who hold State jobs.'

"Startled, I asked, 'How can you be so damned sure?'

"She said, smiling slightly, 'Can't you guess?'

"I paused. I was not shocked, and yet . . .

"She said, 'Does it show?'"

"I said, 'Not in bed.'"

"Then she was outraged again, declaring, 'Communist bastards, committing you, but not themselves. How typical. Sticking someone else in the line of fire, while they brag about their own convictions.'"

"I felt sick now, and bewildered. I said, 'I didn't know you were a member of the Communist Party?'"

"'Not any more,' she replied emphatically. 'I'm getting out.'"

"'Did you sign?' I asked."

"She stared at me as if I were out of my mind and retorted, 'Of course not. I was given specific orders not to. Because I work for the State.'"

Alex halted, as if what followed was too painful to recall. But Harold, who was listening intently, urged, "Go on! What happened with her? Did you still screw her?"

"I tried, but I wasn't worth a damn the rest of the night. Together, we were an intricate sexual mixture, and now I wasn't sure I could trust her either. Then I was distracted and disturbed by what had happened at the theater. It became an unsuccessful and frustrating evening."

Harold was surprised. "You're telling me you let that stop you?"

"It amounted to that," Alex said, still feeling ashamed.

"I would never let such things bother me," Harold said. "Alex, a woman could ruin you. Distract you, and you're done, impotent."

"It's not quite that easy."

"What happened at the rehearsal the following evening?"

"The play was cancelled. The Committee said it was naive and possibly subversive, asserting sympathy for a character on the Right."

"Even after you signed the petition?"

"I asked Artie about that and he said I had done it too late."

"Didn't your friend who asked you to sign speak up for you?"

"He disappeared."

"Did you ever see him again?"

"Once. After I was fired."

Harold was shocked. "Fired? By whom? You never told me."

"Shortly after I signed the petition a government investigating committee raided the offices of the Communist Party, seized those nominating petitions and gave them to the State and all those who had signed those petitions and worked for the State were fired."

"Without a hearing? You were an All-American quarterback!"

"I had a trial. By those who fired me. They were the judges."

"It must have been an important news story."

"The day I was fired there was a multiple murder and it got the big headlines. And by the time I was tried *my* war had begun and the trial was stuck in the back of the newspapers. Moreover, the Communists were our allies now."

"Then you must have been reinstated," Harold declared impatiently.

"Everybody was except those who signed the petition. Sixteen of us. We did not get our jobs back. We were told we had violated public confidence. But thirty who were fired were reinstated, although they supported Communist positions, for they hadn't signed the petition."

"Couldn't you tell the judges what you told me?"

"I couldn't expose my girl friend. It could have ruined her."

"Some people wouldn't respect you for sleeping with a girl who was a Communist."

"It's no different," Alex assured a worried Harold.

"You should have called her. This was no laughing matter. What happened to her? Did she appreciate what you did?"

"She stopped seeing me. I had a crucial responsibility, she told me, to satisfy her sexually, and I had failed her."

"What about your friend, Ira? You said you saw him again."

"At another theater, during an intermission, while I was on trial. I approached him, to ask his help, and when he saw

me he vanished into the crowd and although I stood outside
the door when the play ended there was no trace of him."

Harold said determinedly, "I would have grabbed him."

"It would not have proven anything. Besides, it was
evident that not everyone who signed the nominating
petition was a Communist."

"Why not?" Harold asked belligerently. "It isn't evident to
me."

"Over fifty thousand signed the petition to put the Communist Party on the ballot, but the Communists received
only five thousand votes."

Before leaving, Alex had to read some of the telegrams
Harold had received. Harold was insistent; his columnists
must be practical.

Alex read: "You have stripped your country of its honor.
Do you want our boys to run away in the presence of the
enemy!" But these were sane comments compared to the ob-
scenities that dominated most of the wires.

Then there was one from Coach Butch Borborg in which
he wired Harold Hinton: "If I had known that Alexander
Grant signed a Red petition I would not have played him."

As this caused Alex to laugh, Harold realized Alex hadn't
conceded anything important and exasperated, he blurted
out, "Why don't you tell your story to the newspapers?"

"I can't. I would expose innocent people. The girl."

"She wasn't innocent," Harold declared. "She was a Communist."

Alex was silent. He was sorry he had confided in the publisher.

Harold said, "You would be well advised to take a
vacation."

Alex said, "If I do that now it will look as if I'm running
away. And I've already written a column for Monday.
Nothing like Friday's," he added, seeing Harold frown. "It's
a birthright memo for sons."

"I will read it before we release it."

"Harold, would you like to play tennis later?"

"I can't. I have a very important engagement the rest of
the day."

There was a knock on the door and as Alex said good-bye he added, "Harold, it is a little late to question my sincerity."

"It is not your sincerity that worries me, it is your judgment."

Harold opened the door and Graham Graves stood there. Harold said hurriedly, "You know each other, of course."

"Of course," said Alex, but Graves didn't say a word.

Graves, in his bitterness, couldn't greet this betrayer. Grant had put him in a very embarrassing position. After the disaster of *The Game* the President had rejected his invitation to play tennis and after *Who Has Measured the Blood?* Victor Winner hadn't spoken to him for twenty-four hours. And now there was that blasted petition! He couldn't allow Grant to screw him again. Only his suggestion that the President invite Harold Hinton to dinner with a few other important newspaper tycoons for a special briefing on the Pacification Program had evoked some of the old warmth from Victor Winner. Bringing this invitation in person, which was also a sign of presidential favor, perhaps not all was lost.

Alex said, "Harold, thanks for the advice, I will think about it."

Graves ignored the columnist as he presented the President's invitation and the publisher replied, "Thanks, Graham, it is kind of the President to ask my advice. It is more than some of my employees do."

Alex walked off, thinking, I am a fool, trusting anybody. He could hear Harold telling Graves, "I'm looking forward to having dinner with the President with great pleasure. Do you think we could play tennis later?"

# Survive

Survive
    to become seed
Survive pollination
    to become prenatal
Survive the prenatal
    to be born
Survive birth
    to live
Survive life
    to die
Survive death
    or find out


STYMEAN KARLEN

# Survive

Shipmen was upset. The appearance of the petition in the newspapers had not accomplished the desired results. Grant's column had appeared as usual on Monday and while *Birthday Memo* had been less incendiary than *Who Has Measured the Blood?* Shipmen didn't trust it. He felt this list of instructions a father gave his son on how to achieve manhood, although written jokingly, was a defense of the quarterback.

Imagine, he thought angrily, suggesting a permanent draft deferment card, half burnt. A list of protest methods. A manual on surveillance.

Some of the other ideas, too, disgusted him. By now the columnist's treachery, he could not think of it as anything else, was an obsession with the investigator and to correct it was a matter of honor. The columnist's behavior had become a personal insult to his religion.

So Tuesday, to prepare for a discussion with Spleeno Bludgeon about the situation, Shipmen consulted his computers in the hope they would find something more damaging than the petition. This new dossier, he resolved, must be truly incriminating. And as he felt the presence of his computers he began to feel better. They reminded him, not everything is going badly. Several other portions of the columnist's past were being investigated and there were some encouraging developments. Then the Monday meeting with the President had been hopeful. He felt he had created a convert. He could recall every detail.

He sat next to Victor Winner, on his instructions, while Graves was switched around, a few chairs away from the President now. The foreign policy advisor had become Mister Softly. Graves didn't talk at all during the conference, and smiled only when the President thanked him for suggesting that Harold Hinton was a sensible dinner guest and invited him to a ceremony Tuesday night to honor a hero of the Pacification Program. But then, Shipmen noted, the President invited *him* first. It was consoling. Even more consoling, after the meeting ended Victor Winner drew him aside and conferred with him privately.

The President said, "I knew Alexander Grant was not to be trusted. Congratulations. When did you find out he was a Communist?"

"In the newspapers, sir, when you did."

Victor Winner smiled knowingly. "No one will believe his columns now."

"I hope so, sir."

"Keep up the good work, Roger. Did his column appear today?"

"Yes, sir. I'm sorry to say."

Victor Winner frowned, then said, "We must be patient. Some situations take time. You will have new material for Spleeno soon?"

"Yes, sir. I am working on that at this very moment."

"Fine. The petition must have done some good."

"Yes, indeed, sir. I heard that six affiliates of the syndicate refused to carry one of his columns and that four are leaving it."

"So I heard, too."

Shipmen was surprised. He was alone with the President, except for two Examiners in the doorway, and this was a great honor.

"Roger," the President reminded him, "I have sources, too."

"Naturally, sir. I'm just one of many humble servants."

"But one of my most important ones, too." Then the President did something which made a profound impression on Shipmen. He handed the investigator his personal intelligence summary and said, "Study *P I S*, Roger, it should be helpful, give you some new ideas."

Shipmen's hands trembled as he took the precious folder from the President. He knew very well what was in it; he could tell by the color of the paper and the lettering. Now he knew that he was a person of consequence. He said emotionally, "I'll do my best, sir."

. "I know you will. I would take a hand myself in this situation, but I am too busy. If I read all of my intelligence reports I would not have time for anything else. That is why I need relaxation so much. Roger, would you be free for some tennis later this week?"

"Yes, of course, sir. But ..." Shipmen couldn't hide his surprise.

"Not with the columnist. Harold Hinton is here to observe and to evaluate, and he loves tennis. He is almost as good as we are."

"Who would be our fourth, sir?"

"I haven't decided yet. Graves's game is undependable, but he may steady down. But Harold is definite. He has accepted my invitation already. He will be at the ceremony, too. As my personal guest."

Victor Winner was a genius, thought Shipmen, no wonder he had become President.


Yet *Hush* and *Hush-Hush* differed with the personal intelligence summary, for it didn't agree with their own. An exasperated Shipmen shouted at them, "I ask for two opinions and you give me six!"

The computers were more helpful when he asked them, "What books does the quarterback read?"

*Hush* and *Hush-Hush* stated, "His bookcase contains Bernard Shaw, Che Guevara, Sean O'Casey, Karl Marx, Tom Paine, and other revolutionaries."

Shipmen was so heartened by these findings, which confirmed his own suspicions, he programmed the columnist. With Alexander Grant in his *Subversive* file, new information should be forthcoming.

The computers replied, "His credit rating is dubious. He

has no credit cards. Or insurance. Or stocks. His lack of faith in the economy is suspicious. But most suspicious is his interest in sex. It is a very serious thing. Quite disturbing. He has been married three times, he has had many affairs. All inquiries suggest that he is attracted by females as a moth is attracted by a flame."

Shipmen halted his computers. They were editorializing. Yet, he reflected, sex was where the columnist should be most vulnerable. But one fact was not clear: did Grant fancy himself a Don Juan or was he a Don Juan? If he found this answer, he should find the fatal weakness.

Shipmen was excited, for he had begun this line of inquiry already. He had a feeling that if he could find the right match to ignite the bonfire, *the situation*, as it was classified now, would be resolved favorably. He was pondering this when he received an urgent telephone call from the military doctor. He replied irritably; M.P. was shattering his concentration just as he felt he was achieving a solution.

M.P. was too inspired to notice. He blurted out, "I have unearthed vital information. The Demolisher was a student at the university."

"Are you certain?" This was hardly a great step forward.

"Yes. I never give up. When I examined him in my medical computer, *The Crapper*, it revealed he had flunked his chemistry course. I checked those who had flunked chemistry and I found him."

"Where?" Shipmen was annoyed. M.P. was becoming too vain to trust.

"Freshman chemistry. He failed. He was in the same class as Grant."

"That could be useful." Shipmen was more interested now.

M.P. said triumphantly, "And his name is Gary Ginger."

"Were they friends? Or, at least, did they know each other?"

"I don't know yet. There were two hundred and seven students in the class. It was a lecture course."

"Then how could he have failed?"

"I will find out."

"Ginger—Grant, Gi—Gr, they must have sat close to each

other. We always sat alphabetically. Or have they changed that, too?"

"That's still the same. There must have been collusion."

"What else did you learn? I'm a busy man, Doctor."

"Give me time. Please!"

"There isn't much time. You have an exceptional opportunity to serve your country. Examine The Demolisher again. Have it appear to be a court of law. He is still in the university hospital, isn't he?"

"Yes. You left four Examiners with him, sir."

"Good. The President expects every soldier to do his duty."

This wasn't as easy as Shipmen thought, M.P. told himself. But he was accustomed to obeying orders, and so he arranged a hearing which would have the form of a courtroom trial and which would imply that grave consequences would afflict The Demolisher if the culprit didn't confess.

He held this inquiry—it was what he called it for the hospital records—in a bare, white conference room that was stark and forboding. The four Examiners sat against the wall like a jury; The Demolisher was placed in the center of the room and seated in the most uncomfortable stiff-backed chair that M.P. could find; then M.P. ensconced himself in an armchair on a raised platform, so, as both judge and interrogator, he was above everybody else.

Then M.P. asked in a staccato manner, "Where are your parents?"

The Demolisher was equally staccato—whatever M.P. did, he could do better, "That is not the point. They have nothing to do with it."

"Where do they live?"

"That is not the point. That is not why I am here."

"What organization do you represent?"

"Myself."

"Who are you against?"

"The world. That is not the point."

"When were you born?"

"I wasn't. That is not the point."

"What else did you flunk?"

"What did you flunk?"

"That is not the point!" M.P. was becoming desperate. He was supposed to exert the pressure, not the culprit. "What books do you read?"

"What do you read?"

"But your name is Gary Ginger!" declared M.P., feeling triumphant again, and better. "You can't deny that!"

"My name is The Demolisher!" He was outraged. He had flunked his chemistry course, but he had succeeded as a demolisher. Once they called him Gary Ginger, he lost his identity, he was back on the old weary treadmill. He couldn't return to that role, to failure, it would be better. not to have any role to play than to return to that.

M.P. shook his head wonderingly. "I don't know how you can be so ornery. You are only a down-and-out, a freak. You ought to be proud to be called by your name."

"Do you know what skill it takes to construct an anti-personal device?"

"You were in the same class as the quarterback."

"I was in the venereal detail."

"You must have known James Grant."

"I don't know anybody. That is not the point."

"You were a decoy."

"You are a liar. But that is not the point."

"Why did you blow up the storeroom?"

"That is not the point."

"If you don't answer these questions you will be cited for contempt."

"That is not the point. That won't change anything."

"You will get a sentence."

"That is not the point. My dynamite sticks will be getting the sentence, not me."

"What is the point?"

"I'm living in a mixed-up world. Send the world to prison. And yourselves. I don't know who you are. I don't know who I am. I learned to hate. I learned that in the war. And I can't stop!" he screamed.

"That is not the point."

"I see it now, you jerks! I exploded the wrong target! I

should have exploded myself! Where are my dynamite sticks, they'll blow me up!"

The four Examiners had to restrain The Demolisher from smashing himself against the wall, and M.P. was proud he had the foresight to hold the inquiry where there were no windows, otherwise the culprit would have lacerated himself so badly he would have become a hopeless witness.

The Vice-President wasn't interested in reading Shipmen's new dossier. "You can take care of the details," he assured the investigator. "When a Communist like Grant copulates, you can't expect me to be there. That's your business. Have you been invited to the ceremony, too?"

"Yes." Spleeno, amazingly, had given him a good idea. Who did the columnist copulate with? That could be useful.

Spleeno added, "No wonder his son behaved so stupidly. Those college radicals can't even balance a check book."

"Yes." He must pursue this idea before Spleeno diverted him.

"I always speak with sincerity, it is the only way." If he could only control the intelligence of the students, he reflected, he could achieve his political destiny.

Spleeno was honored that the President shared his love and respect for ceremony, especially for military ceremony. He felt this was a vital bond uniting them. It was understood Victor Winner must always be in the center, but this didn't bother Spleeno, it was enough that the President included him. He was proud he had been invited to the true count ceremony, honoring a hero of the Pacification Program.

It was impressive, he thought. He stood behind the President, while Shipmen was on the right and Graves and Hinton were on the left. He had lightened his gray, sparse hair so that it was brown and younger, and he wore his mouth-definitely-up-at-the-corners-decent-good-fellow smile.

He was surprised that the hero, Private Bobby Blaber, was so insignificant-looking, child-sized and sweaty-faced and ordinary.

But Bobby Blaber had achieved the greatest true count in

the Territory and his memory was phenomenal, he could remember every one of them. He possessed total recall. He was not introspective, but he had pride. His job had been to pacify and he had: two hundred and fifty-five times.

And as the President pinned the medal on him and said, "It is heart-warming to meet a young man who knows his duty," and as he replied, "Thank you, sir, I was only doing my best," he thought gratefully, it had been a good year. He had been the smallest kid on the block, wherever he had lived, and he had lived in many towns and cities, for his parents had moved frequently, his father never able to hold a job; but nobody would kick him around any more, or tease him, not even about his size. Christ, he hadn't made any mistakes in the Territory. He had never let up. He had learned fast that the only good enemy was a dead enemy. He had never cheated. Every child and civilian he had included was thoroughly dead. He had made sure of that.

Now the President was shaking his hand and congratulating him and he was glad he had had such good aim, for so was the Vice-President and other dignitaries. One of them, a newspaper publisher, Harold Hinton, suggested, "When you settle down, if you would like to write an account of your experiences, I am sure we could publish them."

"Thank you, sir." He would need a job when he was discharged. Only he could just about sign his name. "I'll consider it."

"I wish you would. We need more patriotism these days."

"I quite agree," said the President. "This young man was not afraid to involve himself. We all owe him a debt of gratitude."

Spleeno saw Victor Winner smile encouragingly in his direction and he added, "Private Blaber, we have learned from you what our duty to our country is and we will always appreciate it and seek to emulate it."

Victor Winner's smile was so fixed, Alex noticed, watching the ceremony on television, he wondered if the President ever removed it. It was his best-dressed face, he thought, the most carefully chosen part of his meticulously chosen wardrobe. Yet when Victor Winner turned to address Harold Hinton as the sanctified public ceremonial ended the President's smile shone with special enthusiasm.

But Monday's column had appeared on time and no one seemed to be offended by it. There were a number of letters defending *Who Has Measured the Blood?*, including one from Christine Lister, but not a word from James. A few of the letters that supported him, said, "You were an All-American quarterback, you couldn't have been a Red."

He turned off the President, for the latter was putting on his strong, executive face: level-eyed, thin-lipped mouth, rigid jaw.

All of a sudden the telephone rang. Before Alex could say hello, James shouted, "Will you get your wife off my back?"

"Where is she?"

"In my rooms," James said woefully. "She is supposed to hate cold weather. What is she doing here?"

"How should I know? I haven't spoken to your mother for over a year. We have been divorced a long time."

"You are still my parents. She wants me to return to the team."

"But she always says she is afraid you'll get hurt."

"Not any more. Now she says it will keep me out of trouble. That it will show my remorse. But I don't feel any remorse. Will you hurry up here and get her to mind her own business? Before she drives me nuts."

"I'm busy."

"What is it, a babe?"

"I'm working."

"Sure!" His son laughed, obviously not believing him.

"James, what did you think about the petition?"

"It was stupid. Everybody knows the Communists can't be trusted."

"It was thirty years ago."

"Besides, nobody will pay any attention."

"Some newspapers already have. They've dropped my column."

"I told you that you couldn't play ball with them. But you tried."

"I wrote *Who Has Measured the Blood?*"

"Clammy, Alexander, clammy. I'm no Lady Godiva. Who was she anyhow?"

"It doesn't matter." Alex sighed. "What do you mean—clammy?"

"Wet. Teary. Sentimental. But it might wake up a few people."

"Thanks."

"Why? Your style is still wooden and the article was clumsily written."

Alex was silent.

"You're not offended, are you, Alexander?"

"Isn't that your intention?"

"I don't want you to be always in-between. Will you get here as fast as you can? Rita is as prying as some of these snoopers around here."


This time Alex didn't drive all night or rush. He left the next morning and drove leisurely and arrived at the university just before evening. James arranged for the three of them to meet at a small suburban restaurant where it was unlikely they would be seen or overheard. However, as they sat in a secluded corner Alex was asking himself, what subject will Rita choose, I have none.

Rita's buxom beauty which had aroused Alex when she was twenty was gone. The youthful blouse she insisted on wearing accentuated the heaviness of her breasts, and her tight skirt caused her buttocks to bulge. It were as if her flesh had multiplied, but little else. Her once pretty brunette hair was dyed a silver-blonde, and her features were no longer pert and oval but sagging and square. And he had never loved her with all of his love and she knew this and had never forgiven him. From the first moment she saw him, she was critical.

"Why didn't you stop James?" she demanded.

"Would he have listened?" Alex turned to the menu, asked, "Rita, would you like a drink? Some wine, or perhaps, champagne."

"There is nothing to celebrate," she snapped. "My son is

in trouble, his father, too. Why didn't you tell me about the petition?"

"It was in the newspapers before I married you."

"You know I didn't read the newspapers."

"Anyway, that's not why you've come here, is it?"

"You should talk to James and keep a better watch on him, instead of running around so. The next thing you know, they will question me."

"Have they?" cried James, coming out of his protective silence.

"You are too young to know about such matters," she said. "Eat some food. You've lost weight lately. Running around naked. How could you?"

James said, grinning, "Rita, it is the *Bare Ass Principle.*"

"You're not being funny. You could jeopardize your future here."

"Oh, they've let me back in school, as long—in their words—I behave myself. As long as I don't undress in public."

"Shame shame shame."

But she wanted me to run around naked, Alex remembered, when we made love before we were married. Suddenly he felt he was surrounded by soundless colorless odorless sightless senseless sensations.

James said, "Fact is, I wanted to improve my image. After all, I am one of the few people who looks good naked."

"You could have caught your death from the cold. If you had played in *The Game*, you could have been at the reception the President gave for the hero of the true count. Don't they teach you anything at the university?"

"I've learned a great deal. I haven't been the same since."

"I'm surprised you didn't commit the worst of indiscretions and relieve yourself right on the field. I saw it on television, with friends and neighbors. I'm glad you went to the bathroom before you stripped. You always had good self-control, not like your father."

"I ran out of waiting."

"What?" Rita didn't understand him.

". . . out of patience."

"Couldn't you have consulted your father first?"

"No. He always teeters on the edge of sincerity."

Alex said defensively, "I voted for Peace but I got Pacification."

Rita said, "And all I get from my son is 'Hi,' and not even cordially."

James said, "You have it down pat, Rita. You're lucky."

"I talk to you. I always did."

"Is that why you came?" Alex asked. "To tell us how we neglect you?"

"Order me something, and then we can talk."

When Alex did, as he used to do when he courted her, she was pleased and she ate the roast beef with relish while no one spoke. But when she finished she could not endure her son's silence. The moment she was done with her dessert, she burst out, "James, I bear the awful responsibility of motherhood and you behave as if I am your worst enemy. Yet until you were five you always wanted to sit on my lap and you held my hand wherever we went. You were very affectionate then. You enjoyed my love. But when you began to see more of your father, you changed. Then you even seemed uncomfortable with me."

James said, "Rita, you have a splendid imagination."

"And now you are filled with such high-flown principles."

"Rita, you are impossible."

"I'm your mother. Be careful, darling, you do have a res- ponsibility to me, also, even if you don't feel any to your- self." James looked puzzled and she explained, "I devoted many years to you, I don't want it to be wasted. If I were your father after your disgraceful exhibition on the football field I would have spanked you."

"He's too old."

Alex refused to accept the challenge, even verbally, and was silent.

Rita said, "I express myself and you get excited. You didn't have anything to do with blowing up that building, did you?"

"No, Rita."

"You can call me mother. I am, you know."

"Yes, Rita." But James lost his smile.

"Now run along. I want to talk to your father."

"Rita, I'm not twelve."

"I know how old you are. I was there when it happened. Which is more than I can say about your father."

Alex said, "I was away fighting a war. *My* war."

"I know where you were. James, don't you know any girls? Your father always did. Is this what all that ridiculous involvement with social causes has done to you? And there are some things that you are still too young to discuss. Will you excuse me?"

"Is that why you came to see me?"

"Your father's car is outside. Alex, give him the keys to your car."

"He has a car, Rita."

"He prefers yours. He always liked to drive it."

Alex handed James the keys to his car, and James said, "Rita, I could hear you better if your voice wasn't so loud," and then he was gone.

Rita said tearfully, "Whatever he needed I gave him. But I did want to talk to you. Are you sure we can't be overheard?"

Alex glanced around the small, intimate restaurant. There were a few couples sitting nearby, but none of them within hearing distance. Champagne had come, but neither of them touched it.

"Well, at least," she said with sudden nostalgia, "we are together."

"Rita, what did you want to discuss with me?"

"Alex, are you under surveillance?"

"I don't know. It is possible. Why?"

"I am. At least, I think I am."

"Because of me?"

"I think so. A few days ago a man visited me at my apartment and said he was writing an article about the important columnists in the country, including you."

"What did he want?"

"He asked me about your political opinions, but when I said I didn't know them, that we never discussed politics when we were married, he said, 'Grant must have been interesting to know. Was he as exciting a ladies' man as he was supposed to be? How did he perform in bed?'"

"What did you answer?"

"I was so surprised, I blushed and stammered, 'What has this to do with his column?' and he said, 'Reader interest, Mrs. Grant.'"

"Was there anything special about his appearance?"

"He was burly, middle-aged, with a high hairline, short sideburns, and a crew cut haircut. Almost like a soldier's. Yet he wore a dark, dreary, depressing gray suit that corporation people wear, although he had a heavy, square face."

"Like an examiner?"

"Yes. He asked questions as if it were his profession. I wondered whether he really was a writer."

"Did you ask him for whom he was writing the article?"

"He didn't let me. His next question was almost an accusation. He asked, 'Do you think Grant is as sexually exciting as he is supposed to be? Grant never writes about sex. Or anything amorous.'"

"'That is not his field,' I answered.

"'That is what I mean,' he replied. 'Some men who profess to be most potent are often hiding their impotence.'"

"I almost exploded then: You—impotent? How ridiculous! But I managed to keep my emotions in check, although I was very angry, this stranger was so aggressive and then he asked all sorts of questions such as, 'What books do you read? What politicians do you admire? Are you extravagant?' I felt so hemmed in, I wanted to flee, but I was afraid. He was very authoritative. Then he asked me, 'Are Grant and his son close? Do they have the same views?' and I shrugged and answered, 'They are father and son.' And suddenly he caught me completely by surprise, asking, 'What are his bathroom habits? Does he spend an unusual amount of time there? Has he ever done anything that you could consider strange? Extraordinary?'"

Alex said, "I hope you laughed in his face."

"Nothing of the kind. I was so shocked I forgot my fear and I shut my door on him."

Alex asked thoughtfully, "You have no idea where he really came from?"

"No. But that is not all. Several days later another stranger sat down beside me at my pool and said how much he admired your columns and that you must have been quite a man to know intimately, and were you as exciting as your reputation? And did you still believe in Communism? It was the day after the story about the petition appeared and I replied, 'It is none of your business.' To my surprise, he agreed, but after a few minutes of small talk, mostly about what beautiful weather we were having, he mentioned you again. He asked me, 'Did you know Grant when he wrote a play for a Communist theater?' and I excused myself."

Alex said, "He sounds as if he started out with the conviction that I was already guilty. Although I am not quite sure of what."

"There was something odd about him," said Rita. "Despite the fact that the temperature was in the eighties and everybody else around the pool were in their bathing suits, including myself, he wore a heavy, dark, unpleasant gray suit, just like the other man had worn."

"Had you ever seen him before?"

"No. And I know everybody in the apartment house. Then when I telephoned James and you, I couldn't get either of you and I heard a funny buzz on the line. Do you think they tapped my telephone?"

"I don't know why they should involve you."

"So you are being investigated?"

"I'm not sure yet."

"Is it because of what James did?"

"Possibly. And because of what I did."

"What did you do? Now really, Alex, words never hurt anybody."

"Keep out of it. If anybody asks about me, tell them the truth, that we haven't lived together for years and are virtually strangers."

"But we are not. And we will never be, actually."

Rita was overwhelmed with nostalgia. Although she told

herself that her reasons for coming north were to stop James and to warn Alex, in her heart she was hoping for a reconciliation with Alex. She assumed he must have loved her, for when she was twenty he had pursued her with passion. And while she had allowed Alex to caress her perfect breasts and her voluptuous buttocks, for many months she had kept his hands from straying. Her excuse was: He had no intention of marrying her and she was afraid she would become pregnant.

But one night Alex persuaded her to use a contraceptive, for it was becoming impossible to resist him.

She never forgot this night. She refused to allow him to see her naked and as he approached her, naked, too, she couldn't look at him. She was afraid to see his penis, but when she felt it against her, warm and firm, she was seized with an uncontrollable craving. And as he inserted his penis into her, she was certain it was the largest penis she would ever know, and she realized her notions about sexual intercourse were wrong. Instead of being ugly and awful, she was afraid she would never experience this ecstasy again.

Then one night she panicked. She was still undressing in the dark, and Alex was talking about moving away to look for another job and she was sure it was a girl and she could not endure the idea of losing him. She didn't use her contraceptive and a month later she tearfully informed Alex there had been an accident, she was pregnant.

Alex looked so ghastly, she never forgave him.

She accomplished her purpose however, he proposed to her and soon after they were married. But now that their sexual experiences were no longer illicit they were not exciting. Spitefully, she retaliated by talking during their sexual encounters, which he hated, it distracted him. And when he returned from *his* war to an infant son, he showed little interest in the child and then they separated. She resisted the divorce, but finally, when he refused to see her at all unless she gave him a divorce, she consented. Once James was old enough to play tennis and football with his father, Alex became interested in him and they became friendly, although she sensed James didn't completely trust it.

Living without love didn't make sense. Tonight, she was willing under any conditions. She blurted out, "Alex, we have known each other a long time, we shouldn't waste it." Damn, he was not listening!

Alex would have liked to have changed his feelings for Rita, but it was too late, it always had been too late. Her superb breasts had been the trap. He was grateful that she wasn't talking now, just sitting and thinking. He never could endure her when she was talkative, especially when he was about to enter her. And Wally hated it. Wally got limp; Wally couldn't bear indifference. But had her pregnancy been an accident? He had never been sure, but he had never forgiven her. And had she told James? She must have, he decided, why else did James have a chip on his shoulder against him? Thinking of this, Alex's detachment left him.

Rita was reaching for his hand and he pulled it away.

"We have many things in common. We could still love each other."

"No," he said. "It won't work."

"I'm not asking for anything that is not coming to me."

"This is ridiculous. We haven't had sex for years."

"It would please James."

"I doubt it. He knows it would only be a marriage of convenience. Rita, did you ever tell him that he was an accident?"

"Alexander, I would never betray you!"

Except to preserve herself, he thought. Just as she felt he had seduced her, he believed he had been victimized by loneliness. "Even for James I cannot exhibit domestic virtue. It would be false and he would know it. But I do appreciate your efforts to protect me."

"I didn't want James to know. Especially about the sexual inquiries." But perhaps she had been hasty, Rita reflected, answering the queries. During one of the questions it had popped out of her that Alex didn't like her to talk while he was making love. She had not meant to expose him, and in a way she had not, she consoled herself, for she had added immediately that he was very virile. Now that she confessed this to herself, she felt better, for she knew confession was good for the soul. "Alex, I wish the public knew how fortunate they are to have a columnist like you to read."

"Did you read my last two columns?"

"No. But you must keep up your good work. Everybody where I live knows you are a nationally syndicated columnist."


James interrupted them, declaring irritably, "Your car won't start."

Rita said, "Why don't you use your own?" She was annoyed by the interruption. "Can't you see that we are talking privately?"

Alex stood up and asked, "Is it out of gas?"

"I don't think so. It just won't turn over. It's dead."

The three of them trooped out to the car as if they were about to attend a funeral, but Alex was relieved to find the source of the trouble. The wires on the battery were disconnected; he wondered if someone had done it deliberately. The car had run properly until now.

Alex corrected the wires, said, "Okay, James, it is working again." He turned to Rita. "Thanks for your help. It was considerate. But I think you ought to go home. James and I can take care of ourselves."

James smiled with relief, but he didn't say anything.

Rita asked, "Alex, do you think the wires on the car were disconnected deliberately?"

"It is possible. James and I will take you to the plane."

"But I have no intention of leaving."

Alex said, "I am returning to the capital."

James said, "And I am going back to school."

Rita said, "Promise me that you will not protest any more."

James said, "I promise nothing."

"Why doesn't he marry, have children, do graduate work, that would keep him out of trouble!" But when no one answered her, Rita asked imploringly, "You will both take care of yourselves?"

"Of course!" They said it with one voice, for once in agreement.

But it was not until the next morning she was able to catch a plane for her home in the south. Alex drove her to the airport in his car, which was functioning perfectly since he had adjusted the wires on the battery, and James sat on the other side of her. Afterwards, he took James back to his rooms. His son did not ask him to come in, although James did say, "I'm sorry I had to interrupt you last night."

"We weren't talking about you."

"I didn't think you were. There was a special gleam in Rita's eyes when you appeared. You are not going back together, are you?"

"Do you want us to?"

James laughed, almost stridently. "Do you?" When his father failed to answer, he added, "How did you two ever come to marry?"

Alex started to say it was an accident, then he caught hold of himself and replied, "At twenty we do many things we wouldn't do later."

"Don't lecture me! You were over thirty when you married Rita!"

Alex changed the subject. "Do you think they are watching you, too?"

But if Alexander assumed this would create a collaboration, James told himself, he was wrong. James said, "Probably. It doesn't matter. There are a couple of new characters in several of my classes."

"With crew cuts and critical eyes?"

"No! Their hair is the longest in the class and their style is very much with it. I also hear they discovered that The Demolisher and I were in the same class when I was a freshman."

"Did you know him?"

"In a class of over two hundred? Not likely!"

There was an expression on James's face that said, Well, what words of wisdom are you going to bestow on me now? and so Alex said, as he started his car, "Be seeing you. Take care."

James had walked away, intending to make the first gesture of departure, and he was surprised by his father's brevity and quickness to leave. He turned and said, startled,

"Yeah." When he saw his father was really leaving, he added, smiling, "Take care. You, too. And thanks."

"What for?"

"Getting Rita off my back."

"But she is your mother."

"And you are my father." James repeated that, as if it were a litany. Yet as he saw that his father was really going without another word, he shouted after him, "Don't let them get you down, Alexander."

"I'll try."

"After all," it sounded like a warning now and it came with a great effort, "We got to survive."

# The Handle on the Door

The handle on the door
Would ask for nothing more
Than to play its role
To open and close the door

But the handle on the door
Resents the hand on itself
That has all the power and even
Christened it after itself

The handle on the door
Plans one day to throw off
The hand on itself
And open and close the door

And then to re-christen itself


STYMEAN KARLEN

# The Handle on the Door

Alex repeated James's parting words to himself many times the next few days as he sought to use them to guide his column. For the first time, he felt his son could truly care for him and it was an emotion he longed to encourage. He had written two moderate columns, *The Coming of Winter*, and *The Common Cold*, and matters were going more smoothly. James was back in school, the football season had ended, for which he was thankful; The Demolisher was still in the hospital and there was no proof the young man had known James; there was no evidence of anyone spying on him; Rita had returned to her home and he was continuing to support her, although unwillingly; his last two columns had been received without criticism, and there were many letters defending him and deriding the story he was a Red. But there was no comment from his son.

He sat down at old Iron Face to write his next column, not sure what to write, which was normal. At the instant of starting he preferred to play tennis, or for the telephone to ring or any merciful interruption. Nothing happened. Yet he had time, he consoled himself, it was only Friday morning and his next column was not due until Monday.

He stared at his battered tennis sneaks and he remembered Rita's constant complaint, "Alexander, you ought to throw them away. They'll disgrace us. Everybody knows you can afford new ones."

But he liked old sneaks, he was comfortable in old things.

He hadn't played since he had lost to Eric, which added to his frustration.

He turned on the news in the hope this would cue his column and he heard the President announce: "Pacification is continuing indefinitely. And to protect it I am ordering an excursion into a new Territory."

He shut off the radio. If the news would only go away!

History was safer. Alex typed that on old Iron Face, adding, for she was resisting him, keys bumped and tangled and the ribbon was balky, "I can write about history with an amused tolerance."

"Dismally," she replied.

"It's easy to be tolerant about conditions we don't have to endure."

"That's an old address."

"But I could indulge in wry disparagement about the past which, if I wrote it about the present, would be bitterly resented. In the Capitol existence must be regarded as a success, otherwise it is a criticism of the Capitol itself, which was erected as an expression of success."

"And not save any lives?"

"I can't save any lives!" He banged so hard on old Iron Face he almost broke a key. If he maintained an urbane stance, spoke in generalities, no one would be offended, he told himself, and he would be regarded as a minor Montaigne, but if he mentioned the crumbling behind the facade, if he dissected public officials, if he called his column, rightfully, *Bullshit and Blackmail*, it might not even be published.

"You're not relevant," old Iron Face said.

"That's possible," Alex answered. "But what is?"

"Stop evading. You're still afraid."

"I don't want to lose."

"Neither does the President."

"I listen to you."

"A very good idea."

"But . . . ?"

"Can't you write without using but yet still maybe perhaps. Must you always equivocate? Please? Perform? Pander?"

"Old Iron Face, you sound like you are speaking for somebody else."

"I am speaking for myself. Your situation is a matter of conscience."

If he used that as an excuse, he thought, he would be laughed at. To say he was seeking to write a column of conscience was to invite ridicule. He would be accused of using jargon, of debasing the language. Stridency sold. But conscience? It would be a waste.

Old Iron Face declared, "Even if I have to be your conscience myself."

But that didn't mean he and his conscience were close friends.

"You're still depending on yet but perhaps. You have no ear at all."

"You're as critical as James," he retorted.

Old Iron Face didn't answer. Her ribbon stuck.

This time Alex didn't address her, but said to himself aloud: "I don't have to see the blood, I can be color blind, too, like Roger Shipmen and Graham Graves and Spleeno Bludgeon and Victor Winner. I could amuse, get rich, and let other matters alone. Better to be a rubber stamp blotting up trivialities. Plunk. Plunk. Plunk."

There was still no reply from old Iron Face and he walked over to his mirror. Some days he didn't mind what he saw, but this morning, although his weight was good and his skin glowed with health and there was no gray in his hair, he wasn't reconciled to himself. This was one of those unfavorable days when he saw his petty vanities about his age, about being a self-made man. No wonder James felt competitive. He was taking himself too seriously. Pacification was full of reasonless reasons.

He felt better when he played Mozart's Jupiter Symphony. It was one of his favorites and the record had been given to him by James as a birthday present, and it should relax him, give him good thoughts. He fixed old Iron Face's ribbon and prepared to write once more. As he listened to the Jupiter he recalled it had never been played in Mozart's lifetime and he stopped feeling sorry for himself.

He braced himself before old Iron Face, hoping she

wouldn't talk back this time, adopted a tone of self-mockery, titled this prospective column, *Lifestyle*, writing that much of protest grew out of such diverse elements as students wanting to be both Huck Finn and Buck Rodgers, but once again the *c* became *f*, and he wrote Fuck Finn and Fuck Rodgers, then the keys stuck again, the ribbon tangled, and the roller skipped.

Yet when he retitled the column, *Blackmail and Blunderbuss*—although he still preferred *Bullshit and Blackmail*, but there was no point in antagonizing Harold Hinton—old Iron Face worked perfectly.

He wrote: "Pacification must not be offered as a bribe for victory. We must protect each life, one life, any life. The stone never campaigns and has to be President. What is grander than a snow-capped mountain! It never extols itself as a leader of humanity. Man must stop murdering his image in other men . . ."


The telephone rang. Ordinarily, Alex would have been grateful, but now he was annoyed, he was absorbed by what he was writing, then he was excited, it could be James calling, James wanted him, it was better than not being wanted at all, and he was surprised by how nervous this made him. It was Harold Hinton.

Let down, he asked, "What is it, Harold?"

"I'm still in the Capitol."

"I hope you're enjoying it?" Was the publisher staying on to keep an eye on him? Then Alex decided this was being vain.

"The President and I have developed an authentic intimacy. He has solicited my views. He thinks I can make a major contribution."

"Has he discussed me?"

"Alex, you are not that important."

My column might be, however, he thought. "Does he listen, too?"

"We had an extraordinary tennis match. He has a fantastic knowledge of the game. He told me that he only drew with you, but he won with me."

"Who played against you?"

"The same pair you couldn't beat, Shipmen and Graves."

"So Graves is out of the doghouse?"

"That was my doing. The President is pleased Graves brought us together. But I called to congratulate you for being moderate. Maybe you don't need a vacation. We must have compassion for the President. Most people don't realize how much he has on his shoulders. Keep up the good work. Your last two columns were fine. I'm glad you listened to me."

"Did any of the affiliates who threatened to leave return?"

"Yes. Several of the outlets reconsidered when we submitted those columns and have decided to stay with us, at least, for the time being."

"Despite the petition?"

"Apparently your football record convinced them you weren't a Red."

"Suppose I say something critical about Pacification?"

"You mustn't beat a dead horse. Although I don't think Graves will forgive you for what your son did. He feels you are responsible."

"Does Shipmen feel the same way?"

Harold laughed.

"What's funny?"

"He asked me if you were as much a Don Juan as you are supposed to be."

"What did you answer?"

"I said it was probably a rumor to get women readers."

"Thanks."

"Don't be sensitive. You did confess to me that after your Communist girl friend told you that she was a Communist, you were impotent."

"Did you tell that to Shipmen?"

"Of course not! Would I betray you?"

Alex didn't reply. He felt as if he had been stripped.

"One doesn't have to look under covers to know what is taking place beneath them. You paralyze too easy. But I won't tell anybody."

"Is that all?"

"Alex, I didn't call to critize you."

But to warn me, Alex thought. "Why did you call, Harold?"

"I appreciate your co-operation. Is that Mozart in the background?"

"Yes. The Jupiter."

"One of my favorites, too. Alex, a man who loves Mozart can't be all bad. You're too smart to get hurt in a foolish cause."

Alex was so tired. He wanted to stop, not write another word, no one would give a damn, but he couldn't quit. He never could quit, he thought, it was stupid, but that was the way he was. He reviewed what he had written. Then he changed the title from *Blackmail and Blunderbuss*, to *A Matter of Conscience*. He hoped that would sound more moderate.

Old Iron Face didn't argue with him as he wrote out his thoughts: "How much responsibility does one have to possess for another person? Is there a time when authority must be questioned? At this moment I admire other species, but not man. Yet if I embrace this flame it will scorch me. I wonder when the body count began, probably when Caesar started his commentaries."

He reread this, put it in his file for future reference, and returned to what he had been writing when Harold called and decided to use "*A Matter of Conscience*," for his next column, Monday's.

Senator Upshaw was calling for action. The elderly, white-haired veteran of many legislative wars stood in the senate cloak-room, which he felt was his own private territory and where he expected other senators to listen to him—not like the senate chamber where they listened only for the sake of appearances—and shouted, "I knew Grant was a Red! They are on our doorstep and he writes we must halt Pacification! How obscene can you be!" In his rage he waved a newspaper with one hand as if it were toilet paper that he was going to use to wipe his ass, while he scratched his crotch with the other.

He became so irate that Cotterick, who disagreed completely with him, whispered, "Parry, calm down, you'll get a heart attack!"

"I bet you put him up to it!" The seventy-year-old Upshaw yelled back.

"Put him up to what?" Cotterick was puzzled.

"His filthy column, *Who Has Spilled the Blood?* A constituent sent it to me. It appeared a few days ago. Did you put Grant up to it, Silas?"

"I didn't know he wrote this column. I've been out of the country. I have been speaking to our friends and allies abroad. Privately they tell me that we should get out of the Territory, but none of them will say so publicly. They're afraid to offend the President."

"They're smart," muttered Upshaw. "We ought to impeach Grant."

"He is not a public official."

"That doesn't matter. I would be happy to do it."

"Parry, can I read the column?"

"It won't change anything." Upshaw shook so with rage his flesh beneath his shirt vibrated and Cotterick wanted to recommend a bra, but Upshaw would never forgive that, that would be personal. "If you live long enough you hear everything. Declaring Pacification is obscene. I wonder how he would feel if his daughter was screwed by a Red."

Upshaw was so involved in his rage he didn't notice Cotterick deftly extracting the newspaper from his trembling hand. He screamed, "I have an open mind, but we ought to throw this traitor into jail!"

Eric Losell, entering the cloakroom to interview Cotterick, was intrigued by Upshaw's anger. This was not unusual, but Upshaw was so furious he was becoming apoplectic and there could be a story in that.

Upshaw held forth on the iniquities of pacifists and how dare they complain about Pacification, they were infringing on the natural and inalienable right of patriots to kill. After a few minutes of this tirade, Cotterick, who was trying to read the column, couldn't endure any more. But when he started to interrupt Upshaw, Eric said, "Senator, old Parry, he really believes all this."

"I know," said Cotterick, "but somebody has to answer him."

"Why don't you do it in public? The senators might not listen to you, but the voters will. Grant's column is quotable." It would make a fine story, Eric thought, and he would have the edge on everybody, even Grant.

Cotterick glanced at Upshaw, who was still denouncing meddling pacifists, and he realized no one could argue with him at this point. Upshaw refused to look at anything but the flag which hung over the entrance, as if it were his impregnable conscience. His expression neither gave nor asked quarter; his face was as righteous as a biblical prophet, his handsome features florid and unsmiling, his eyes misty. Cotterick thought Upshaw was about to cry and suddenly Upshaw declared, "Those sentiments in this column are so sickly they are nauseating. People always want something for nothing!"

Cotterick retreated into the men's room, to get privacy. Eric followed him, but entered another compartment so he would not disturb Cotterick while the Senator studied *Who Has Measured the Blood?* for quotes.

The senator was grateful to Upshaw for calling his attention to this column. Some of it could have the kind of impact he longed to make. He had been intending to issue a similar statement for some time, and now the time seemed ripe and he liked the way it was said. It was worth using, at least in part. He called over to Eric, "Do you have a pen?"

Eric handed it over a toilet partition. "I was right, wasn't I?"

"Possibly?"

"Can I quote you, sir?"

"After I do."

Upshaw was still holding forth when they emerged from the men's room. He was shouting, "I'm not going to allow any columnist to intimidate me."

Cotterick's office issued a news release that he would be uttering an important statement and soon after, when there were the most viewers, he announced on television that he was thinking of running for President.

He was asked, "Why?" and he replied, "Too much blood has been spilled."

"But why have you come to such a decision at this time?"

"I haven't come to a decision. I am considering it. Pondering."

"Why are you considering it, sir?"

He had just seen how he looked on camera and he thought, I look fine, rugged enough to be virile, yet moderate enough to be trusted, and so sincere no one could accuse me of being superficial. He replied, "I am deeply concerned about our policy in the Territory, yet every time I ask the President when he is going to end Pacification, he extends it. Just yesterday he announced he is ordering an excursion into a new Territory."

"What is your remedy, sir?"

"*The body count is an obscenity and Pacification must end now, before it ends us. We must speak for the young people who cannot speak for themselves.*"

"Thank you, sir."

"I intend to repeat that over and over until the President listens."

Alex turned on the news when Eric told him that Cotterick was going to make an important announcement. Cotterick was a friend and this should be interesting, but as Alex heard his own words coming back at him he shivered. The senator sounded like a noble knight, but he had no wish to be a hero. It was difficult enough now to survive. He wondered if Shipmen would assume he had written this intentionally for Cotterick.

The telephone interrupted his reverie. To his surprise it was Marcia.

He said, "I thought you were angry at me."

"Don't be silly. I really did have a headache last week. I'm delighted to find you in. I hope I didn't disturb you."

"You don't mind about the petition?"

"Alex, you are not a Red. You are much too good in bed. I thought with all the strains you might want to spend a quiet weekend in the country. I'm worried about you. You sound tense, on edge."

"I can't come tomorrow, but Sunday would be fine."

"Lovely."

"Marcia, you won't change your mind, whatever happens?"

"What should change my mind?"

"I've done some things Shipmen and Graves didn't like."

"It is natural for a parent to defend a child. I would do the same."

"Did you read my column, *Who Has Measured the Blood?*"

Marcia hesitated, then said, "No. When did it appear?"

"The Friday before you cancelled our last engagement."

"I told you, I had a splitting headache. I'm not interested in politics. I'm flattered when important men are attentive, but it was for your sake I gave the dinner party."

"Did you hear Cotterick on television just now?"

"No. Was it interesting?"

"He quoted me."

"Many people quote you. Even my son. Stanley says you got it bad."

"Got what bad?"

"Sincerity. But I love you for it. It gives you such genuine emotion."

"What time should I come, Marcia?"

"For supper. Then we will have a whole evening to ourselves."

"Fine." Alex hung up, feeling better. He would be free of politics, at least for a few hours.

Spleeno's telephone call was one of the most urgent Shipmen had ever received. Friday night was usually quiet and he settled down for a satisfying evening with *Hush* and *Hush-Hush*, delighted to be with them, for they were not people with people's wayward ways, but always used their wits and were his own dominion, precious to him because no one else shared them. Yet Spleeno wanted to talk to him at once.

And not on the telephone, he noted, this was evident

from Spleeno's insistence he come to his office. Did the Vice-President think his telephone was being tapped? Such conceit, it was not worth tapping.

But Shipmen knew this simple truth would be accepted ungratefully.

He arrived at Spleeno's office, apparently breathless, to indicate he had rushed all the way—although actually, he had driven from door to door—and the Vice-President said, "Roger, you are out of condition. I hear the President and Harold Hinton beat you."

Shipmen felt trapped and angry, for he could not explain. He had learned his lesson in the match with Grant and so, while Harold was a much weaker player than Grant, this time he made sure the President won. But the Vice-President would use such a confession against him. He shrugged and said, "The President played exceptionally well. As usual."

Spleeno looked skeptical, but he didn't pursue the subject. Instead, he said, "I wanted to talk to you here. Where nobody could hear us?"

"You think we are under surveillance?" Shipmen sounded surprised.

"You never can tell."

Shipmen smiled knowingly to himself. If he wished to put Spleeno's office under surveillance, the Vice-President would never find out. He was proud he possessed the best wire-tapper in the business, no one was safe from his electronics expert, The Eavesdropper. Only this was not necessary here. He knew Spleeno's thoughts. They were carefully stored and catalogued in his data banks. He could afford to profess humility in Spleeno's presence: he owned a precise, up-to-date, complete dossier on him. He held all the details within his reach: Spleeno's credit rating, bank records, income tax, medical chart—"etcetera, etcetera, etcetera," he said to himself—all of Spleeno's flaws, wherever the Vice-President was vulnerable. Shipmen preferred adverse information. He didn't believe in entertaining conjecture; he had to know. It was his compulsion to learn everything about anybody he was investigating. He was sure there was always something he could unearth to damage a subject. Any person. Reassured, he relaxed despite Spleeno's tension.

Spleeno's face darkened. "Roger, we are in a real crisis. Did you hear Cotterick's statement earlier in the evening?"

"No. Is he still criticizing Pacification?"

"Worse. He is attacking the President."

"Should I look into his file?"

"That is not my department. Or the President's."

Shipmen nodded understandingly. What the President or Vice-President didn't know could not be held against them. If he were in their position, he thought approvingly, he would have assumed the same stance. But what was done unofficially was fine. If it worked.

Spleeno said, "I'm glad you know what to do. But keep us out of it. Cotterick quoted Grant word for word. About obscenity, blood—awful!"

"Did you hear it, sir?"

"Graves did. He digested it for the President. The President is very upset. Victor says Grant's words are a contagion that could ruin the country. He is a real troublemaker. You must accelerate. Does he have any strange bathroom habits?" As Spleeno saw Shipmen's eyes light up, he added hurriedly, "Don't tell me, tell the public."

Spleeno had given him another good idea. He said, "I'll check."

"A morals' charge is always hard to disprove."

Shipmen nodded.

"What about the son? Has anything new developed on him?"

"It is being worked on."

"I thought by now you would have proven he was collaborating with The Demolisher. The timing is more than a coincidence, it is a very useful coincidence. If the son is discredited it will rub off on the father."

"Right."

Now there was no danger of getting mixed-up. Shipmen had his goal precisely set. But as he worked with his computers later, he became so absorbed in improving his information on his subjects he forgot why he was investigating them. He loved this research. It involved him in a way nothing else did. *Hush* and *Hush-Hush* were perfect for his needs, they had no principles, only results. What returned him to the reason for his investigation was another urgent call from Spleeno, asking, "Have you found anything new? Don't tell me what, but have you?"

Shipmen felt guilty, a rare emotion for him, and he said, "Soon."

"It would be useful if it were in time for tomorrow's press. That's where Cotterick got his information. Cheap bastard, stealing it from somebody else. Is the columnist as sexy as he is supposed to be?"

Sometimes, in spite of himself, Spleeno was wonderful, a genius. Spleeno, with all his fumbling, reminded him of the clues he needed. "It is quite possible the columnist will be obsolete after tomorrow."

"Thanks. That will be appreciated."

But as Shipmen focused on the material he processed about Grant's sexual life, he realized he would have to use the by-products of it if he wanted to succeed. If only Grant's last two wives had not died, he thought regretfully, they could have been so valuable. No one was quite as spiteful as an ex-wife. Even the first wife, although she had been disappointing—for she had been reluctant to talk about her sexual life with the columnist—had revealed several useful clues. Women always gave something away, he said to himself contemptuously, it was safer to remain celibate and to masturbate.

Answering the telephone Alex heard, "Did I wake you up?"

"No," mumbled Alex, as he yawned and got out of bed. But Harold had this morning. Saturday was the only day he slept late, and last night he had worked past midnight rewriting *A Matter of Conscience*. He still wasn't satisfied with it, but he had said some things he felt should be said. What was Harold frantic about now?

"I must see you. At my hotel. Can you get here immediately?"

This wasn't a request but an order and Alex said, "As soon as I dress."

"So I did wake you up! You were sleeping!" It was not an apology, but an accusation. "Did you write a column for Monday?"

"Yes. That is what kept me up so late. Finishing it."

"Bring it along!" Harold hung up, extremely abrupt.

Alex dressed hurriedly, pausing only to gulp down a cup of coffee, and he drove as fast as he could to the hotel. Harold was alone, pacing up and down his long living room, as vigorous as ever, but today anxiety and irritation etched new lines on his face, and he looked more fat than chunky, his ruddy complexion was florid, and he had forgotten to touch up his brown hair and the gray showed. Harold was drinking, too, which was unusual, and was being dynamic.

He blurted out, not asking Alex to take off his coat or to sit down or to have a drink, "More affiliates are cancelling your column. I received half a dozen wires just this morning. They woke me up!"

"Why are they cancelling? Did they tell you?"

"Several reasons. Some of them objected to what Cotterick quoted. They said it was inflammatory. Did you put him up to quoting you?"

"No. I've not seen or talked to him for several weeks."

"Then deny it."

"I can't. I did write *Who Has Measured the Blood?*"

"Repudiate it. They are your words really, not Cotterick's."

"How can I?" If he did, James would cut him off completely and that was a prospect he must avoid. "Besides, I like what I wrote. It's true. Is there anything else, Harold?"

Harold stared at him a moment as if he were a lunatic, then said, as if Alex had committed a crime, "Haven't you read today's paper?"

"No. I told you that you . . ." Alex halted, this would infuriate an already infuriated Harold even more. "What's wrong now?"

"Most of the new cancellations were about this." Harold

handed Alex a morning tabloid as if it were infected with leprosy. "Two affiliates even called me long distance to discuss this with me. They were shocked and horrified. How could you behave so disgracefully?"

Harold's hand trembled and Alex wondered what degradation he had caused his publisher. Then he saw the picture which dominated the front page of the tabloid. It's prominence made the emphasis unmistakable.

Alex felt drums pounding on his head. It was the loudest, most disagreeable noise he had ever heard. He longed to close his ears and eyes. This must go away. He just wanted to write. Just give me another chance, he thought, but Harold was forcing him to look.

It was a large picture of himself emerging from the women's lavatory at the stadium, slanted so the most conspicuous item were the words, "*Ladies Only*," and next in prominence, himself.

"A fabulous picture," he mumbled. What else was there to say, he thought. Worse, the angle was such that his identity was plain, a genuine close-up, and he had blinked when this picture was snapped and in his surprise he looked guilty and it implied—for it had taken him as he was finishing pulling up his fly—that he might have been exhibiting himself in a gesture of indecent exposure. He thought ruefully, I couldn't have done any better if I had posed willingly. He said apologetically, "Life does have embarrassing moments. I had to go."

He handed the tabloid back to Harold and the latter refused to take it, stating, "That is not all. There is also a news story."

"Do I have to read it?"

"I did. Sit down!"

"May I take off my overcoat?"

"It is your coat."

Alex discarded it, but he didn't stop sweating. And while he sat down, his eyes blurred and he couldn't find the place Harold was pointing to. He prayed that the story would be at the bottom of the page, in the smallest, most inconspicuous corner, then he remembered that in this tabloid everything on the front page was over-emphasized.

"Here!" Harold was so curt he almost snarled. "The story is at the top, on the right, next to the picture."

Alex stalled, replying, "This is a bootleg picture."

"But it is you, isn't it, coming out of the woman's lavatory?"

"I guess."

"That is what Upshaw said. On the senate floor. There was a filibuster going on last night which he interrupted just before midnight. Then when he got the floor he demanded an explanation of your behavior. It is a national news story."

"I'm not that important. Upshaw is much too flattering."

"Surveillance is always important."

"Did they take any pictures of me putting out my garbage?"

"Alex Grant, you can tell a great deal about a man from the shaving lotion he used. Why did you go in there?"

"I had an intense longing. To pee."

"That is not what Senator Upshaw implied."

"I'm surprised they didn't have a T.V. camera there."

"You must read it. You owe that to yourself, and to me."

But Alex felt he was reading his own obituary while he was still alive.

"Senator Upshaw declared on the senate floor Friday night that a matter has been called to his attention by concerned citizens, whose identity cannot be revealed because of national security, which, he feels, is his sacred duty to bring before the country. He stated, 'I do this with deep regret, for I do not want to harm anyone, but I have taken a hard look at my conscience and I have come to the conclusion that in the interests of national security I must reveal what I have learned.'"

Alex paused, wondering how much longer this story was, and Harold motioned imperatively that he read on. The remainder of the story was on page two and when he saw that it covered most of it he shuddered.

"Senator Upshaw added, 'Several weeks ago, at one of our best universities, a young man disrupted one of our most sacred institutions, *The Game*, by exhibiting himself lewdly in public. And now, it is revealed, his father may have done the same thing. As you can see from the picture I am holding, and which I am releasing to the press as soon as I finish, one of our columnists and the boy's father, was detected emerging from a *Ladies Only* room. Now this may be of particular significance, for it is known there was a men's room nearby, and it happened just a few minutes after his own son exhibited himself and expressed himself with indecent gestures on the football field before thousands of innocent spectators, and the son is fortunate that we have been merciful and he is not in jail right now on a disorderly conduct charge.'"

Alex exclaimed, "But that is not true, Harold. The only gesture James made was for peace."

Harold said, "That is not the point. Upshaw has much more to say."

Alex returned to Upshaw's speech. "The senator stressed, 'The son has compromised himself and it is known the father supported him.'"

"Naturally," said Alex, as if he were having a dialogue with Upshaw.

Harold said, "The senator doesn't think it was natural."

"That is only one man's opinion."

"Now it could be many people's opinion."

"I don't have to read this slander."

When Alex refused to go on, Harold picked up the tabloid and read aloud: "The senator pointed out another significant fact."

Alex said, "The newspaper is editorializing."

"Hush!" Harold continued, "Upshaw said, 'This photo was snapped by an artist. Every detail is clear. Authoritative sources inform me that reliable observers saw the father come out of the *Ladies Only* room, although national security insists their identity must remain secret.'"

Alex cried, "So I am to be damned by anonymous witnesses!"

Harold ignored him. "'My fellow senators, what has forced me to bring this distressing affair to your attention is that men who use women's lavatories, especially when men's are available, are often deviates, exhibitionists, or homosexuals. Such men often indulge in many disturbing practices. They may solicit, or perform an indecent gesture, or worse, exhibit themselves with indecent exposure, as the son did. These men are sick or not in possession of their faculties. I am not saying the father involved himself in any of the perverse things I have so carefully enumerated, I am not saying he exposed himself, like his son, or performed any act of perversion. But the fact he was in the *Ladies Only* room, perhaps even loitering there, as if peeking through a keyhole, especially since it occurred immediately after his son's perverse behavior, causes many of us to wonder about his sense of responsibility. Whether his words can be trusted? These questions must be asked. It is my duty to my country. Where the security and well-being of my country is concerned I must take the most arduous steps, no matter how painful they are.'"

"Harold, please!" interrupted Alex, "He's way off. He's rambling."

Harold was inexorable. "'Fellow senators, the columnist is lucky he was not arrested on a morals' charge, or for trespassing. Clearly, he didn't enter the women's lavatory because he had a sore throat. Certainly, after what his son did, it is plain the family has some odd habits. The father likes to write about responsibility, but he has the responsibility to explain why he used the women's lavatory when the men's was available. It could have been a perverse impulse that led him there. It surely causes one to wonder about his integrity. Not that I am accusing him of anything, except that his behaviour is a matter of public importance. I am not saying he indulged in abnormal behavior, but it is known he has been suffering from fatigue and distress over his son's indecent exposure.'

"'This raises the question of whether we can trust his word. All of us are subject to frailty, but certain failings cannot be tolerated in a public figure. A columnist has an obligation to maintain the highest standard of conduct, to take every sensible precaution against wrongdoing. Lapses of self-control, even if they are not forms of sexual perversion, must be condemned. His laxity cannot be tolerated.'

"'And I haven't even mentioned his gravest error, that he signed a Communist petition. We know that anybody who supports the Reds is not to be trusted. It is no wonder he opposes Pacification. Like so many who are against our country's ideals, he would like to see our beloved country defeated in order to justify their opposition.'"

Alex was so outraged he couldn't answer.

"'Fellow citizens, I believe—and I am sure you share my view—that this columnist has lost the confidence of the public. If he truly wants to serve his country he should resign. We must restore morality to our press. He is a bad apple and all of us know what should be done with rotten apples. I will boycott any newspaper that carries his column and I recommend to all of you that you do the same. Thank you.'"

There was silence after Harold finished reading, as if both of them needed it to collect their thoughts, and then Harold said mournfully, "Alex, you are ruining me. No one will trust you any more."

"Do you?"

"It is very embarrassing."

"Harold, there is nothing to prove!"

"Caught coming out of the women's lavatory! How could you?"

"I told you. I had to go."

"Like the petition? Upshaw is right. You have no self-control."

"I could sue Upshaw for defamation of character."

"Contesting his assertions would be more embarrassing than ignoring them. And he didn't actually accuse you of abnormal behavior. Besides, you wouldn't have a chance. He said it on the senate floor, where he has immunity. Why did you loiter in the women's lavatory?"

Alex stood up, put on his overcoat, said, "Thanks for warning me."

Harold strode to the window and stared at the Capitol which dominated the horizon, noticed that the sky was growing hazy, and thought, Snow will be coming soon and there will be no more tennis, at least outdoors, which was sad, and he said abruptly, "Upshaw is one of the most influential men in the country. His speech could be very harmful."

"Even though nothing was proved?" Alex paused in his departure.

"Many people will still read Upshaw's speech because he said it and most of them will believe it." Harold poured himself a brandy and soda and while he didn't offer Alex a drink, he added, "Graves sent me some vintage wines. He has excellent taste." Drinking nervously, Harold said with an anxious air, "You've worn yourself out. That is why you went into the women's lavatory. If you had done what I suggested and taken a couple of weeks' vacation, all this could have been avoided. When you went into the lavatory were you stoned?"

"I wish I had been."

"Too bad. That would be excusable." Harold got another idea. "Or were you protesting, like your son? Or for yourself?"

"I was doing neither."

As Alex reached the door, Harold asked, "Where is Monday's column?"

Alex handed it to him and Harold stuck it in his pocket.

"Are you going to read it?"

"Later."

"At least, could you tell me this afternoon what you think about it?"

"I can't. I have a tennis appointment. With the President."

"Today?"

"Yes. But don't worry. I'll send it to our central office by teletype if I decide it can be published."

What Alex recalled most vividly after the door closed was that Harold had not shaken his hand. Harold had regarded it as if it were unclean.

Neither of them noticed an item in the tabloid about The Demolisher and the quarterback, which said: "A ranking official of the government, who must remain unnamed, has stated on the highest and most reliable authority that there are significant indications that Gary Ginger and James Grant knew each other, for they sat next to each other in class. The timing of their protests indicates a conspiracy. They were both aimed against the President and came at virtually the same time. But further investigations are being conducted, for while James Grant has been allowed to return to class, Gary Ginger is still undergoing medical treatment. He has speech problems. He may have been stunned by the explosion of his bomb. Or by what he did."


This item was sent to the tabloid by the military doctor. He had to do this—to prove to himself and to Shipmen that he was succeeding.

All Friday afternoon he sought to question The Demolisher. This time, recalling the difficulties of the previous examination, he conducted the inquiry in the patient's hospital room and although he stationed Examiners at the door and the windows, so the young man could not jump out and hurt himself, he tried to conduct this situation with some of the amenities, in the hope this would induce the patient to talk. And while M.P.'s insistence still made it an interrogation, he started off as if it were an interview, using a conversational tone of voice.

But the instant he called the subject Gary Ginger, the subject froze. Even when he returned to addressing him as The Demolisher and sat close to him to show his confidence in him, and then eyeball to eyeball, he realized this was not a fallow situation. A tape-recorder was in the room but The Demolisher was like a statue.

M.P. asked in his best fatherly manner, "Is there anything you want?"

Silence.

"Steak? Lamb chops? Lobster? I love lobster."

Silence.

"Do you need a girl?"

And still The Demolisher stared blankly into the distance.

"Money?"

Silence.

"Were you a hyper-active child?"

Silence.

Growing desperate, M.P.'s voice rose in pitch and intensity. Now he felt like a father admonishing a naughty son. "Gary, you must talk to me. I represent the govern-

ment. I speak on their behalf. Come on, let's go, or you will
only make matters worse for yourself."

Silence.

"You could be accused of conspiracy. You and the
quarterback did protest at the same time."

Silence.

"Did anybody help you?"

Silence.

Suddenly M.P. got an idea. The true count ceremony
honoring Private Bobby Blaber was being replayed on television and M.P. ordered a set wheeled into the room and
then he put on the program. He was just in time, he thought
exultantly. The President was pinning a medal on the hero,
but damn! The Demolisher wasn't looking! Didn't he have
any feeling of patriotism? Gary Ginger was staring at the
blank wall.

M.P. nudged The Demolisher and when he didn't
respond the doctor pushed his face around so he had to
look. At that moment the network, to make sure the viewers
saw what contribution Private Bobby Blaber had made to
society, flashed the figures at the bottom of the screen,
across the President's midriff: "*Private Bobby Blaber
achieved the greatest true count in the Territory, two
hundred and fifty-five.*"

It was working, the military doctor thought triumphantly,
there was a conscious expression in The Demolisher's eyes.

The Demolisher was saying to himself, Big Deal, I got
more, I must have got at least three hundred, I hit a lot of
villages, and I didn't need civilians and children. Then his
face went blank again and he was looking at nothing.

"Turn the set off," M.P. said regretfully. "Everything is
clogged. His speech, his vision, his hearing."

But as the set was wheeled out of the room The
Demolisher spat at it.

At least, M.P. thought gratefully, he can react. He asked
urgently, "Why did you do that?"

Silence.

"Was it aimed at the President?"

Silence.

"Are you jealous of Private Blaber? You could have been in his place if you behaved differently. Is that it?"

Silence.

M.P. lost his temper. "Don't you realize what we are doing for you? If you weren't here, we could rent this room for a hundred dollars a day. Aren't you ashamed of what you're costing the government?"

The Demolisher sat mutely, staring blankly at the hospital wall.

"You must take notice! You must admit ... !" M.P. halted, exasperated.

The Demolisher thought, I admit nothing. Not that I am alive, not that I am dead. Not that I hear, see, feel. There is nothing to hear, see, feel. If I am not The Demolisher, I am nothing. Nothing.

But when the newspaper item appeared the next day M.P. felt better. He was sure he had displayed ingenuity after all. If he had not gone far enough, he had gone fast; he had been the bright boy in his family, and he was one of five brothers. The item also gave him the courage to call Shipmen later that morning to report there was progress. While his item was not as prominent as the Upshaw story, it was near the story.

He was surprised that Shipmen was impatient with him. Shipmen said, "I haven't much time. I have a tennis appointment with the President."

"Did you see my item, sir?"

"Yes. Why?"

M.P. didn't want to feel apologetic, but he did, mumbling, "The item should prove that a conspiracy does exist at the university."

"Conspiracy?" Shipmen sounded puzzled, which was unusual.

Feeling pleased that he had accomplished this, M.P. explained, "A conspiracy because The Demolisher and the quarterback had a common cause, to discredit the President."

"Congratulations."

M.P. wondered whether Shipmen was being sarcastic, but

Shipmen was his superior, so he replied, "Congratulations yourself, sir."

"On what?"

"I read Upshaw's speech. That should take care of the father."

"I had nothing to do with it. And neither did the President. Has The Demolisher revealed anything?"

"I think he is losing his mind. He doesn't talk at all anymore. I hope I get something out of him before it is gone completely."

Success! Shipmen repeated that to himself after he got rid of M.P., Upshaw had broken the story beautifully while he was sleeping and The Demolisher was a minor item now and not worth a headline. There was only one problem: he wasn't certain whether he should call the Upshaw speech to the President's attention. Victor Winner might lose his concentration and he hated to lose his concentration on the tennis court. Yet the President should know what he had accomplished.

After the tennis match, which was played at Graves's mansion, the President suggested that the contestants and Spleeno, who had been invited to be their audience, have a drink in the converted club house before they showered. He was caught up in the exhilaration of winning. His pale green eyes gleamed and his tight, thin mouth grinned and Harold had never seen him look so pleased. Many Examiners hovered protectively outside the Tudor brick house, while Graves, as if it were one of his natural functions, became the bartender and the President sat in a black leather chair which was six inches higher than any of the others, skillfully arranged by Graves so Victor Winner was above everybody else.

Nobody ordered a drink until Victor did. When he asked for a vodka martini, the others did, too, although it wasn't their preference. Spleeno and Shipmen sat on his right, Graves and Harold on his left.

Victor said, puffing out his scrawny, rawboned chest,

"We sure beat you down today. Six to one. You were lucky to win a game."

Harold said, "Sir, they didn't always seem to be concentrating."

"Perhaps. None the less, I really put it to them."

Spleeno said, "You did, indeed, sir. I never saw you play better."

Harold had a moment of terror. He could hear himself saying, Sir didn't play that well, I made most of the points, when Graves and Shipmen didn't make errors, which was on almost every shot, if I didn't know their great feeling for Sir, I would have thought they were throwing the match. But fortunately, no one could hear him.

Shipmen said, "Sir, your strokes were the boldest I've ever seen."

Graves added, "To be truthful, sir, you were simply too strong for us. If I were really precise, I would say overpowering."

"Now! Now! I wasn't that good! Harold won a few points, too!"

"Thank you, sir." Harold felt humble, although he was not a humble man.

After all of them praised Sir on the soundness of his tennis tactics, each of them seeking to outdo the other, he said, "I appreciate that all of you are being completely honest, but we must not exaggerate, I know I'm a born competitor." But now that they agreed with his own appraisal of his athletic skill, Victor wanted to talk about Upshaw's revelations. Sexual titillations always amused him and he possessed as much curiosity as the next man. Sir said reflectively, "I wonder how he made All-American. After what Upshaw disclosed it is hard to believe. Imagine, opening a newspaper and finding out he was that way."

Harold asked, "Sir, did you read the entire speech?"

"Oh, no! I'm too busy. Graves did. He compressed it for me. But I wish I had the time," the President said regretfully.

"I gave the high spots," Graves said modestly.

The President said, "I wonder where Upshaw got his information."

Shipmen shrugged, said, "I haven't the slightest idea, sir."

"Neither have I sir," said Graves.

"Do you think anyone ordered it done, sir?" Harold asked.

The President glanced questioningly at his aides and no one knew who had ordered it done. Or if it had been ordered? Shipmen denied that, and so did Graves, and Spleeno said, "I would never think of such a thing, and a senator, especially one as honorable as Upshaw, would be above such an act. It must have been a vindictive woman. An ex-wife perhaps, or even," Spleeno smiled now, "an ex-boy friend, sir."

"I wondered about him after our tennis match. He wasn't good in a crisis. I should have known he was unstable from the way he hogged my shots. Harold, you know him best. Did you know he was limp wristed?"

"Sir, I would be ashamed to say I am a close or an intimate friend. I would have to say I am not really close or intimate."

"One must be careful who they associate with. Especially a President. No wonder he is against Pacification. I have a deep sense of compassion but his behavior arouses indignation. Loitering in a women's lavatory!"

Spleeno said, "And there is the picture to confirm it, sir."

"Yes," said Victor Winner, "whoever took it—and this doesn't mean I approve of spying or prying—demonstrated foresight. I wonder if he had a rendezvous there. Certainly he must be regarded with suspicion. Now he is a definite security risk. Yet he is not a young man."

Harold said, "I'm sorry, sir, but I'm not sure I . . ."

" . . . understand." Sir beamed at him beneficently and explained, "It raises the question whether he prefers girls or boys."

Harold said, "Sir, he has a reputation for being popular with women."

"Perhaps he is ambidextrous."

"Sir, he told me there are moments women make him feel impotent."

Shipmen said suddenly, "You are sure?"

"Do you doubt me?" Harold grew indignant.

"No, not at all, that fits in with information I was given."

The President changed the subject. "Harold, have you lost many affiliates since his behavior of the past few days?"

"What behavior, sir?"

"His son's scandalous exhibitionism, his prejudiced support of it, the revelation that he was a Communist, and now this! Ugh!"

All things he was responsible for, Shipmen thought with gratification. But this was not the time to take the credit.

"Sir, at least six, and maybe more. I don't know for sure yet."

"Too bad. But I'm sure some will return, that it is a temporary loss."

"I'm not sure, sir."

Spleeno said, "Forgive me for suggesting it, Harold, I have the utmost confidence in your judgment, but perhaps you ought to keep a closer watch on what he writes. *Who Has Measured the Blood?* was deplorable."

"I have. Since that column. I have Monday's column in my pocket."

Sir asked, "Have you read it?"

"No. Would you like to read it, Mr. President?"

"Graves, digest it." While his aide read it to himself, he said, to show he could be one of the boys, too, "Dumb S.O.B., I would rather have pissed on the women's lavatory than be caught pissing in it." Everyone laughed as he expected. "Graves, what do you think of the new column?"

"People will watch with interest whether this appears or not, sir."

"Do you think it should appear, Graham?" asked Shipmen. He sensed that Graves might be allowing his scruples to get the better of him.

"That's up to Harold. A matter of conscience, as the title says."

Harold turned to Sir, asked, "What do you think, Mr. President?"

"I never interfere in other people's business."

Graves said, "Sir, now that Grant is being discredited, I doubt it is necessary to censor him. No point making him a martyr. It could cause a storm in some quarters, be advantageous to opportunists like Cotterick."

"You think so? After the Red petition and the women's lavatory?"

"Sir, he is also a famous football player with a fine war record. This could rebound in his favor, if he uses these things properly."

"Sir, I wouldn't·worry about that," said Shipmen, "There are other things developing ..." He halted. There was a warning glint in Sir's eyes. He turned to Harold, said, "You will do the right thing."

No one wanted to take the responsibility, Harold thought irritably, or to subject themselves to risk. Yet as he saw all of them staring at him, he realized that while he could lord it over the columnist it was impossible with these men, they possessed one trait in common, no matter how respectful they were to him, they were men who lived for power, who believed in it as they believed in nothing else, and who knew how to use it. He took the column from Graves, read the title aloud: "*A Matter of Conscience.*"

"Something we all approve of," Spleeno said spontaneously, without thinking. Then he saw the President frowning and he hurried to add, "But he hasn't any. Any man who ..."

Sir cut him short, "We know, Spleeno. Harold, why don't you take a poll of his readers? It will help you understand what they are thinking. Polls have helped me make some of the most vital decisions of my life."

"Thank you, sir." Harold stuck the column in his pocket.

"Did you enjoy the true count ceremony?"

"Yes, sir. I was honored that you included me."

"It was a poll that told me to go through with the award. First we verified that Private Blaber was authentic, we checked his service carefully and discovered he had kept his records meticulously. But what finally convinced me was a poll which showed that eighty per cent of the voters surveyed, expressed a deep, devout admiration for Private Blaber. So we made the rational choice. One mustn't overlook anything."

"But sir, suppose most of the polled support the columnist?"

"I want you to make up your own mind."

"Thank you, sir. I'll think it over."

The President stood up, signalling it was time to go, and to Harold's surprise Graves interrupted his departure.

Graves said, despite Victor Winner's obvious annoyance, "I think, sir, I may have found an answer to one of our most serious problems."

"Problems?"

"Perhaps I use the wrong word, sir, in referring to the True Count, but our latest poll shows that fifty-one per cent of the voters polled are against it."

The President paused. "What do you suggest?"

"If we could count rifles, sir?"

"Rifles?"

"Yes, sir. Then we wouldn't have to count civilians and children. That has been creating a rather sticky situation, sir."

Victor Winner turned to Harold and said forcefully, "You see, my friend, we need big themes, something to give our programs a major thrust. A strong game plan, a winning game plan."

Graves continued meekly, "Do you approve, sir?"

"It is original thinking. Use your intuition, Graves." Then as the President saw Shipmen's annoyance at the possibility that Graves might be surpassing him, he said abruptly, "Roger, do you have a file on me?"

"Sir, how could you ask?"

"I bet you have one on Harold."

Harold had the strangest feeling as Shipmen said, "Sir, Harold doesn't have to worry about a thing. Any facts that come in about him, I will personally see to it that they are kept out of anybody else's hands, on my desk." Harold wondered if Shipmen was tapping his mind.

The President smiled blandly, said, "Thank you, Harold, for playing with me. We are a good team." He dismissed everybody but Shipmen.

As Shipmen said, "Sir, I hope you don't think I've been disloyal, that you're being watched, I'd lay my life down for you," Sir thought, there was something charming about the investigator's craving for power, like a child who wanted a cannon instead of a gun, and he replied, "I know. Do you have a complete file on Harold? Oh, don't tell me, he should support us, but just in case . . ."

"Don't worry," said Shipmen, sighing with relief, "You're protected, sir."

"Good."

Nothing essential had altered, Shipmen thought, regaining some of his confidence. He must only tell the President what the President wanted to know. What Victor Winner didn't know wouldn't embarrass him.

"I'm glad, Roger, you are a member of my team. Graves tells me that Upshaw's remarks appeared in all the newspapers, the evening papers, too, and that there will be a spill-off on Sunday."

"Sir, I have no personal knowledge of how Upshaw got his material. I just have to keep track of what goes on. I do my homework."

"I understand. Next time, perhaps, you will be my tennis partner. You might even make a great pacifier." Sir shook his hand with such fervor Shipmen stood at the bar in reverent silence long after he was gone. Harold, when he returned to tell Shipmen they were flying back in the same helicopter, was astonished by the depth of Shipmen's emotion.

Shipmen thought, I have spent countless tedious hours going through trivia, enough to boggle my mind, but it has been worth it, *Hush* and *Hush-Hush* are marvelous, they have never given me an incorrect reading.

Boy scout. Bat boy. Bell boy. Bus boy. Alex had done all these things during his growing up and always Wally was vital. But then it was natural, he thought, blood pumped through his penis and it sweated quickly and his fortunes rose and fell with it, and no one would mistake his penis for his adam's apple, yet Wally was as individual and unique as any part of him, and women had enjoyed Wally and some had loved Wally, exclaiming as they fondled Wally, "How handsome! How warm! How smooth! How vital! How interesting!" Several had teased him that Wally was his third leg, as sturdy as oak and yet as pliant as birch, but never before had Wally embarrassed him so much or betrayed him. Yet Wally had lived many lives in one.

But Wally was no help now. He sat in front of old Iron Face after his meeting with Harold, waiting for a telephone call from Harold that he knew would not come, and Wally felt limp. Would his writing be ruined, too, he wondered. He put down what he was thinking and a key stuck.

He halted, looked at old Iron Face, and said, "Well?"

"Well?" she replied.

"That's no answer," he said.

"It's not an answer," old Iron Face said. "It's a question."

Maybe he ought to call Wally his council of ten.

Someone slipped a note under his door with the statement, "*Traitors Beware!*" printed in large red and black letters and ran.

Two reporters who knew him were at his door asking his reaction to Upshaw's speech, "Do you want to deny it, Alex? We know you wouldn't do anything like that? Do you want us to quote your war record? Your football career?" He answered, "Thank you, fellows. No comment. Excuse me." He shut the door politely but firmly.

Eric Losell telephoned, but he was in no mood to discuss the affair with him either, although he tried to be courteous. However, when Eric pressed him, he had to say, "No, I won't issue a statement."

Eric said, "Alex, what you ought to do is get a piece of tail and get caught in the act. That would put Upshaw in his place. And make you a hero."

"Thanks, but I've already developed that side of my nature."

"I know, but some people will wonder now."

"So they'll wonder. Would you like to play tennis Monday?"

"Monday . . . ?"

"Yes, Monday." Why was Eric hesitating? "It's when we always play."

"I can't. Not Monday."

"Later in the week?"

"Let me call in a couple of weeks. When things calm down."

Sunday, when Alex still hadn't heard from Harold about his column, he felt he ought to call him. Then he decided it would be humiliating. He had never done so before and the syndicate had been publishing him for years and if his column didn't appear, he wouldn't be destitute. But he knew he wouldn't find a better income, and not knowing what was going to happen on Monday made it impossible to write anything for Wednesday. He fondled old Iron Face but she didn't respond.

And there was Marcia. Surely she would cancel their engagement now, yet after Upshaw's insinuations he wanted to see her more. Only he didn't want to drive an hour to her country retreat and not find her there.

But when he telephoned Marcia, she greeted him warmly and said, "I'm looking forward to it. More than ever." He was surprised she didn't mention anything else, but said, "See you soon," and hung up.

He put on a Mozart sonata and a minute later there was a knock on his door. He was surprised to see James there, an odd expression on his son's face.

When Alex recovered from his surprise, he said, "You should be proud of me now. I've finally got the kind of recognition you said I should."

"I'm not a child, Alexander. Don't use self-pity on me."

"What do you want?"

"Do I have to stand here all day?"

Alex opened his door wider and James strode in.

"For a moment I thought you had someone here."

"Those stories are greatly exaggerated. Is there more trouble at the school? I saw something in the papers about you and The Demolisher."

"A lie. A rumor built into a lie. Alexander, are they trying to screw you because of me? Everyone knows you are masculine."

It was the first time James had visited his apartment and Alex asked, "Why did you come here? You must have driven all night."

"Temperature changes. Goes up, goes down. What's the music?"

"A Mozart sonata. I play Mozart when I want to clear my head."

"Do you ever play the record I gave you?"

"Sometimes."

James noticed that Alex's fist was clenched, a familiar gesture of intensity, and he sensed his father's nerves were strung like taut wires and once off guard, there was panic in him. He had never seen his father so tense; at least he was human. James glanced at the paper in the typewriter and asked, "Is this tomorrow's column?"

"No. It is over there. A carbon. The publisher has the original."

"Can I read it?"

"You better. I doubt anybody else will. I don't think my publisher will allow it to be published."

"Isn't it good enough?"

"Read it."

After James did, he said, "It is certainly not revolutionary."

"My publisher is privately liberal, but publicly noncommittal."

"Don't start preaching. Your eyes are bleary. Who knocked your hat off?"

"I don't wear a hat."

"So I noticed in the picture. It is quite a good likeness."

"Do you believe it?"

"People believe what they want to believe. Alexander, have they been investigating you, too?"

"For some time."

"On my account?"

"I suspect by now it is on my own. Who has been investigating you?"

James asked, "Do you think you are being bugged?"

"I don't know. I don't think so."

"We'll see," said James. "I'm becoming an expert on surveillance devices. Loose wires. Small objects like sea shells. Let me check." James went through the entire apartment with a thoroughness and skill that amazed Alex, examining each wire, every inch of space, tapping the wall, paying special attention to the telephone and the bathroom, saying, "They got a thing about bugging johns. They seem to think things take place in johns that are especially incriminating." After he finished and found nothing, he said, "It looks clean. I guess they figured they had enough on you without bugging you."

"What about yourself, James?"

"Examiners have been interviewing and checking neighbors, friends, and fellow students for weeks. They say they know me, or that they are an acquaintance, or an insurance man or a salesman interested in whether I am a good prospect, and two said they were pro football scouts, trying to find out if I have the character to play pro football. I know they are Examiners because of the questions they ask. They even questioned the janitor who works my dormitory about my bathroom habits, and whether I am interested in girls or boys. He was so shocked, he told me. I didn't make a big thing about it because I didn't want to worry you, and besides, I'm not the only one they are watching and checking."

"Does the university know?"

"They say they don't, but we have campus guards now I'm sure are Examiners." James smiled but his tone grew more serious. "However, I hear they don't like to interview professors. Professors are unreliable."

"This must give you an awful feeling."

"You get used to it." James shrugged. "I think they even checked my laundry and what I eat. I bet·they gòt your doorman on their payroll. He made sure he got my name before he allowed me to come up. After all, one of my pals on the football team was offered three hundred bucks—they called it expenses—to keep an eye on me and to report if there were any other radicals on the team."

"What did he do, James?"

"He took the money and told them that half the team was unreliable, particularly on pass defense. The campus is loaded with new guards. My dorm has four. Last year there was one. And I'm a sensitive subject, which means, a suspect. Whenever I see a campus guard staring at me I assume he is an Examiner. Some of them stare all the time."

"Why didn't you tell me this before?"

"I didn't want to worry you. I figured you had enough on your mind."

"Or you didn't trust me?"

"Join the gang, Alexander. But I'm not supposed to know I'm being investigated. Yet there always seems to be a hand on my door."

"You're a little late, James."

"You've been a little late a long time, Alexander." But when he saw him wince, he asked, "Weren't you wounded and decorated in *your* war?"

Alex nodded.

"Why don't you use it?"

Alex shrugged.

"How did you get wounded?"

"In the rear. I didn't get my ass down."

James burst out laughing, sat down, then remembered something and bounced to his feet.

Alex asked, "What's wrong now? I believed in *my* war. I still do."

"Why did you marry my mother?"

Alex didn't answer.

"Oh, don't be gallant, I know you didn't love her. Was it because I was on the way?"

Alex wished he didn't look guilty as he said, "Did she ever discuss this with you?"

"What's the difference."

"Would you have held this against me?" Alex was afraid of the answer, and yet the answer was of vital importance to him.

"I never saw you until I was half grown-up. I never felt I knew the real Alexander Grant. What will you do if your column isn't published?"

"What I know best. Write. Someone will publish me. I hope."

"You must make some sense or so many people wouldn't read you. Even at school. Even some of the bearded characters, although occasionally you blow my mind. You still modify too much."

"Did you believe Upshaw's insinuations?"

"You want to believe them, you believe them. You haven't even been tried."

"The accusation is enough. They don't need a conviction."

"If you would like to come back to school with me, throw a football around, play some touch football. You could take off for a few days and I ..." James halted, as if he didn't know how to finish.

"I'd like to, but ..."

James's expression turned sour. "That's the way it always is. I never really felt you gave a damn until I made the football team. Fucking football!" He started for the door. "I knew I shouldn't have come."

Alex grabbed him at the door. "James, please! You must listen!" His son paused, but he didn't talk. "I didn't think football was such a big deal. I was grateful it paid my tuition, got me attention, even helped me to get a couple of good opportunities eventually, but it wasn't that important. If it was, I would have played pro football. I had offers."

"I'm sure you did."

Alex had a desperate need for James's affection but his son was so stiff. He cried out, "It didn't matter to me whether you played football or not, it was simply a way of bringing us together."

"Yeah?"

"I would love to go back to school with you, but I have a prior engagement and it wouldn't be fair to break it."

"A woman?"

Alex blushed and didn't answer.

"I'm grown-up. You can tell me. A married woman?"

"Yes. But she is a widow."

"I never did believe there was anything wrong with you. When I read it, I said, Oh, no, not Alexander! Have you known her long?"

Alex shrugged.

"Are you in love with her?"

Alex hesitated, then shook his head reluctantly, "No."

James stepped out of the door, then turned and said, grinning, "Have a good day."

# *Form a Habit*

Form a habit
And it will form you
In its own quality

STYMEN KARLEN

# Form a Habit

Sunday evening was beautiful. Alex enjoyed driving through a country which was still saturated with the tang of autumn. The red, brown, and scarlet leaves reminded him that this season was his favorite time of the year, when he felt most vital. He was pleased, too, about James's visit and he tried not to feel any more guilt. It was a relief to be away from the worries of the moment and as he came closer to Marcia's retreat his anticipation grew. The air was cool and the sky was clear and reflected the exhilarating glow of the sunset in a multitude of brilliant and constantly changing colors. Alex was grateful that nature was co-operative and he decided not to ask Marcia any questions, but simply to enjoy this evening. And yet, within himself, there was a determination that this evening would be his own answer to Upshaw.

Marcia was waiting for him at the door of her spacious cottage, standing under the imitation Tudor turrets, and as she heard the car approaching, she stepped outside to greet him. Alex had never seen her look more attractive or enticing. She wore a slim black sheath, which fitted her tightly, with a very low-cut neck, and she carried a glass of champagne in her hand.

She offered him a sip and it was sparkling and cool.

She said, "I've kept it on ice. I love champagne, don't you?"

"Indeed!" He was delighted to see that she was in a party mood.

Marcia took his hand, squeezing it amorously as she did, and led him into her dining room, and Alex was prepared to feel drunk with sensual sensations, particularly after the slanderous implications about his masculinity. Soon he thought, he would feel complete again.

"Alex, dear, I had cook prepare a buffet supper before I gave her the night off," she said as she showed him the lobster salad, the caviar, the shrimp, the cold roast beef and the champagne. "They say roast beef and lobster are good for virility. A kind of aphrodisiac. Or do you think that is an old wives' tale?" When he appeared embarrassed, she added, "But that wouldn't matter to you. You won't need it."

"Did you hear what Upshaw said about me?"

"Alex," she said impatiently, "I told you I don't read the papers."

"Never."

"Seldom. They are too depressing."

"But you do know what Upshaw accused me of?"

"There was something on T.V. about it, after a lovie I was watching. I wish they didn't give so much news. The news is bad enough as it is. I prefer lovies."

"Lovies? What are they?"

"Movies about love. I love love, don't you, darling?"

"Yes. What did you think about Upshaw's remarks?"

"Alex, you are determined to talk about it. Why don't you ignore it?"

"How can I?"

"Alex ..." Her tone became soothing, caressing. "I know you. I know how ridiculous such charges are. You don't need reassurance, dear boy, you are a lovely lover. Now eat so you won't complain later."

However, he was on edge again and it caused him to lose his appetite and he nibbled rather than ate. If Marcia noticed, she didn't say anything, but ate heartily and sipped another glass of champagne.

Suddenly she was laughing at the wry expression on his face and saying, "Nobody who knows you would ever believe it and I still don't."

Reassured, he followed Marcia into her bedroom. It was decorated in pink, a delicate perfume scented the air and the boudoir stirred his senses erotically. She motioned to Alex to undress, and as he did quickly, she excused herself and hurried into the bathroom, ostensibly to prepare herself for their sexual party. Then Alex waited. As minutes passed, he wondered uneasily what was happening. This was not like Marcia.

Marcia retreated into the bathroom, to review what Shipmen had told her. She remembered every detail, for he had gone to great lengths to stress the importance of what she was doing.

He said, sitting in the art gallery of her spacious colonial house, where they were least likely to be observed, "I made a special trip just to talk to you."

"Is it that important? I know my husband's business is, but I know nothing about chemicals."

"Yes," he repeated, "that important." He leaned forward, like the eighteen-inch-high Thinker he was sitting near, and said with special emphasis, "Marcia, you are a patriotic citizen. Alex is not. We have to bring him to his knees and we know he is vulnerable to impotence."

She interrupted indignantly, "Roger, you are assuming . . ."

He halted her. "I'm assuming nothing, dear. But you and Alex are friends. He is attractive, you are, too. Any man would be honored to receive your affection. And you will be doing this for your country."

"I don't know whether I am worthy," she replied humbly.

"I'm not sure I am either. But since the President has entrusted me with vital duties I do the best I can. As I'm sure you will."

"This is for the President?"

"In a sense, yes."

"What do you want me to do, Roger?"

"If you can render Alex Grant impotent, maybe in defeat he will recognize his loyalty to the President."

Marcia said, "I have begun to worry about his patriotism."

"That is what concerns us, too. Instead of repudiating and denouncing his son's shameful exhibitionism, he supported it. But it is no wonder. Now that we have discovered he signed a Red petition it is obvious where his sympathies lie. Upshaw's speech verifies our suspicions."

But still she hesitated.

"You will be performing a great service."

She felt quite noble, then the thought of giving up Alex was painful suddenly. No man satisfied her more thoroughly than he did.

Shipmen, afraid she would equivocate, said softly, "We have been reviewing draft deferments lately. If you want to save your son's, I would like to, but it will take considerable effort."

"I'll do my best," she said suddenly. "Since it is my patriotic duty."


Once she memorized her instructions she returned.

Alex said, "I was wondering what happened. You are still dressed? Why did you go into the bathroom?" He hadn't heard anything.

"I was getting ready."

"Ready? You're not even undressed." He gazed at her suspiciously.

She said, "I will be. Soon." She smiled at him enticingly, thinking, How can I distract him, arouse him, and then frustrate him, making a pigmy out of a sexual giant without arousing his suspicions, which would be fatal. Then she was sure she knew the answer. She said coquettishly, "The longer you wait, the better it will be."

"For a moment, I even thought you might be bugging your bathroom."

"Alex, you are nervous. But I'll make your wait worth it."

He was puzzled by her obvious attempt to be seductive. Hitherto, she had been natural, almost professional in her sexual practicality. But he dismissed his doubts as she took off her clothes as if she was performing a sexual strip tease.

"I hope you are not in a hurry," she said.

"No," he said, although he was and becoming more so with each article she discarded. "Take your time."

"No one will interrupt us," she said comfortingly.

"Stanley is back in school and I told all my friends I was going away for the weekend."

She stood close to him now, clad only in a bra and panties, as he lay on her bed waiting nakedly while Wally swelled.

"Help me, will you, Alex darling?"

She turned her back so he could unbutton her bra and she pressed close to him as he did. He could hardly restrain himself now. Wally was thick and long with urgency, and yet suddenly she pulled away.

"I have to be neat," she said. "I can't leave my bra on the floor. It could capture dust, or some infectious disease."

But as she saw Wally pointing erectly in her direction she returned from her closet where she hung her bra.

"Your wang has an interesting shape," she observed.

"Wang? Where did you ever learn that expression?"

"From my husband, Ernie. He was proud of his wang. Are you?"

"Well, in a way, yes."

"So was Ernie. He said he had a big one. Do you have a big one?"

"Marcia, you never mentioned your husband before."

"You never asked me. Alex, do you think size has anything to do with virility? Ernie said that . . . ?"

"Marcia!" he cut in impatiently, "do you want me to take off your panties?" Her breasts dangled in his face, and he never could resist breasts, and he wished she wouldn't talk about Ernie. This was the first time Wally was erect since Upshaw's remarks and he didn't want Wally deflated now. "Right now, please?"

"Yes." She snuggled close to him as he pulled off her black panties. But as he gently pushed her into the bed she recoiled at his touch.

"What's wrong now?" he asked.

"I forgot something." She ran into the bathroom, but this time she returned quickly, although she didn't get back in bed, but stood over him, enticingly, seductively, very near to him and yet in a way, very far.

He asked apologetically, "Did I do something I shouldn't have done?"

"Never mind."

"What did I do now to upset you?"

"Are you hungry? You ate very little."

No, he wanted to shout, but he whispered, "Only for you."

"I knew you wouldn't run out of energy no matter what they said."

"Please, Marcia!" Wally was growing soft.

"All right, if you are in such a hurry. But we have all night."

She pouted as she lay down beside him and as he tried to enter her, distracted by her petulance and still disturbed by what Upshaw had implied, Wally softened completely and he couldn't enter her. He didn't move then, furious at her, at himself, at these bastards who sneered at his virility, and her conversation made matters worse.

"I didn't believe those silly insinuations. You're not improper, you've never been. I'm a woman of the world, I understand such things."

Couldn't she ever stop talking? Wally was utterly limp now.

"You are sure you are not hungry, Alex?"

"No."

"Would you prefer a drink?"

"No."

"They say champagne is an aphrodisiac."

"I don't need an aphrodisiac!" Alex's voice rose angrily.

"I know. I just want to be helpful. How about some beer?"

"No." All he needed were no distractions, he thought irritably.

She was silent, then she asked, "Maybe beer would be better?"

"Silence would be better!"

"Losing your temper won't help. It never helped Ernie."

He grabbed her and Marcia, perhaps afraid, perhaps anticipating, he couldn't tell, lay quietly while he struggled to enter her. Wally seemed ready once more, only she wasn't moist and he couldn't penetrate her and yet in his need to prove he could, he bruised Wally, who promptly softened. Imagining the most erotic woman he had ever known, Wally hardened, and this time he forced his penis into her vagina, but she was so narrow, so tight—had she contracted her vagina deliberately, he wondered?—and Wally was terribly uncomfortable again and softened.

Exasperated, he didn't move, not knowing what to do next.

She rolled over until she was close to him and she said, "I dearly love your masculinity, Alex, but you are upset."

"I'm not upset!" he shouted.

"Oh, yes you are. Like Ernie used to be. Men take their wangs too seriously."

"No, I don't!" Was she trying to provoke him, he wondered.

"Lay here quietly and you'll be normal soon." She halted his reply with a kiss and as it aroused him, he thought, possibly she is right.

Wally was just becoming erect again when she sneezed.

"It is the wind," she said, but when she ran to the window, instead of closing it as Alex expected, she opened it wider. "That will clear the air. And the fresh air should help you, stimulate you, darling."

Marcia returned to his side, but the wind blew dust into his face and he sneezed now, too. Suddenly a handkerchief was more important than anything else. It was ridiculous, he thought, but he couldn't make love while he was sneezing. By the time he found a handkerchief, Wally was useless once more. This couldn't go on much longer, he knew, Wally was not a battery that could be recharged continuously. He reached for Marcia and as she squirmed away from him, he lunged after her, knocked her toy Panda which stood on her night table upon his head, bruising that, too, and as he bent over to pick up the toy which had fallen on to the floor, he jostled the floor lamp by the bed and it careened against the wall with a crash. "Adjust the lamp," she ordered, but Alex ignored that, and chasing her the width of the bed, he finally caught her. He fell on top of her, determined not to allow Marcia to get away from him or to repulse him any more—it was becoming a matter of honor—and the bed teetered and sagged, as if a spring was breaking. Yet Marcia, instead of being surprised, said, "See, what you did to the bed. With your lack of self-control. We could end on the floor."

Nonsense, he wanted to retort, but tonight he had to prove something. So he tried to appease her, saying, "I'll fix it later. It'll hold us."

"No! You must fix it now! I can't make love on the floor!" She jumped out of bed, but when she saw his startled look she said, "Don't worry, dear, I'll be back. I have to go to the bathroom."

Waiting for Marcia to return and this time she was even longer, Alex remembered when Wally was the most co-operative of friends. Whether it was Ellen with her pale blonde hair and her parents' sofa which they used as their bed, or his second wife, Cathy, beautiful and bright and in-satiable, or Louise, who he married after he found Cathy in bed with his best friend and for a few months they argued and loved and laughed and loved, and finally, she was too talkative, also, almost as garrulous as Rita, and they parted.

But none of these women or any of the many who followed or who occurred in-between complained about Wally or resisted Wally. He stopped confusing sex with love, with anything beyond the moment, and Wally fitted their grooves, their dancing hips, their laughter and their excitement, cunning in his attractiveness, skillful at provoking orgasms, and making believers out of non-believers.

Now, staring at the wall while he heard her performing her bowel functions in the bathroom, he wondered if she had to be so loud, it corroded whatever erotic impulses remained in him, and he noticed she left the door ajar, which she never had done before. Was she playing a game with him? If she was, he could play, also.

Marcia returned wearing a sheer silk red nightgown which he could see through and he felt she was taunting him, and when he asked, "Why aren't you naked?" she replied, "I got cold, waiting for you." Yet she did get into bed beside Alex and ignored the spring and cuddled close to him.

"As an expression of confidence," she assured him.

Gradually Wally responded and just as he was about to

enter her and he nudged her with a firm Wally to alert her,
she asked, "Do you love me?"

He kissed her hand, her cheek, her mouth, but she drew
away.

"You don't really love me? You just want me."

"Marcia, you never asked me this before."

"You never gave me a chance."

Why was she so talkative, so distracting? Did she believe
Upshaw?

"Would you marry me, Alex?" she asked suddenly.

"Marcia?" He recoiled without thinking, as if he had been
hit.

"Am I that repulsive?"

"It isn't that, but it was never a factor in our friendship."

"Always but! I'm something to discard when you are tired
of me."

He was so distracted he didn't recall what had started this
argument.

"I'm still cold. Alex, could you get more blankets?"

"Where are they?"

"In the closet next to the bathroom. I think."

He stumbled on one of her high-heeled bedroom slippers
as he found the blankets in the dark—not wanting to turn
the lights on or she would use that against him, too—and he
twisted his ankle so painfully he could hardly limp back to
bed. He cursed. He wouldn't be able to play tennis for
several weeks, and she assumed he was snarling at her.

"You're a brute," she whimpered, "You used to be
marvelous, but no more."

"Marcia, I'm not any different than I ever was."

"Your knee is sticking me."

"It's Wally."

"Does he have to be so rude?"

He almost pushed her out of bed, but the smell of her
perfume, the smoothness of her skin and the firmness of her
buttocks aroused Wally and he was ready to let bygones be
bygones and he pressed close to her—for the last time he
swore, whatever happened—and she laughed.

Startled, he sat up abruptly and bumped his head on the
floor lamp.

As it fell to the floor, she said, "I warned you to fix it. Pick it up."

"Pick it up yourself."

She was motionless, determined not to heed him.

But she was also within reach and a little off guard, and Alex, with a last desperate effort pulled her to him. And as Wally pushed against her pubic hair, swelling despite all her rebuffs, she had a wild yearning for Alex to shove Wally as hard, as far as Wally could penetrate. Her flesh quivered with desire and reminded her of Wally's ability to make it last. They did fit skillfully and excitingly. Sweat trickled down her body as her urge quarreled with her reason. Alex put his hands on her shoulders and unable to endure being tantalized any more, she pumped her pubic hair into Wally with the most sensual writhing motion she knew. Then, as he was about to enter her, she remembered. She couldn't. She could lose far more than the joy of this moment. But as she withdrew and the exquisite sensation was gone, her frustration was almost unendurable. Yet she had no choice and she knew it. Although it was the last thing she wanted to do, she laughed loudly and contemptuously.

As she expected, Wally could not endure it. Wally assumed it was ridicule. The more she laughed, the more limp Wally became.

Alex said, "I don't see anything funny."

"You ought to face it. You've lost it." She must hit him hard, she thought, so she wouldn't weaken.

"If you hadn't talked so much?"

"Talked too much?" She pointed at Wally. "Look at him! That is your answer. You must face facts, you tried hard enough, but whenever I was ready something went wrong with you. Ernie was right."

Poor Ernie, he thought, but he replied, "You kept interrupting me."

"That wouldn't bother Ernie. Maybe Upshaw was right."

He stared at her suspiciously, wondering, could she have been put up to this? He asked however, "How was Upshaw right?"

"His photo indicated you made an indecent gesture."

"But you said you didn't see the newspaper story. How did you know about the photo, Marcia?"

"I didn't see it. The T.V. news mentioned the photo."

Now he was sure that she was lying.

"I know you could be innocent, but after tonight I wonder."

Could she have been part of a frame-up, too, he asked himself. He started to dress.

"After what happened tonight, Upshaw's charges make sense."

"You believe them?"

"You must face facts. You're sick. You need a doctor."

"Is that why you responded to me so passionately a few minutes ago?"

"I forgot myself. I was remembering the past."

"Then why did you stop?"

Irritated that he was asking her the questions, she snapped, "You were sweaty. You smelled. You needed a bath. You didn't expect me to make love to you in this condition."

But as he put on his pants he recalled she was the one sweating, and for a moment she had almost overwhelmed him with her passion. Hardly the behavior of one who was revolted, he thought. He smiled, and asked, "Who put you up to this, Marcia? Shipmen? Graves?"

"How dare you! Get out before I have you thrown out!" She wrapped herself in a dressing gown and pointed to the door.

Instead, he put on all the lights in the bedroom and continued to dress leisurely and said "You have Examiners downstairs to throw me out? Were they taping our conversation and behaviour, too?"

"You're very nasty. No wonder you are impotent."

"Only with you. And only tonight. Are there any Examiners here?"

"I told you that we are alone. But you insist on not trusting me."

"Why should I after *Marcia's Complaint*. Who created that?"

"*Marcia's Complaint*? What is that?" She was truly puzzled.

"You impersonate a woman, but you are not one really.

"I am more of a woman than you are a man!" she retorted furiously. "Upshaw was right and Shipmen ...!" She bit her tongue. "Go, or I will call the police!"

"And create another scandal, that this time will involve you. You won't call anybody, except perhaps Upshaw or Shipmen." He sighed reflectively, "And you almost got away with it." Alex was completely dressed but she insisted he remain one more minute.

Marcia stated, "I know far more about sex than you do, I am far more experienced and sensitive to the nuances, particularly of style. This, you have on the best authority, for I am telling you myself. But you betrayed me. You should learn the truth about yourself. You are sick."

She was still talking as he left, and he realized the more she talked the more she believed it. But was he so dangerous, he wondered. It was unpleasant enough when they sought to seduce him and then to attack him, but to try to discredit and to degrade him, that could destroy him. After he checked his car to make sure everything was working safely, he drove with extreme care for it was very dark on the road. And when Alex reached his apartment he didn't feel safe until he was inside. Everything was as he had left it and he went at once to old Iron Face. After Marcia, he would listen to anything she said.

# If You Don't Believe in Something

If you don't believe in something
you'd better believe in something
Nothing is nothing to believe in
And you'll have nothing to believe in
So you'd better believe in something

Hold on
If you don't hold on to something
you'd better hold on to something
Nothing is nothing to hold on to
And you'll have nothing to hold on to
So you'd better hold on to something

If you don't believe in
you'd better believe in
If it's something or nothing
Something or nothing is something
to believe in
Or you won't have something or nothing
at all


STYMEAN KARLEN

# If You Don't Believe in Something

The column did not appear on Monday. Alex searched for
*A Matter of Conscience* everywhere, but there was not a
trace of it in the local newspaper which published his
column. Neither was there an apology or even a word of
explanation. He assured himself that he was not really
surprised, and yet, now that it had happened, it was a
shock. He sat staring at old Iron Face and for once she was
silent, too.

Then suddenly he had to act. He telephoned the hotel
where Harold was staying and he was informed that his publisher had checked out early this morning and had not left a
forwarding address. Next, Alex called the main office in
another city where Harold preferred to be most of the time,
and they wanted to know who was calling.

When he gave his name he was told, "Mr. Hinton isn't in,
and we don't know when he will be." The secretary hung up
abruptly.

Growing angry and desperate, Alex called back and insisted on talking to Harold's private secretary, whom he knew.
Today however, Angela was formal, which confirmed what
he sensed, and when he asked, "Where can I reach Mr.
Hinton," she replied, "He is on vacation."

"Where?"

"He didn't say. He left word that he was not to be disturbed."

"Did he leave any message for me, Angela?"

261

"I don't think so, Mr. Grant."

"Look. Will you please?"

He waited what seemed to be an interminable time and then she came back and said, "There is something about you after all that he left on his desk to be submitted to all the affiliates in the syndicate."

"Is it confidential?"

The secretary read: "It is with deep regret that I accept the resignation of Alexander Grant. It is a very sad day for me and for the syndicate. But since he says his decision is irrevocable we cannot argue with it. Yet it will be impossible to replace him."

They were both silent for a minute.

Then she mumbled, "I'm sorry."

"Thanks, Angela." What else was there to say, he wondered, I'll be seeing you, it's a dirty trick, I'll call back, I don't believe it, I must change his mind. Alex said nothing and hung up.

He was still sitting and staring at old Iron Face, feeling as futile as he had felt in a long time, he had the same sense of shock he had when he had learned how the Communists had betrayed him with their petition, when the telephone rang. He was trying to decide what to write, or whether to write, or to submit elsewhere, he had no desire to be an unread writer, but maybe Harold was calling back after all, maybe Harold had changed his mind and realized that many readers wanted to read him still, that many readers cared, or it was more bad news, and he hesitated. But Alex knew he had no choice. He picked up his telephone, hoping for the best and expecting the worst, but his heart was beating faster, and it was one of the last people he expected to hear from, the university's military doctor.

M.P. was agitated. "Alexander Grant?" he asked portentously.

"Speaking."

"I have terrible, terrible news."

Who died? flashed through Alex's mind. "Is it my son?" he asked.

"Yes."

"What happened? Has he been hurt? Seriously?"

"He seized a building. Infiltrated it, occupied it."

Relieved, Alex wanted to laugh. He said, "Lots of buildings are being seized these days. That is nothing unusual."

"This is. This is no laughing matter. He has seized our re-evaluation center. If anything happens to our computers it will be a tragedy."

"Has anybody been hurt?"

"Not yet. Why didn't they keep him under better surveillance? Your son infiltrated our re-evaluation center when our backs were turned, disguised as a guard, told the guard on duty that he was being relieved, and when the guard went to the toilet your son locked him in."

"Was the guard hurt?"

"Only his dignity. He had to escape out the back window. It was very small and he is rather fat. But that is not the point. Do you realize what your son has done? It could start many such seizures."

"Who is helping him?"

"He did it by himself. The re-evaluation center is small, with just two computers. But they are vital to the university. These computers contain a vast store of information about our students which is essential to the welfare and safety of this great school. It is a crisis. Nobody knows how to proceed."

"Does my son have any weapons?"

"He claims it is a non-violent seizure. But I don't believe him."

"Assuming however, that he doesn't have any weapons, why haven't you taken this center from him? Since he is unarmed? Alone?"

"We don't dare!" M.P. yelled angrily and unhappily. "Our computers are very sensitive. We can't use tear gas because it would injure them. They can't stand any temperature or atmosphere changes. And the doors are six inches thick and can only be opened from the inside and your son threatens to destroy all the information in the computers if we attempt to take the re-evaluation center. It is just a little building."

Alex sighed. He was in no mood for a new cause, and yet

James must have a reason for what James was doing. "What do you want me to do?"

"Your son says you are the only one he will talk to. Maybe you can persuade him to give up the re-evaluation center without ruining the data banks. Before he kills all my work! Something has to be done!"

"It will take time to get there. Even if I fly."

"We've connected the telephone from the re-evaluation center to you. You can talk to him now. Maybe you can change his mind."

"Put him on."

The instant James and Alex were connected, Alex had no chance to talk to his son, for James exploded in a torrential burst, as if an enormous store of emotion had to be released before it overwhelmed him.

"Alexander, I did it for Sid Virgin. Sid Virgin and I are holding this building. They got two computers here with data banks on everybody who attended this university and the information goes way back. I expected to find my name on file, but what got me is putting Sid Virgin's name here. I could almost take anything else, Alexander, but not this. They have Sid in their suspicious file because I mentioned him in the hospital examination, they have me and The Demolisher and Sid in the same file.

"They have put Sid under permanent suspicion, in a kind of jail, forever. These computers have tried me and The Demolisher and Sid without a hearing, as if we confessed. A trial without jurors or a jury or even the right to appeal. Can I hold the computers in contempt?

"Everything I said in the hospital they put down, and a lot more. They must have stolen and photostated Sid's last letter to me, where he said Pacification stinks. How else could they have gotten it, for it is here, too. Lots of wrong information, too, like I am a suspicious character because I read Karl Marx and Sigmund Freud. This is underlined in red, to indicate this makes me untrustworthy. Christ, they were assigned to me in class!

"They have something here even about you. Quite a file, and this particular item says, 'Alexander Grant must be stopped.' Only when you read carefully do you realize that somebody said it about you when you were playing football. But whoever dug this item up, got confused, took it seriously, and misread it. It is in the suspicious file, too.

"And what crimes did I commit? They have a dossier on me—Wow! Length of my hair, my legs, my penis, yes, my penis. Why don't they examine those doctors, M.P., P.P., and G.P.? What about their penises?

"I ought to hold these computers in contempt. Full of gossip about whether I drink, smoke pot, how many times I have protested, and where and when, and who was with me. Girls I know. Fellows.

"You should see these computers, Alexander. Polished and shiny and perfectly placed to receive the right temperature, the right air, the right affection. I wish they took such good care of me.

"They got enough stuff here to fill the newspapers for years, and they didn't even print your column this morning. But they publish garbage about you using a women's lavatory as if you violated a dozen mothers, as if no normal man ever did what you did—didn't they ever get caught short!

"Now there is another excursion into a new Territory and when we question it all we get is heartburn. Well, this is my excursion into a new Territory and it is just as legal. If the President doesn't like being frustrated, why should I feel frustrated.

"You had better get me while you can, Alexander. I brought food with me, and they are not going to take this building away from me, not as long as I can destroy their precious data banks. If you really want to talk to me come up here. I'll talk to you here, not there. And bring old Iron Face. Now you will have something to write about. You might even get this published."

Alex heard the receiver slam down on the hook like a period.


M.P. called back. "See what I mean. Simply outrageous behaviour." But who would have paid any attention to

James, Alex thought, if his son had not behaved outrageously. He said, "I'll fly up. At once."

"Hurry! Our patience is running thin. Something awful could happen."

"Yes," said Alex. But it was James he was thinking of, not M.P.

James would not have wanted to speak to him, Alex told himself, as he grabbed old Iron Face and rushed to the airport, unless his son needed him. His son, however James expressed it, was casting his need before him and Alex knew that his son must be answered. If he didn't now, he had a feeling, he wouldn't get another chance. And it was no use praying or weeping or hoping or wondering, but to go as fast as he could and however he got there.

It was just before twilight when Alex reached the grounds of the university. The sun was still in the sky and the weather was unusually mild and pleasant for late autumn. A perfect Indian summer afternoon, he thought, to remind him of the beauty of nature before winter set in.

The re-evaluation center was on the outskirts of the sprawling university, within sight of the stadium and the blown-up storeroom, and the taxi he took from the airport found it without any difficulty. But to get close to the building itself was not easy.

The entire area was enclosed by a high barbed-wire fence and at the gate he and his taxi were stopped by four men in civilian clothes. He sensed they were Examiners, for all of them wore somber dark gray suits and they looked like ex-football players, over-age and over-weight for such strenuous activity, but muscular enough to handle most physical situations. And like all Examiners they wore the same expression on their square, rugged faces—accusation.

They told Alex to get out of the taxi and demanded to know his business. They refused to allow him to move on until he gave them his name and he told them the military doctor had asked him to come.

Then, staring at Alex intently, they ordered him to walk the rest of the way, with them as his escorts. And when they saw old Iron Face, they regarded the typewriter suspiciously.

"It is not a bomb," he said, "but if you wish to examine it . . .?"

"Don't be wise," one of the Examiners retorted "If I had my way, I wouldn't let you get any closer. Like son, like father. Check it, Buddy Boy. You never know."

The youngest Examiner, who looked like a rookie, removed the case and examined old Iron Face with the utmost suspicion, saying contemptuously, "It's awful old. Gimme the creeps to use it."

But he found nothing incriminating, although he put old Iron Face back in her case so roughly Alex was afraid he would break her.

However, once old Iron Face was safely in her lodgings Alex felt better. With her, at least, he could express himself.

The Examiners walked Alex down the road a few yards, marching on each side of him so he was surrounded and several times they bumped into him, deliberately, he was sure, to frisk him for any hidden weapons.

When they reached the anxious and impatient M.P., the leader said, "Here is your pigeon. I hope it works, but I doubt it."

"It has to work," M.P. said querulously. "I can't take a chance with these computers, they contain essential information, and if we storm the center he could break them. What took you so long, Grant?"

"Distance, Doctor."

"Well, you haven't far to go now." He pointed to a small building a hundred yards away. "Maybe you can talk some sense into him."

Alex noticed that a lovely, green meadow with fertile grass was the approach to the re-evaluation center. Almost like a meditative gateway to revelation, he thought. Then he knew he must be practical; he must, somehow, get James out of this building before anything was destroyed. Even incorrect records, he said to himself ruefully.

M.P. interrupted his reverie by dismissing the Examiners. Alex was surprised, until he saw a group of university guards standing near by. At first he thought that they were college students, for they were mostly nice looking young

men, but now they were trying on their plastic masks and
flak helmets and they were becoming an entirely different
kind of an animal and he shivered. He saw about a dozen
other people by the guards and M.P. explained, "College
officials, and a few government observers. The government
supervises this re-evaluation center."

"Is it really a spy bank?" Alex asked. "As my son said?"

"My dear fellow," said M.P., "Your son exaggerates."

"But does it contain secret information about all the
students?"

"You do research when you write. Come, we haven't
much time. It will be dark soon and then it will be too late."

Before Alex could ask any more questions, he was diverted by Eric Losell, who was holding a microphone attached
to a trailing wire. Startled, he asked, "What are you doing
here?"

"I'm reporting this situation for the news media. I was
chosen from a pool of newspaper men because of my experience and because I know you."

So they really want to pick my bones clean, Alex thought.

Eric added, "Alex, you get your son out and nothing is
damaged, it could help you. You could still play ball. It is
not too late."

"It is never too late," Alex replied, "until it is."

Eric was puzzled, but Alex didn't bother to explain.

M.P. pulled him in the direction of the re-evaluation
center, saying, "Persuade your son to leave peacefully, to
promise that he will not damage anything, and we will drop
the charges."

"What charges?" Alex halted.

"You don't seize university property without raising
serious issues. The least arraignment would charge that the
defendant acted disorderly, obstructed justice, molested in-
valuable equipment, and interfered with the safety of the
government and with the public interest."

Before Alex could question M.P.'s accusations, James's
voice boomed out. But where was it coming from? There
was no visible sign of his son. He saw that he and M.P. had
walked closer to the re-evaluation center than anybody else.
They were alone now, apart from all the others, and only

about fifty yards from the center, he figured, as he used to figure on the football field when he was about to pass.

"Don't come any closer," James said, "or I'll burn the files."

M.P. said, "He must have a bullhorn. You can hear them a long way. I'm glad nothing is taking place in the stadium now."

"Get yourself another bullhorn," said James. "I'll need an answer." M.P. led Alex back to the guards, got a bullhorn, and Alex had to ask one of them who looked no older than James, "Do you know my son?"

"I never mix in students' business."

"You haven't been watching him?"

"That's what I said. Nothing wrong with my ears. I know what I said." All the guards were frozen now. M.P. shoved the bullhorn into Alex's hand and said, "Tell your son everything will be all right and go to him."

Alex took the bullhorn and walked toward James.

"Wait a moment, Alexander. You forgot something."

"What, James?" He called back through the bullhorn.

"Old Iron Face."

Alex hurried back to where he had left old Iron Face, picked her up, mumbling to her, "I'm sorry," and started toward the re-evaluation center again, the bullhorn in one hand and old Iron Face in the other. But he had travelled only about halfway when James's voice halted him once more.

"That's all, Alexander. Don't come any closer."

"But you said you wanted to talk to me."

"The only person I will talk to is my father."

"I'm your father."

"That depends."

"James, what do you want me to do?"

"Discard your uniform. Your coat, your ties, your socks, your shoes, your pants, your shorts. Everything."

"Why?"

"There are lots of reasons. Anyhow, I don't have to explain. Approach me nakedly and I will let you in. Otherwise, no."

"Nakedly?" repeated Alex, not certain he was hearing correctly.

"I call it *The Bare Ass Principle*. Remember. If you approach me nakedly, carrying nothing, except old Iron Face, I may let you in."

"May?"

"That depends on how you approach me. Other things."

"What other things?"

"Don't you ever take a chance, Alexander?"

Alex hesitated.

"No guts, Alexander?"

"Why do you want me to bring old Iron Face?"

"Maybe she is the part of you I can trust. Maybe she will find a story here. Maybe she isn't a weapon. Maybe, maybe, maybe, what's the difference! Either you do as I say or nobody gets in, not even you."

"What about the bullhorn?"

"You won't need it. Once you get started I'll give the directions."

M.P. grabbed Alex's bullhorn and shouted back, "I've never heard such drivel in my life!"

James replied, "Like the drivel in these data banks. It will be easy to burn them and to damage the computers." He held a flare in the window to demonstrate he could do just that. "Alexander, if you want to talk to me face to face, I will only do this if you walk toward me nakedly, and alone, with only old Iron Face."

M.P. mumbled in a sudden change of mind, "You have no choice, Grant. Look, he will burn our data banks if we ignore him."

A flare flamed high in the window of the re-evaluation center and Alex hesitated. He couldn't expose himself before all these people, and it would add fuel to the fire Shipmen had lighted under him, and yet he knew that if he didn't heed James now there would not be a second chance.

M.P. urged, "You must do it. Think of the computers."

Yet what his son was asking was impossible.

"*The Bare Ass Principle* is easy. Unless you are afraid. Unless you are too old. Unless you got arteriosclerosis. Or something to hide."

"I'm not too old!" he shouted back. "And I have nothing to hide!"

"Then undress." James was inexorable. "It will be the essence of non—violence. You won't be carrying arms of any kind."

Suddenly M.P. changed his mind and screamed through the bull-horn so James could hear him, also, "Don't! We'll surround him from the back. We'll get in, somehow. No matter how much force we have to use."

"No!" Alex grabbed the bullhorn from M.P. and called to James, "Wait! I'll do it!" If he didn't believe in something, he couldn't continue, he had to believe in his son, he had to believe in something. He took off his coat, but paused when he came to his pants.

James said, "Alexander, it is not hard, when you get used to it."

Alex hated the pressure of all the eyes. M.P. retreated from him as if he had the plague and everybody was staring at him. The human body should be beautiful but rarely was. He felt numb. His knuckles were white. Yet they couldn't say he had soft legs or a fat stomach. His chest was compact and he didn't need a tuxedo to prove that, and his penis was in the right place. He shuddered. After what Upshaw insinuated, stripping was the last thing he should do.

James said, "I guess you are scared. I guess you weren't as good a football player as they said."

Alex felt his son really was saying, I was half-grown-up before I actually knew I had a father. I was brought up by a mother I didn't respect, a father who was absent. I had to become defensive to protect myself. There was no one I could depend on. Alex started to take off the rest of his clothes.

He heard Eric whispering to him, "I think you are nuts."

Once Alex started to undress it wasn't too difficult until he reached his shorts.

As he halted again, James shouted, "It's okay, Alexander, your jurisdiction extends to your ass."

But this was worse than even his fear before *The Game*. Not only did Alex have a football stomach now, with nervous cramps, he thought he would perish from the cold. The sun was almost down, the air was getting chilly, and everybody was staring at him, as if no one expected him to take this final step and disrobe completely.

James declared, "I didn't think you would do it. I never really felt you were noticing me until I became pretty good at football. And even then I wasn't sure."

Alex dropped his shorts to the ground, although he was shivering. He turned so he faced James and no one else and picking up the bull-horn, which M.P., in his agitation, had dropped to the ground, he called, "Is there anything else you want me to do, son?" He couldn't give up his relationship with James, with the one person who mattered.

"You heard my instructions. Walk toward me with old Iron Face. I'll let you in if you do it properly and if no one interferes."

Alex dropped the bullhorn, picked up old Iron Face, but then he couldn't move.

He heard Eric urging, "Hurry, Alex, I have a deadline to meet."

Alex imagined Eric broadcasting that he was using foul language and gestures too dirty to mention, and Shipmen, Graves, and Harold repeating this, and congratulating themselves that Alex Grant had fallen into the final trap, and exclaiming, "We've won!" Victor Winner would say, "Now the public will truly believe me!" And Shipmen, sitting in his roost like a vulture, perched for the kill someone else had performed, would feast on his carrion and continue to use other people's blood.

What Eric was thinking actually, Why didn't I think of this? Everyone is going to want an account of this. Harold will never be able to keep this from his affiliates. They will want an eyewitness and who is a better eyewitness than Alex. As he saw the scar on Alex's ass, unable to resist a good story, he broadcast, "The father hasn't started yet, but we are all waiting. I can see the scar on his behind. It is a war wound. Grant got it in *his* war when he saved his sergeant's life. After he recovered, he was decorated. The war wound is unmistakable."

So Alex stood in the middle of the meadow, his clothes at his feet, wishing he could be invisible. Then, not hearing what Eric was saying, he bent to pick up his shorts and

James said, "Alexander, you have nothing to be ashamed of. I thoroughly approve of your contour. No wonder women like you. And you move well. Maybe you were a pretty good football player after all." Alex edged forward. "Remember, The Demolisher still lingers in the hospital and they got Sid Virgin here. You have to speak up. For me, for Sid ... even for The Demolisher. Doesn't anybody care about why he did it? Is that unconstitutional?"

Although Alex had a muscle cramp in his leg from the cold and his nervousness and he thought he was going to crumple to the ground, he managed to walk forward. Display your penis in public, he thought, it was the only way to get attention. Yet he felt he was still auditioning, for James was still instructing him.

"You're doing better, Alexander. Better. This direction. Sid Virgin and I will hold this building until you get here."

If he could only run it would be a little easier, thought Alex, but as he started to hurry there was a warning from James.

"I won't open the door if you run."

The people behind Alex became a gray blob and he wasn't sure whether it was cloudy or it was growing darker. If he were only a bird to fly to the re-evaluation center in an instant. He estimated he was about forty yards away now, or perhaps a little more. The grass scratched his bare feet. He thought, The grass didn't care whether he was male or female, naked or clothed. Yet this world was his as much as anybody else's. No more, but surely no less. He saw the start of a late autumn moon in the sky, and now he knew twilight was near and soon it would be dark and much colder. He walked a few feet more and no one spoke, not even James, as if that would break the spell of this deed. He wished he could feel exultant, wanton, and dance across the meadow like Isadora Duncan, only he couldn't dance. But he couldn't feel sorry that he was born. There were times when he loved his naked body. Closer to the re-evaluation center by another ten yards, he was moving very slowly, as if his feet could hardly bear this burden, and he was remembering a summer at camp where he was one of the swimming instructors. His best time was the hour he was off-duty and he paddled up the seven-mile-long mountain lake where no one else ever went, and on a little deserted island he lay naked on the beach and felt as free as the wind. The waves of the mountain lake lapped over his body and gave him an invigorating and wonderful sense of well-being, and the sun soaked him warmly and stirred him sensuously, and there was only the smell of pine and the sway of the birch and he was young and he felt he was at the beginning of things and so much seemed ahead of him. Nature glowed in his heart and this was his island, a hundred yards long and wide, and he didn't have to step shyly for anyone.

Who had said, "Naked came I into the world,
And naked must I go out."

Cervantes, who probably had taken it from the book of Job, but that didn't matter, it was true. Each man was bound to his body and to hide it was to hide himself. Yet there were people watching him now who could not have been more surprised if the oak at the gate had started to walk. But only man, of all the species, worried about nakedness. For this moment, at least, he was the center of this world.

He was almost at the re-evaluation center now.

James said, "You're doing fine, Alexander."

He could touch the re-evaluation center, when M.P. announced on his bullhorn, "Grant, if anything is damaged, if one file is violated, both you and your son will pay for it."

Alex gripped old Iron Face tighter, glad now that he still held her. When he got inside he would issue the following statement: I am convinced James Grant is neither a bomber nor a conspirator and that he has rejected all acts of violence. It is his anguish over the Pacification Program and the body count which led to his non-violent resistance against violence. I join him in this. I share his views." He would type this on his own dossier, and the idea caused him to smile.

He heard James speaking, this time without a bullhorn, this time only to him. "Alexander, I'm not doing this to embarrass you."

"It's cold. Can you let me in?"

"In a moment. I have to find the keys. Thanks for coming."

"Okay." James grateful was more awkward than James critical. Yet it was good to feel wanted. He realized, too, that until now, a part of him had been untouched. It could have been buried with him, his unused center, never expressed, if James hadn't touched it.

"I've got the keys. I'll be down in a moment."

Then Alex noticed a curious thing which, for this moment at least, outweighed in importance the cold. While he was walking across the meadow Wally had swelled and now Wally was firm and straight and erect. Suddenly he felt reassured, and content. No one else could realize that Wally's good health mattered so much to him, but it did.

James opened the door of the re-evaluation center and said, "Come in."

As Alex warmed his hands so that he could use old Iron Face and he saw the two computers, he asked, "What are you going to do now? Destroy the files?"

"How can you be so violent? Of course not."

"What then, James?"

"Your son inherited some common sense. Rewrite them. Correct them. Yours and mine and Sid Virgin's. Those we know."

"And The Demolisher's? He shouldn't have bombed the building but no one cares why he did it."

"You are the writer in the family. You figure that out. Hell, you must be frozen. Here." Before Alex could protest, James took off his pants and jacket. "I have shorts underneath and now you are a guard, too. We had better hurry. They won't leave us alone much longer."

"Then you are not going to destroy the two computers?"

James shrugged. "What do you think, Alexander?"

"You're the boss."

"Leave them alone. It isn't their fault, but the way they are used."

Alex sat down before old Iron Face and as James handed him Sid Virgin's dossier and he placed it into his typewriter, he found himself writing, "Lads must live if we are to justify our ways to our fellow men. To grow used to be a destination."

When he saw what he had written, he said apologetically, "Old Iron Face has a way of taking over, whatever I try to say these days."

James read it, then said, "It's not bad." He looked outside and added, "They are still standing there, the guards, the Examiners, the university officials, the government representatives, the military doctor"—and Shipmen, Harold, Graves, Marcia, Spleeno, and Victor, reflected Alex—"staring, staring, aghast. Didn't they ever see a man naked before? We know they admire themselves in the mirror."

"I guess it is a different mirror. Their mirror. James, do you mind if I sign your name to what I am writing, as well as my own?"

"I will be honored."